An attempted meeting with  d
Bullet is injured. They are rescued by   lo
reluctantly allows them to stay at hi   ce
even though he is her third soul bond.

Grace seals her bonds with Bullet and Riot, and hunts down Wild to find out why he's avoiding her. It turns out, Wild has encountered the gods before. In a moment of arrogance where he claimed to be stronger than Death himself, the God of Death snatched him up and spirited him away to the underworld, kicking his ass in front of the deities who reside there. Thanatos stole Wild's voice and has haunted him ever since. Worried that he'll pass this curse to Grace, Wild runs.

Meanwhile, Bullet is in increasingly bad shape, and is warned by Nyx to make the most of the time he has left. Riot's deal with Viper is dissolved after Viper discloses information about Grace to Mercy when he helped her escape town, breaking the terms of the original agreement. Riot, Bullet, and Grace drive to a sacred waterfall, hoping to have a productive conversation with Gaia. Gaia learns of the prophecy, and nearly buries them all in a landslide. Wild has followed them from a distance, and is led to them by a divine voice, freeing them all from the dirt and taking an unconscious Grace back to a motel and calling a daimon doctor to attend to her.

Bullet learns the full extent of Wild's history with the gods in the dreamscape, telling the others when they wake up. Thanatos appears, bedecked in sequins, and takes them to the underworld to meet Hades and Persephone. They wish to see the Olympians restored to power, and offer their support. Grace is introduced to the soul of a daimon who recently passed into the underworld, who she later discovers is Dare's mom. She was murdered in her home by agathos, and Dare struggles with the aftermath in the upperworld, enraged at Bullet for not telling him, at Riot for abandoning him, and at all agathos for the violence and suffering. He throws himself into the street wars between agathos and daimons back in Milton and eventually picks a fight he can't win. He's found by Mercy's abandoned soul bond, Dice, who takes Dare back to his sister's house where Dare recuperates, helping Rogue out with baby Quinn until Onyx can convince him to get his act together.

Persephone gives Grace a mysterious pouch as a parting gift, as well as removing the block on her memories of the dreamscape with Bullet. They all come rushing in at once—Grace remembers everything. The four of them make their way out of the underworld through a cave, finding themselves in a remote corner of Greece. They eventually stumble upon a community of agathos and daimons living together, alongside Kakodaimonistai—humans who drink a hallucinogenic and can know about the other kinds of mortals who inhabit their world. Vasileios, the daimon leader of this ragtag group, invites them to stay, and once they hear Grace's story, they are all eager to help in the hopes of improving the lives of agathos and daimons. They make offerings and prayers to the Olympians to strengthen them through belief, hosting an orgy in Dionysus' honor.

DARE NOT

DARE NOT

STATE OF GRACE 4

COLETTE RHODES

CONTENT WARNING

Violence, Drug References,
Sexual Content, Grief

Do not go Gentle into that Good night

-DYLAN THOMAS

THE STORY SO FAR

Our angelic agathos, Grace, met bad boy daimon, Riot, outside a club in Milton—a daimon town she'd moved to in a bid to escape her overbearing parents and community. At age 25, Grace had expected to feel a pull towards her four agathos soul bonds by now, but it never came. Instead, she felt pulled to Riot, even though a connection between agathos, worshippers of Anesidora and servants of humanity, and daimons, worshippers of La Nuit and designed to lead humans astray, shouldn't be possible.

Grace's parents found out about Riot, and had Grace taken from her job at a shelter and dragged to the basement temple in Auburn for a cleansing ritual to break the connection. Riot was given instructions by the psychic daimon, Bullet, on where to find Grace. With assistance from one of her fathers, Riot rescues her from the agathos attempting to do a cleansing ritual and praying to bond her to recently widowed agathos men. They drive to Bullet's place, where Grace encounters her second soul bond for the first time.

While Riot is stuck working for the daimon, Viper, as part of a deal to keep Grace hidden, Grace gets to know Bullet. Bullet, as an Oneiroi, has known Grace her whole life. He has visited her dreams every night, and had thousands of "first meetings" with her that Grace doesn't remember. He teaches her about the true origins of the gods La Nuit (Nyx) and Anesidora (Gaia), and their feud. Grace is given a prophecy and tasked with bringing 'forth the Second Age of Heroes.'

Wild and Grace seal their bond, while the tentative feelings between Wild and Bullet grow. At the same time, tension comes to a head between Bullet and Riot, when Riot grows frustrated with Bullet's decision to keep Dare away. A plane crashes off the coast of Greece, which they later find out was carrying Dare, and the relationships grow more fraught, but there's no time to reflect on it because Gaia has set a plague of giant scorpions on Athens. Gaia possesses a local Basilinna, speaking through her body on live television, telling the humans that they enraged Gaia with their disrespect. Exposing agathos and daimons to the wider world, promising it will be made wonderful again when the daimons and their influence are eliminated.

Their group of allies rallies around Grace, and they all head into Athens together by bus. The scorpions won't attack the agathos, so Grace and the other agathos run off on their own, heading for the Temple of Zeus. Some enemy agathos have lined up in front of the temple, and Grace's side livestream what they're about to do. Grace steps forward alone, pulling out the pouch Persephone gave her and dropping the sharp seeds into the earth, little scratches on her hands mixing her own blood in with them. From the "seeds" grew a hundred Ancient Greek soldiers—the Spartoi—armed with spears and shields, who quickly dispatched the scorpions.

PROLOGUE

25 YEARS AGO

"It's a girl," the doctor pronounced cheerfully, holding up the bright red, squalling creature that was apparently, my daughter.

A daughter.

The bonds buzzed with excitement—Chance and Creed's, more than anyone—and I tried to temper my irritation before they caught onto it. It was the kind of thing that would upset them, and then I'd never hear the end of it. The bundled-up infant was placed on my chest, and I gave the doctor a brittle smile, my arms moving mechanically to hold the girl in place.

Grace. That was what we'd agreed to call her if we had a girl.

A swell of bitterness arose at my unanswered prayers. I'd begged Anesidora for a son. A son who would always love me, who would always feel some sense of loyalty to me. Even if he found his soul bond one day, she was only one woman. There would still be room for me in his life.

All I'd asked Anesidora for was a boy. It wasn't that much to ask, and I rarely asked for anything else. Why couldn't she have given me this *one* thing?

The girl in my arms would have many soul bonds, as agathos women did. What was the point in raising her, only to give her to her bonded when she reached maturity and never see her again? What was the point in investing in her future, when she'd only turn her back on us eventually? It was a waste. *She* was a waste.

A daughter was no *use* to me. To my family.

"Give Grace to me." Chance's voice was quiet and cold, the expression on his face making it obvious that I hadn't hidden my anger as well as I'd hoped to. I didn't protest, lifting my arms slightly so he could take her from me, while Earnest and Valor leaned in close, stroking my hair and whispering reassurances in my ear. Creed gave me a long, unreadable look, but the disapproval radiating through the bond made his feelings perfectly clear.

There was no point trying to appease Chance or Creed. They were perpetually let down by me, even though I was Anesidora's own gift to them. Perhaps their ungratefulness would lessen, now that I'd given them a child. Neither of *them* cared that it was a girl. They weren't smart enough to realize how pointless raising a daughter was, and I doubted they'd figure it out until she encountered her first soul bond. I made a note to myself to make them grovel for my forgiveness for the disrespectful looks they were giving me now.

"What can we do for you, my love?" Valor murmured, eager to soothe my irritation. "What do you need?"

1

I looked around the spare bedroom of my home in dismay, hating the clutter and assortment of things the agathos midwives had scattered everywhere. The baby had barely been here five minutes and she was already disrupting the neat order of my home.

Despite the number of people in the room, *no one* was paying me any attention. A few hours ago, I had been the center of everyone's focus, but now the baby was out, all anyone was interested in was *her*.

"I want to be alone to pray," I announced loudly, cutting a glare at Chance who was cradling the baby in his arms while Creed leaned over her, cooing like an idiot.

Embarrassing.

The birth team had made claims of patient confidentiality, but agathos traded in gossip. They'd probably leave here and tell the entire Auburn community how pathetic two of my bonded had been over the baby.

"You want to be... alone?" one of the midwives echoed, glancing between me and the baby. "If you'd like some quiet bonding time—"

"Alone," I repeated in a louder voice. Was that such a complicated request? "I want to be *alone*."

"Of course," Valor agreed quickly, pressing a kiss to my sweat-covered temple before ushering everyone out of the room. Chance and Creed walked out with the baby, and I supposed I'd need to remind them later about watching their emotional responses. They only had to experience *my* emotions, I had to experience it from all four of them. The least they could do was to be considerate of how they were feeling for my benefit.

I was too uncomfortable to move into a more respectable position, so I remained on the slippery but waterproof tarpaulin covering the bed, leaning back against the pillows with a thin sheet thrown over my legs for modesty, resenting both the indignity of childbirth and the fact that I didn't even have a son to show for it.

How many times would I have to do this to get a boy? It had been nice in the beginning. Everyone had treated me with such care and excitement when they found out I was expecting, but pregnancy was far

more miserable than I'd expected it to be, and my bonded hadn't truly appreciated how much I'd suffered.

Why was Anesidora punishing me? I'd done nothing to deserve this.

"Anesidora, Sender of Gifts," I began, tempering my anger and keeping my tone even. "Great *Mother*. I thank you for safely delivering me through the trial that is childbirth. I cannot understand why you saw fit to give me a daughter, but I suppose I have to trust that you know what you are doing and it will all make sense in time. It would be a kindness of you not to bring her soul bonds into her life during her teenage years, so she can at least be a daughter to me for that long," I added bitterly. I'd met Valor at age sixteen, and we'd moved into the flat underneath my parents' home in Saskatoon while we finished high school. I'd barely spent any time with my family from that point on. "Perhaps you aren't really listening and this is all in vain. To be an agathos is to sacrifice, after all, to be a woman, even more so—"

The baby made a shrieking sound from whatever room it was they'd taken her to, and I glared at the closed door at the intrusion into this moment of peace between me and my goddess.

"She'll learn," I muttered under my breath. "Someday, she'll make a simple, straightforward request that goes ignored, and she'll know what it is to truly be an agathos woman."

I blew out a long breath, getting my prayer back on track.

"While I consider pregnancy and childbirth to be an unpleasant and degrading process, I pray that you will ease my suffering by giving me sons from now on. I trust that you will do what is right and just, Anesidora, and only ask that you consider what a wonderful mother of boys I would be, and how well I would raise them to follow your light. *Láthe biōsas.*"

CHAPTER 2

"*You* are *mine*."

Grace's words hung in the air, too good to be true. I'd waited for so long, *wanted*, wondered, and here I was. Grace was mine.

My head spun with the overwhelming crush of emotion, of relief. Or maybe it was something else because my head was spinning *a lot*.

Grace climbed off Riot's lap, chewing the inside of her lip as she slowly approached me, glowing in the lamplight. Fuck, she was pretty. Even prettier than I'd thought based on the pictures and videos I'd seen—golden brown skin, shiny black hair that hung halfway down her back, a delicate heart-shaped jaw, and full soft lips that seemed in contrast to her solemn, world-weary eyes.

Opal eyes. Agathos eyes. They were a strange swirl of teal and lavender, flecked with gold. The same odd combination of eye colors that had glared at me in hatred these past few months while I defended my town and my kind from the angry agathos who'd raged against us. The same colors that my mother had probably seen before she died.

She's not like them. It's not the same.

Right?

Grace lifted her hand as though she was going to touch me, but froze in place, hesitating.

Not on my fucking watch. Wariness of agathos aside, I was going to make sure Grace knew she could touch me whenever she wanted. I was *desperate* for it. I closed the gap between us, the ground feeling weirdly unstable under my feet, and lightly cupped her elbow, running my hand up and down her arm, relishing the feel of her silken skin beneath my palm.

Moving slowly, giving her time to tell me to fuck off if she wanted to, I moved my other hand to her hair, brushing my fingers through it and baring her neck to me. Agathos weren't big on tattoos, so it didn't surprise me to see all that bare skin, but fuck if I didn't want to put my mark on that blank canvas. Would she let me?

Riot watched us from the bed, leaning back against the pillows, his entire body my practice ground for working with color. Bullet was downstairs, inked in tarot cards he'd seen in his visions that he'd only entrusted me to execute.

Grace and Wild had to wear my ink too. I needed that to happen, it was essential to my being.

"I want to kiss you," Grace whispered. "I want it so much, it's a little frightening. Is that okay?"

"That is the best thing I've ever heard." I closed the distance between us instantly, brushing my lips urgently over hers. I needed this like I needed oxygen, and I didn't care that I was probably coming off embarrassingly eager. I *was* embarrassingly eager.

Grace didn't hesitate, softly sucking my lower lip into her mouth, running her fingers through my hair, and holding my head firmly in place. It was more assertive than I'd expected her to be, but maybe she needed this as much as I did.

Though, maybe it was *me* doing that. To be a Philotes was to be a walking aphrodisiac. I hadn't expected my gifts to work on an agathos, but there was a definite hum of energy between us, a sexual chemistry that felt tangible. Maybe I was just romanticizing things because Grace tasted like sweetness and felt like a dream, and there was nothing wrong in the world while my lips were against hers.

No, life felt perfect. Wondrous. Warm and fuzzy and sort of hazy around the edges.

"You're so hot," Grace whispered, her lips moving against mine, hands cupping my cheeks. *Hell yeah, I am.*

Probably the Philotes magic at work again.

Riot chuckled. "You're bold today, Gracie. Is Dare bringing out your naughty side?"

"I don't mind," I told her, my tongue feeling weirdly thick and heavy.

"No, Riot, he's literally *hot*," Grace said, her voice taking on a decidedly more urgent, less sexy tone as she pressed her hand to my forehead. "He's burning up."

"What?" I laughed, moving my hands to Grace's shoulders to keep her steady as she swayed. "No, I'm fine. I feel great. We should kiss more. You just need to... stay... still—"

"Fuck, Dare!" Riot cursed, diving off the bed and hooking an arm around my waist before I flattened Grace. *Whoops.* She dragged one of my arms over her shoulders, and the two of them clumsily flopped me onto the mattress on my back, the impact making all of my injuries flare to life once

more. The adrenaline that had gotten me out of bed and through the agonizing drive to this place was fading, making all my aches and pains rise to the surface.

Gods fucking damn it.

I didn't want this. I wanted to have this big, romantic moment with Grace, one I'd barely let myself dream about, but noooooo.

The Philotes touch starvation I'd been fending off for months had been easing off slightly with Grace in my arms, but now it was back with a vengeance, burning under my skin. It hadn't felt this unbearable stateside, but having Grace just out of reach seemed to exacerbate it.

"It's going to be okay," she whispered softly, and I exhaled in relief at the feel of her hands all over me, checking for injuries. Just that small amount of contact calmed my racing heart while making it pound harder at the same time.

Shit, everything hurt.

I'd been in less pain at Jack's place. The adrenaline that had kept me going on the rough drive here was rapidly fading.

"You need a doctor. Or at least first aid. Someone here must know first aid, right?" Grace asked desperately, pushing my overlong hair out of my eyes and checking my temperature again. "Riot, he has a *fever*. What if it's an infection? We need medication!"

I tried to open my mouth, tried to tell Grace not to worry, that no stupid infection was going to beat me when we were finally so close to being together, but the only sound that came out was a very unsexy zombie groan.

"I'll go ask if anyone has medical knowledge," Riot replied instantly, the mattress shifting under his weight as he rushed off the bed. I heard the door shut quietly behind him, leaving Grace and me alone for the first time.

"I'm so sorry, Dare. I'm so, so sorry." Grace sniffled, her probing touch turning soft and soothing.

Another weird set of unintelligible noises came out of my mouth as I tried to soothe her. Grace's distress was so acute, I swore I physically *felt* her anxiety.

"You're hurt from the crash, but you should have never been on that plane," she replied vehemently. "You should have been with us. It's my fault you weren't. These injuries are because of me."

Her fingers ran through my hair again, and even though she was kind of bumping against a sore spot on the top of my skull, I didn't want her to stop. My thoughts were hazy, but there was a weird sense of wrongness about her words that I couldn't explain, even to myself. All I'd wanted for weeks was to meet Grace. I'd felt left out, resentful even. But now that I was here—despite how garbage I felt physically—it felt exactly *right*. Like everything had been building toward this moment, this meeting, this point in time.

Maybe the bitterness would come back later, but for now, it felt as though the Fates had laid out this path just for me.

Through the haze of pain and desire and the strange suffocating press of destiny weighing down on me, I wondered if that feeling was my own, or some weird side effect of Grace's gift. Of Grace, in general.

Before I could attempt to articulate my confusing thoughts, Riot returned with a human I didn't know, as well as Grace's other two bonded.

A *human*. Why was there a human here? I mean, I guessed after Grace's vlog, our kinds weren't as secretive as they once were, but it was still weird.

"Marek is a nurse," Riot said hesitantly, shoving the guy forward and flicking on the ceiling light, practically blinding me.

"A nurse with a very basic first-aid kit," Marek mumbled in a thick eastern European accent, cataloging my multitude of injuries. "Too basic for what he needs."

Riot shot the guy a death glare so impressive, even *I* got chills, and Marek hurriedly made his way over to me, digging into the first-aid kit as he went.

"He's got a fever. Should I get a cool cloth for his head?" Grace asked, sitting up on her knees, all business. It wasn't exactly how I envisioned our first time in bed together to be. I mean, she had been kneeling over me in all those fantasies, but usually with her thighs straddling my face.

"I'll do it," Riot offered, disappearing from the room.

"Please bring back a bowl of warm, soapy water!" Marek called after him, grimacing as he unwrapped the makeshift bandage on my arm. "Oh, this is definitely infected," he muttered under his breath.

Cool, cool, cool. That had been the injury I was *least* worried about. I thought if anything was going to take me out, it'd be the head wound.

Then again, I'd been barely conscious after getting myself cleaned up when I arrived at Jack's place, and he'd basically thrown me a bottle of bourbon and wished me luck. It wasn't like his place had been a paragon of cleanliness.

"What can I do to help?" Grace asked desperately.

"Pray, *Prophêtis*," Marek replied quietly. I watched upside down as Grace blinked at him, the suggestion clearly taking her by surprise. It didn't sound like a great option to me either—surely if the medical professional was suggesting *prayer* as a course of treatment, I was in even worse shape than I thought I was.

I wasn't lying on my deathbed right now, was I?

Maybe that sense of rightness was the light at the end of the tunnel.

"The gods have asked a lot of you," Marek continued. "Why not ask for something back?"

"You're right," Grace agreed, still stroking my hair though her hands were starting to tremble. "They *have* asked a lot of me. Of us. And I'm not going to do a single thing more for any of them until Dare is healed."

Riot returned and Grace laid a cold, wet cloth over my forehead. I sucked in a sharp breath as Marek started cleaning one of the wounds on my arm. *Shit*, that stung. *At what point was the numbness meant to set in? I could do with some numbness right now.*

"Not going to lie," I told them. "I don't feel great about fucking around with all-powerful deities. Maybe that's just a me thing."

"I have no idea what you just said, you sound like you're talking underwater. Or after downing a bottle of whisky," Riot replied apologetically. His hand came down on my good arm, pinning me in place when I instinctively tried to pull away from Marek's painful ministrations. "You gotta stay still, man. Let him work."

I nodded in agreement, but couldn't quite suppress the urge to try to escape the thing that fucking hurt. Bullet appeared over Grace's shoulder, looking down at me with a surprisingly distraught expression on his face. Had he not seen this coming?

"I can see you tried to clean the debris," Marek murmured. "But there's still some in here and the wound is closing. I'm going to need to reopen it to get the rest out."

Wild moved to the end of the bed, enormous hands clamping down on my shins, while Riot gave me an apologetic look, banding a forearm across my chest.

I wheezed at the pressure, trying in vain to get away while too weak to actually push him off.

"I'm sorry, but you need to stay put so Marek can pull the bits of fucking *aircraft* out of your arm." Riot sounded genuinely sorry, though that wouldn't stop me from socking him in the face if I'd had the energy.

Grace was mumbling something next to me, her voice low and fervent, and I did my best to look past the fiery pain in my arm to focus on what she was saying.

"*...I know you can heal him. We were healed in the underworld, I know it's possible. Please, Goddess Persephone, Queen of the Underworld—*"

Holy fuck balls, Grace was asking for help from the Queen of the Underworld? On my behalf?

I was grateful and horrified in equal measure. Marek sliced my arm open, ripping a chunk of something from the wound, and I decided I was more grateful than horrified. I didn't care who came to my aid, I just wanted this pain to stop.

"Deep breaths," Riot encouraged anxiously as my vision wavered.

"Just a couple... more..." Marek muttered. Grace switched tacks, finishing her prayer and starting another, though I wasn't sure who it was directed at. My blood was rushing in my ears, a blissful dampener that filtered out the worst of the panicked sounds of the room.

There was a sudden chill in the air, like someone had opened a freezer door directly above my entire body. Wild's hands disappeared from my legs, and everyone startled, shouting words I couldn't make out. People were moving, and I needed to sit up, to see what was going on. Riot leaned further over me, and Grace shuffled forward on her knees, blocking the doorway from view. She was shaking with nerves but steadied slightly as Bullet stood next to where she was on the mattress, wrapping an arm around her waist.

"Who are you?" Grace asked shakily. "How did you get in here?"

"Do you want me to waste time answering questions, or shall I get on with healing your soul bond?" The voice was strange, almost ethereal. I poked Riot in the back, trying to move him, but he wouldn't budge. "My sisters pooled the feeble remains of their magic to summon me a physical form, and it won't hold for long. If you were either wise or grateful, you'd visit my sisters' living tombs yourself."

Alright, I'm just going to assume I'm having some kind of hallucination.

"Please, just tell us *who* you are?" Grace rasped, hand shaking where she gripped my own. "Please. We're trusting you with Dare's life."

"And so you should. I am Hygeia, there is no one better equipped to heal him."

Grace sucked in a startled breath. *Hygeia?* Was she some kind of goddess?

"Hygeia... the agathos?" Grace confirmed hesitantly. "Like an *original* agathos? How is that possible?"

"With great difficulty, since most of our gifts have been channeled into our descendents. You're acquainted with Sophia, of course. She's been whispering her wisdom in your ears whenever she's been able to. Now, move, if you want me to fix him."

"Dare?" Grace asked softly, looming over me, her long, black hair brushing against my face. "Is that okay? I want you to be healed, but it's your body. You need to decide."

"I am the spirit of good health, what exactly do you think I'm going to do to him?" Did divinities roll their eyes? It *sounded* like she was rolling her eyes.

"Unf," I replied, nodding my head slightly so she'd know it was an agreement.

Grace nodded silently, encouraging everyone to move back so Hygeia could approach. I clung to Grace's fingers for as long as I could, feeling needy as fuck at how bereft I was to no longer be holding her hand. Finally, I got a glimpse of the goddess in question and was struck by how incredibly ordinary she was.

Hygeia was at least six feet tall, slim, and draped in an elaborate-looking dark-blue toga thing. She looked middle-aged, with severe features and frown lines around her brow and mouth, and her dark hair was pulled back into a tight bun.

The only thing goddess-y about her was her haunting voice and Stone Age fashion. Aside from that, she looked very much like the terrifying librarian who'd always caught Riot and me smoking behind the building in high school.

Hygeia glared down at me, cataloging my injuries as though they caused her personal offense. "Mortals can be trying, ungrateful creatures. I could abide Gaia's indifference to them, but I cannot abide her cruelty. We are not quite as bound to serve in the way our descendents are, but we aren't immune from that call either."

And with that strange speech, she clamped her hand down hard on my leg sending a shot of blindingly hot pain upwards from where she touched me. I arched off the bed, mouth open on a silent scream as pure agony traveled through every inch of my body, far worse than the pain I'd been in before.

This wasn't worth it. Nothing was worth this. I tried to find the words to stop it, to tell her to leave, but suddenly the world was spinning, the colors all morphing into a swirl of blissful darkness.

GRACE

CHAPTER 3

Bullet wrapped both arms around my waist, struggling to hold me back as Dare went limp. If I weren't so terrified for Dare, I'd have realized how easily I slipped out of Bullet's weak embrace.

Wild stepped in front of me before I could get to Dare, raising an eyebrow at me before lifting me clean off the ground so I was watching Hygeia work over his back. Nothing about Wild's hold on me was weak, and after a quick struggle, I rested my chin on his shoulder, slumping against him to wait for Hygeia to finish doing what she was doing.

"It's probably better this way," Bullet murmured, stepping up next to me and shooting me an apologetic grimace. "At least he's not in any pain right now."

I wasn't sure I believed that. Hygeia's magic seemed to travel through Dare's veins, lighting them up a disturbing shade of silver that glowed from the inside out. We should have asked more questions, should have found out exactly what she intended to do to him.

Should have found out how it was she even *existed*, though perhaps that was a question I should have been asking myself sooner. Thanatos was an original daimon, and we'd met him, though he resided in the safe haven that was the underworld. There must be others down there, other daimons like the ones from the mural painted on the ceiling of Hades and Persephone's palace.

Had the agathos been here all along? Did they have a realm of their own to hide away in? I couldn't imagine them in the underworld. In my agathos classes, the founders of our lines were treated more as *spirits* than physical beings. There were shrines to them and visiting them was encouraged as a spiritual experience, but we never *worshipped* them, only Anesidora.

Should we have been worshipping them? Or at least paying them some kind of respect? Unease slithered down my spine at the way I'd always felt and talked about my own gift. If Eutychia suddenly appeared, I doubted she'd be happy to see me.

"It was a good thing you got all the shards out of his arm," Hygeia said casually, the silvery light emanating from Dare's body illuminating her in the most ominous way. "I was waiting until you finished that to arrive. You did a not entirely unimpressive job with that, human."

Marek made a strangled noise from the corner he'd retreated to when Hygeia arrived, gripping the wall behind him with both hands, eyes wide with fear.

"Sophia won't be able to speak to you all now," she continued, hand still pulsating with power where it rested on Dare's leg. Hygeia paused for a moment, giving me a guarded look. "Not without your help, at least. Should you succeed in fulfilling the prophecy, the true agathos will be free to walk among mortals once more, in some form or another. The Olympians are not the only deities imprisoned, they're just the only ones in a cell."

I nodded mutely, unsure how to respond to that. Just what kind of world would we be creating if we succeeded in our task? Visions of nymphs sunbathing on rocks and drunken satyrs in the forests filled my head.

"Well, that will have to do," Hygeia announced, the silver fading from Dare's veins as her own form flickered in and out. "I have run out of energy. He will live, as will the sacrifice."

My head shot up, and I wriggled free of Wild's hold. "What sacrifice?"

Hygeia gave me a sly smile that sent chills down the back of my spine. "To be an agathos is to sacrifice, is it not? I'm immortal, I cannot take his poor health onto myself, so instead it went to a proxy. They'll be fine, no need to concern yourself."

She flickered in and out of sight again while icy terror spread through my entire body. Dare's injuries had been *life-threatening,* and the idea of inflicting them on someone else was appalling.

My bonded all felt remarkably calm about this—a reminder of their daimonic nature. The small amount of compassion they'd acquired in comparison to other daimons rarely extended beyond our little group.

"I believe *thank you* is what you meant to say," Hygeia huffed, flickering out of sight. Her disembodied voice spoke, making us all startle. "Sophia has watched over you so far, and she gave everything she had left to get me here. Perhaps you could return the favor—you would be safe with my sisters."

With that, her divine presence vanished with a silent rush of air, sucking the chill she'd brought with her out of the room as she went.

"What the fuck," Riot breathed, rubbing his temples. Marek backed slowly out the door, clutching the first-aid kit to his chest like a shield. "I don't even know where to begin with that. But Dare is okay now. Right?"

"I... I think so."

Dare's breathing was quiet and steady, the wounds and bruises that had littered his skin were gone, leaving behind streaks of dried blood. I moved to the edge of the bed, tracing a smudged line with my finger.

I can't believe I kissed him.

He was mine to kiss, my soul bond, and I'd felt immediately territorial the moment I saw him. But he was also in no state to be making out with, and I should have realized that instantly. The past few days of worrying about him while we tried to track him down after the plane crash had clouded my judgment.

Wild rapped his knuckles against the wall to get my attention before tipping his chin at something out the narrow window. Riot walked around the bed to investigate. It was after midnight, but they both looked energized and raring to go, while I felt ready to go into hibernation.

"I'm guessing that's Dare's ride. Shall we head down and say hello?" Riot asked Wild, a mildly threatening note in his voice.

"Be nice," I reminded them both as Wild nodded, crossing his arms over his chest, biceps straining against the too-small cotton shirt he was wearing. "That might be Dare's friend."

"*I'm* Dare's friend," Riot replied a little petulantly. Bullet and I discreetly exchanged amused looks. Apparently, I wasn't the only one possessive over Dare.

"You should rest with him," Riot continued, sidling up next to me and gently guiding me onto the bed. "Philotes daimons need physical touch, and I doubt he's been getting enough. Besides, you're exhausted."

A brief thought that I *hoped* he hadn't been drowning in physical touch flashed through my mind before I suppressed it, disgusted with myself for my selfishness. I immediately laid down next to my unconscious fourth mate, resting my head on the bicep of his outstretched arm but leaving a couple of inches of space between our bodies, not wanting to overstep when we'd just met.

"I'm sure after he sleeps it off a little, he'll be okay," Bullet said reassuringly as Riot and Wild silently left the room. I looked back at him, noting not for the first time how incredibly exhausted he seemed. He'd always been pale, but his skin had taken on a grayish pallor, his usually sparkling purple eyes were duller than usual, and the dark circles beneath them were beginning to look like bruises.

"You need to sleep too," I replied softly, patting the bed next to me. Bullet glanced guiltily at Dare, but I felt his resolve crumble in real-time through the bond.

He climbed up behind me, shuffling slightly lower on the mattress so his head didn't brush Dare's outstretched arm, before burying his face between my shoulder blades. The past couple of days had been fraught— Riot and I had been so consumed in our worry for Dare that I'd neglected Bullet and Wild a little. Not to mention the tension between Riot and Bullet that I *really* hoped they'd resolve now that Dare was here.

Bullet was relieved too—I could feel his gratitude and affection pouring through the bond.

"I love you too," I whispered, hearing the silent words through his emotions. We were all here, we were all together. It hadn't been an easy journey to get to this point, but we'd made it.

Growing into our new dynamics would take time and patience, but I was determined to see it through. Determined that now we were all together, nothing would tear us apart.

This place is beautiful, I thought to myself, glancing around the blooming garden I was standing in. The white pergola above me provided shade from the blisteringly bright sunshine, lush purple wisteria hanging over the edges slightly obscuring the view.

This was a new dreamscape scene. Bullet had been busy.

"Bullet? Where are you?"

"Right here, Amazing Grace." He appeared in front of me out of nowhere, and I jumped, clutching my hand to my chest. "I didn't mean to scare you—I was seeing if Mercy was asleep. I thought you'd like to check on her."

"Is she?" I asked, not letting myself get my hopes up.

Bullet grimaced, shaking his head. "Either she doesn't sleep a lot, or she's medicating. She is Dare-level difficult to track down in the dreamscape."

"I guess there'd be no use visiting Dice's dreams, I doubt he knows

anything about where Mercy is," I sighed, unnecessarily smoothing down the pale blue sundress I was wearing.

"Probably not," Bullet agreed, cocking his head to the side. He looked so much healthier here—like he had when I'd met him. And he was dressed in dark gray slacks and a matching waistcoat, with a cream shirt underneath, sleeves rolled up to the elbows. The elegant, dressy style he'd favored before we were snatched away to the underworld and spat out on a whole different continent with nothing to our names.

Seeing Bullet here and healthy made the contrast between awake and asleep that much starker.

"I wonder..." Bullet mused, grabbing my hips and pulling me against him, drumming absently over my waist. "Want to go exploring, Amazing Grace? It might not lead anywhere, but by the sounds of it, Mercy is at some kind of agathos settlement and I wouldn't be able to get in their heads even if I did know them. Don't worry, I'll make sure to boot you out of the dreamscape when I feel Dare wake up."

I went up on my tiptoes to brush a soft kiss on his lips. "Thank you."

"Anything for you." Bullet winked. There was a pang in my chest at his easy demeanor, the clear weight off his shoulders at being in this realm versus the discomfort he was carrying around in the real world.

"Don't look at me like that, Amazing Grace," Bullet whispered, pulling me against his body and burying his face in the crook of my neck. "I know I'm being selfish, and I know you can't lie, but can you try to give me your smiles? I want to memorize every single one."

Before I could respond—or worse, cry—the dreamscape was dissolving around us, and I held on tight to Bullet as he carried me wherever we were going, forcing my emotions down so I could focus on the task at hand.

We materialized in a grungy bar—mostly black except for the exposed brick walls, with sad rock songs blaring from a speaker in the corner. Viper sat at the bar in a dark leather jacket and white tee, staring into a glass of amber liquid, the light catching on the two deep scars that bisected one eye.

With his chin-length, slicked-back brown hair, and permanently disdainful expression, I struggled to describe him as 'handsome', but he was certainly interesting to look at. Then again, most daimons were. It was part of how they lured humans into their orbit.

"Well, this place is sad," Bullet announced loudly. Viper didn't so much as twitch, so I guessed Bullet was keeping us hidden from view. "You should know that Viper isn't going to be happy to see me in his dreams. He doesn't explicitly know it was me who haunted his sleep so badly one night that he pissed himself, but he's probably figured it out."

My lips twitched in spite of myself. I probably shouldn't feel as ambivalent about Bullet's nighttime torturing session as I did. It was very un-agathos of me.

The door to the bar opened and I nearly swallowed my tongue when my cousin walked in. It wasn't quite Mercy. It was how Viper remembered her, which was probably why she had a far more somber, wide-eyed look on her face than she usually wore in real life. Well, before everything that had happened; maybe this was what she looked like now, how she'd looked to him.

Mercy used to smile a lot back before life had gotten so complicated.

Viper glanced up at her, clearly fighting to keep his eyes on her face. I supposed, to his credit, he hadn't imagined my eighteen-year-old cousin in lingerie or anything like that. She was wearing fitted jeans with rips at the knees, black converse shoes, and a white V-neck tee, loosely tucked in at the waist.

Not an outfit I'd ever seen her in before, but then maybe she'd worn something like this when he'd driven her out of town? Her thick dark curls bounced around her shoulders with each step, but the most jarring thing was the burn mark on her cheek where the bullet had grazed her at the community center that day.

That scar had never featured in how I remembered Mercy, but it was prominent in Viper's version of her.

"Viper," Dream Mercy said, her voice uncannily accurate.

"You're too young to be in a bar," he replied, turning his gaze back to his glass.

"Oh shit," Bullet laughed. "Did we walk in on the beginning of a sex dream with your cousin? I gotta be honest, Amazing Grace, I'm zapping us out of here if either of them start stripping."

"She's eighteen," I hissed, trying to decide if we should unveil ourselves or leave and pretend this never happened. "How old is Viper?"

"Thirty. And feeling some kind of way about it, apparently," Bullet replied, snorting. I wrinkled my nose as Dream Mercy climbed onto the barstool next to Viper, keeping a notable amount of distance between them.

"Unveil us before this gets even more weird," I told Bullet, elbowing him lightly in the ribs. I didn't know how to feel about what I was seeing—it wasn't sexual, and he'd already informed us in person that they weren't soul bonds, but there was a strange undercurrent of something that I couldn't quite put my finger on.

Longing, perhaps?

The explanation that I was most comfortable with was that Viper felt some sense of kinship with Mercy. It was probably wishful thinking.

Viper's head shot up as Bullet revealed our presence, Dream Mercy flickering into nothingness. The guilty look on his face morphed into a fierce scowl. "Get the fuck out of my brain, Bullet. Take your agathos with you."

"Jealous?" *Bullet taunted.* "Looks like you were just dreaming about having an agathos of your own."

Viper's knuckles turned white where he was gripping the glass. "And spend my days fucking some pillow princess through a hole in a sheet? Sharing her with a bunch of other dudes? Nah, I'm good."

I sucked in a shocked, slightly insulted breath, but Bullet's charming smile didn't falter for a second. "I'm going to trap you in a nightmare so terrible you'll be too scared to ever fall asleep again. Though I suppose I could go a little easier on you if you tell us something useful about Mercy's whereabouts—who she's with, what she's doing, that sort of thing. Something that'll ease my sweet, sexy-as-fuck agathos' mind."

"I don't know anything," *Viper gritted out.*

"Unfortunate," *Bullet replied, taking a step backward and dragging me along with him.* "I wonder if you're still scared of spiders the size of buses trying to eat you..."

Surely, there wasn't any being on earth who wasn't afraid of that?

"Don't be an asshole, Bullet. I already told you that I made a deal with her," *Viper snapped.* "I can't tell you where she's gone or anything she shared with me."

25

"I know how deals work, Viper, though don't pretend like you have a perfect track record at upholding your end of the agreement. You can't tell us what you knew then, but you can tell us what you've learned since."

Viper scoffed. "You're overestimating my abilities. The agathos she's with runs a tight ship."

Harbor? That was who Mercy had mentioned being with. Felix Lyon's brother who'd been sent on an outreach trip to Russia when he'd never found his soul bond, but had somehow ended up in Maine.

"All I can tell you is that she's still where I left her, and that Dice is still looking for her, but he's completely off-track. That's all I know, okay?"

"Boo, you're no fun," Bullet sighed. "Enjoy the spiders, fuckface."

"Bullet!" I gasped as we withdrew, reappearing in the startlingly peaceful spring meadow. "Are you actually going to do that?"

He looked at me, tilting his head to the side, squinting as though he wasn't quite sure what the right answer was. "Do you not want me to?"

"No! Of course not."

"Fine, fine." Bullet groaned dramatically, flopping back onto the grass with an arm thrown over his eyes to block out the sunlight. "I'll leave Viper to his normal dreams. Maybe he'll conjure Mercy up again and they'll pick up where they left off—"

"Okay, just send a few spiders," I interrupted, my face heating. "Regular-sized ones. And not too many, just enough to, you know. Put him off."

"There won't be any sex dreams with your cousin happening on my watch," Bullet replied with a mischievous grin, giving me a salute. "Come on, Dare is stirring."

MERCY

CHAPTER 4

What had I been doing?

Beds. I'd been making beds. Changing the sheets after our last lot of guests—a human family with adorable twin girls—had vacated The Bunkhouse. And then I was going to tidy up The Guesthouse, wasn't I? Yes. The party staying there had requested cleaning services, but Harbor and a couple of the other boys had taken them out on the lake to fish for trout and I'd volunteered to clean up while they were out.

So why was I lying on the floor of The Bunkhouse, feeling like I was dying?

Everything hurt—especially my head—though my arm was definitely hurting the most of all. And despite it being fall in Maine, I was sweating through my jeans and hoodie. I tried to lift my arm, but the agony was too much to bear. Eventually, I managed to turn my head to the side, glancing down the line of my body. The sleeve of my favorite hoodie—the white one with daisies and pastel-colored jack-o'-lanterns on the front that Harbor had chosen for me because he knew I loved Halloween—was stained red with blood.

Great, I thought, my brain hazy. I was never going to be able to get that out. And I loved this sweater. It wasn't like I had a lot of clothes to begin with—all the boys shared, and they'd gone out of their way to get me a few things of my own. And I'd gone and got blood all over it like a total idiot.

You are useless. A stupid, useless imposition. You should have never come here. You've made everyone's lives worse.

"Mercy! No, no, no, what is happening? Pax, get the first-aid kit. Or an ambulance. What do we do? We can't go to the human doctors..." Harbor's panicked voice seemed so far away.

I didn't like when Harbor sounded worried. He'd been so good to me, the *best*. He'd taken me in and given me a job here at the campsite he and some other agathos ran to hide in plain sight from the communities that had sent them away. The boys who'd never felt the pull of the soul bond and so had been ostracized, kicked out to preserve the image of perfect harmony that the agathos liked to pretend they had.

The six of them had accepted me with no judgment, even when they knew I had a daimon soul bond out there, hunting me down, and I'd worked *so* hard to prove to them that letting me stay wasn't a mistake.

And now I was ruining it all, getting bloodstains on the carpet that would probably never come out. We had guests checking in tonight, I didn't have *time* for this.

"I'll clean the floor," I slurred. Why did my voice sound like that? "Don't be upset, Harbor, please. I'll clean the blood."

He abruptly stopped issuing panicked instructions to Pax. "You think... You think I'm worried about the *bloodstains*? Are you serious?"

"I'm making a mess, I'm ruining everything. I don't even know how this happened," I all but wailed. "And I'm so *hot*."

"You have a fever," Harbor replied, his voice softer this time. "Come on, let's get this sweater off. Did you use your gifts?"

"On a stabbing victim?" Pax added helpfully.

"I didn't, I swear." I knew my words meant less than any other agathos' since lying was more of a discomfort than a hard limit for me, but I'd promised Harbor I'd do everything in my power not to use my Hygeia ability. I'd slipped up once, speeding up the healing of a human child who'd fallen on the rocky shoreline and gotten an impressively long gash on their leg. But other than that, I'd been good. I tried so hard. We couldn't afford the attention that an agathos with the gift of Hygeia would bring. "Harbor, I promise—"

"I believe you," he cut in. I stifled a sob as he sliced through the fabric of my hoodie, wondering if I could stitch it back together. Harbor had given me this when I'd had nothing, showing up empty-handed at the gates of the campsite after getting off the bus, begging for sanctuary. The wound on my face had been fresh and disgusting, and I'd been a total emotional wreck who hadn't slept in days, and all Harbor had asked in return for me staying was my story. He'd never judged me, never held my ability to lie against me, defended me when the other guys had said anything about my abilities or my past.

If I could have chosen a soul bond, it would have been him. But I couldn't. I could never have him, and so I treasured the clothes he'd given me and the little things he did for me instead, pretending it meant something more than it ever could.

Hale's voice joined in the chorus of worry as he deposited a first-aid kit on the floor, letting Pax get to work, bandaging my arm up tight, staunching the blood flow.

"These aren't your injuries," Harbor pointed out gently. "It looks like that wound on your leg did, that time you used your gift on the child. Too neat, too clean and perfect."

I nodded weakly. We all knew injuries I'd gained myself didn't look so tidy, didn't heal away to nothingness. The ugly scar on my face was proof of that.

"So, what, someone else's wounds just popped up on Mercy's body out of nowhere?" Hale asked, voice laced with disbelief. He was older than the others, and my ability to lie made him wary.

"Is that so hard to believe?" Harbor challenged, stroking my hair back from my forehead with long, gentle fingers. "Hygeia are rare. Maybe this was Anesidora's doing. Maybe she wanted to heal one of her loyal Basilinna's and used Mercy's gift to do it?"

"You're right. Of course, you're right," Hale replied immediately, his voice deferent. Harbor may have been younger than Hale, but everyone respected him and treated him as a leader of sorts. Not because he was loud and bossy like the agathos leaders I'd known tended it to be, but because he was calm and assertive.

Harbor always knew what to do.

"We saw her cousin grow *Spartoi* just a few days ago," Harbor continued thoughtfully. "Anesidora sent giant, monstrous scorpions out of the ground to do her will. Who's to say she didn't have a hand in this also?"

I swallowed back the same bitter jealousy that rose up every time the outcast agathos here talked about Grace in hushed, reverent tones. It was wrong of me to feel jealous. I didn't envy what Grace was going through— not really. But we were cousins, we'd been as close as sisters, and we were both cursed to be broken agathos, ruined in the eyes of our community.

So why wasn't she as unhappy as me?

I'd watched the viral videos of her taking on goddesses and angry agathos while I hid away here, cleaning cabins and battling nightmares, and wondered how our paths had gone in such wildly different directions.

"You have a fever," Harbor murmured, his palm feeling like a sheet of ice where it pressed to my forehead.

"I'll be okay," I assured him. *Reminded* him. Wounds I inherited from others would heal without medical intervention, though it cost me a little of my own life each time. With each healing, my time here on this earth grew shorter.

I thought being a Hygeia was the worst thing that had ever happened to me. And then I almost got my soul bond killed with my cowardice. I deserved to be a Hygeia. I deserved every day that I lost.

"You were making beds," Harbor mumbled to himself, stroking my hair in the most dreamy, inappropriate way. He hadn't been given to me by the goddess. He'd been given no soul bond at all. I shouldn't let him touch me, but I just couldn't seem to help myself. Harbor was the only light in my life, the only one who didn't look at me and see the scarred, ruined agathos. The one who'd listened to the Basilinna and the Elders and fought back against the supposedly evil daimons, and who'd sacrificed her own soul bond in the process.

I sat somewhere in the middle of failed hero and complete monster, depending on who you asked.

"Making beds, with no one else around," Harbor muttered. "No one should have been able to hurt you. What are we going to do, Mercy? If I can't keep you safe here, I can't keep you safe anywhere."

GRACE

CHAPTER 5

I awoke with a start, immediately shaking off the remnants of the dreamscape as Dare groaned next to me. I had no idea how long we'd been asleep, but it must have been a while. Sunrise filtered through the window, and I could hear the clinking of pots and pans coming from the kitchen below as the Kakodaimonistai shuffled around, preparing breakfast.

Bullet slid off the bed, shooting me a wink as he quietly crept out of the room. Wild stood, having apparently been watching over us from a chair in the corner as we slept. Cute.

'*You okay?*' he signed, glancing between me and Dare.

I nodded as I responded. '*I need to talk to him.*'

'*I'll bring you food,*' Wild replied, before slipping silently out the door behind Bullet. His ability to move quietly despite his daunting size never ceased to amaze me.

"Well, I feel like shit," Dare rasped, massaging his eyelids with his thumb and middle finger. My cheek was still pressed against his bicep, and now that the immediate chaos had subsided, I felt the beginnings of the bond between us starting to blossom with the physical contact. "This is not how I wanted to meet you, Grace. I'm sorry."

"Don't apologize. What can I do?" I asked quietly, wriggling further into his side instinctively. "Do you need me to get Marek back? I'd hoped most of your injuries would be healed—"

"Oh they are, I think," Dare assured me, wrapping his arm around my shoulders and pulling me closer until my head rested on his chest. "I haven't slept or eaten much recently though, and my inner Philotes is acting up," he added with a quiet laugh.

"Can I..." I trailed off, swallowing thickly. I didn't have the best track record when it came to immediate physical intimacy with my soul bonds. For one reason or another, we'd always ended up putting it off. Pretty often that reason had been me and my inability to get out of my own head.

I didn't want to repeat those mistakes with Dare for a whole host of reasons, but especially because we'd missed so much time together already. Guilt that I'd put this off competed with the fresh wave of guilt that I was happy he was here, because it meant Bullet took one step closer to...

No, I wasn't ready to think about that. I wouldn't ever be ready to think about that.

"Can you what?" Dare prompted, shifting slightly so he could look down at me. My hand moved before I'd even consciously decided to move it, tracing the matching rose designs that were inked on his skin, trailing up either side of his neck. Dare groaned, arching into my touch. "Shit, you should know that Philotes daimons are touch addicts, and I haven't been touched a lot lately. That feels really good and soothing, and I don't want to make it weird but I *might* come in my pants if you keep going."

A surprised laugh escaped me, my fingers stilling for a moment, resting over his thrumming pulse. "I was going to ask if I could touch you, but I seem to have lost control of my limbs."

"You don't have to ask," Dare replied, his voice dropping slightly. "And I still feel like total shit, so I'm not suggesting anything more than a cuddle right now, but if you're comfortable with it, I'd really like to take my shirt off. I mean, it's kind of bloody so I don't want to wear it, but also the more skin to skin, the better."

"Oh, of course!" I sat up instantly, while Dare moved much slower, pushing up on his forearms until he could yank his tee over his head and collapse back onto the mattress. For a moment, I stayed where I was, staring down at the canvas of his body and marveling at his extensive tattoos. They were symmetrical, each side of his body a mirror reflection of the other. The designs all seemed to be nature-inspired—flowers, waves, flames, all converging and intertwining over his skin.

"My sleeve," Dare groaned, holding up what had been his injured arm, the design now interrupted by a jagged scar. Just the effort of raising his arm had his muscles shaking, and I hoped Wild returned with food for him soon. "Then again, a scar is better than being dead."

"Definitely better than that," I agreed, lying down next to him again and draping my bare arm over his stomach. Should I take my top off too? Was that too forward? "So, um, tell me about yourself?" I winced at the awkward question.

Dare laughed tiredly. "Right, this is kind of our first date, huh? Shit, look at me, immediately taking off my clothes. Way to be a gentleman, Dare."

I turned my face into his chest, smiling against his skin, letting the sense of warmth and rightness of having Dare here wash over me. This wasn't like the rush or uncertainty of meeting Riot, or the confusion and longing of meeting Bullet, or the frustration that had accompanied meeting Wild. The circumstances were terrible and the guilt was crushing, but being in Dare's presence felt like coming home.

"Would you rather sleep some more? Wild is going to bring up some breakfast soon."

"I'll try to stay awake," Dare replied around a yawn. "I don't *want* to sleep—I want to spend time with you. I've been wondering what it would be like for so long, sleep feels wasteful."

Swoop went my belly, a sudden round of butterflies taking me by surprise. Despite the weirdness of the situation and the fact that after so many delays, Dare had gotten here and promptly almost died during our first kiss, I decided to try to treat this as if it wasn't abnormal. As if we were just two regular soul bonds meeting for the first time, out on a private date away from my other bonded so we had time to get to know each other.

For the most part, I hadn't felt like I'd missed out on any agathos experiences—most of them weren't worth having—but the process of dating a new soul bond and integrating them into the group was one of them.

"How'd you get the name 'Dare'?" I asked, voice muffled by his chest. I exhaled softly as he ran his fingers gently through my hair.

"It's very unexciting—I just couldn't say no to dares when I was younger. It was mostly Riot's doing," he snorted. "Daimons aren't particularly attentive students, and it was a way for us to kill time in high school. My mom hated it. Both the dares and the nickname."

I swallowed thickly, stiffening against him despite my best intentions at the casual mention of his mother. I had to tell him, though. Not just because I was an agathos who couldn't lie, but because I got the feeling that I'd caused Dare a lot more pain than he'd ever let on, and I didn't want to cause him any more.

"I met her."

"You met who?" Dare asked absently, combing through my hair with his fingers.

"Your mother. Ruby. I met her."

Dare's hand stilled, his brows furrowing as he stared down at me.

"When?"

My bonded downstairs must have been picking up on my nerves; pulses of love and reassurance surrounded me from three sides, but it only made the stark emptiness of the fourth spot where Dare belonged stand out in sharper relief.

"The day she died. I met her in the underworld, in the palace of Hades. I didn't understand why Queen Persephone had wanted me to meet her at first, but now I do." I exhaled shakily, remembering the shrewd look Ruby had given me before we parted. "I think your mom knew, or at least she hoped, that you were mine. Or someone's. She said she hoped you found an agathos soul bond of your own one day, and that you'd be good to her."

Dare made a strangled sound and I tightened my grip around his middle, needing to offer him comfort somehow, even though I was the one upsetting him.

"I don't know. That sounds too nice to be my mom," he said with a watery laugh. "Maybe you met someone else."

"Maybe," I agreed. I could have been wrong, but I felt like it was her. "She said... she said that her son was a good son, though maybe not a very good daimon, and that she preferred him that way. And that she should have told him that." I took another steadying breath, my voice wavering as I spoke. I didn't want to cry—this was about Dare, and I didn't want him to feel obligated to comfort me. "She called him a 'mother hen of a daimon.'"

A startled laugh burst out of Dare at that, his body shaking against mine. "Okay, that's definitely my mom, she's been telling me shit like since I was old enough to speak." He shook his head slightly, and I understood his disbelief because sometimes I struggled to comprehend my life too.

"I was always pretty weird for a Philotes daimon—for a daimon in general—and she never quite knew what to do with me," Dare explained, his voice wistful. "I hung around her more than most daimon kids do with their parents. Cared about her more than most daimon kids cared about their parents. It wasn't in her nature to accept that care, she didn't know what to do with it, but she didn't outright dislike it either."

Throwing caution to the wind, I nestled fully into his side draping my leg over his and resting my head over his pounding heartbeat.

"It sounds like she appreciated you a lot, even if she didn't always know how to articulate that. We're a generation of experiments, the Fates trying to figure out what to do with us, how to bring agathos and daimons together.

I'm not sure they intended it to cause such friction with our elders, but it has," I sighed. "Not everyone, of course. Plenty of my old agathos friends back in Auburn seemed to have good relationships with their parents."

"What about you?" he asked, squeezing me close though I could tell that even that small gesture cost him energy he didn't have. "What's your relationship with your family like? You have a lot of parents, right?"

I laughed quietly. "I suppose so. By daimon or human standards, at least. Four dads, one mom. I have two little brothers too. And one of my cousins lived with us; she was like a sister to me."

"Mercy," Dare replied instantly. It was strange to hear Dare say my cousin's name like he knew her, but I guessed gossip spread fast. "Her soul bond, Dice, got me out of a tricky spot recently. He came across me while he was looking for her. He's *still* looking for her."

"I don't know how much success he'll have with that. She made a deal with Viper to hide her." I caught Dare up on that day at the community center, before launching into an explanation of everything that had happened since. Every weird, unbelievable moment that had been my life. Dare listened quietly, occasionally asking questions but mostly just stroking my hair.

"So what happens from here?" he asked when I'd caught him up, finally pausing to take a breath. "It wasn't exactly hard to track you guys down, so anyone with bad intentions could do the same. Not just the agathos, but humans too. I'd like to think you'd be safe from them, but change freaks people out, you know?"

"I know," I sighed. "It would be nice to stay in one place, but I don't think this is it. Vasileios and the others should go back to Leonidio—they *want* to go back there. It's a safe haven of sorts, protected by the gods of the underworld. We're too exposed here. But there's the Spartoi, I don't know what to do with them. And us..."

I trailed off, mulling over Hygeia's words. The true agathos, the originals, had offered us a safe place. While Hygeia hadn't been particularly pleasant, Sophia's wisdom had helped me out of a few sticky situations now, and I trusted her.

More than just being a safe space though, it *could* be a strong message of condemnation to the mortal agathos at how far they'd fallen from the original ideals of the founders of our lines. Yes, they were following Gaia's lead and I could sort of understand why they'd feel righteous in their actions—they were sanctioned by a goddess. Except, it fell apart under the smallest amount of critical thought and slightest application of empathy.

Gaia was scrambling to retain the power she'd fought the Olympians for all those years ago, and promptly done nothing with. When the world around us had started falling apart from neglect, her response had been

to make things worse out of spite, because she felt as though she hadn't received the worship and respect she was due.

Maybe once upon a time, that was true. Us mortals *hadn't* been as careful with the gift of earth that Gaia had given us as we should have been. But disappearing completely and then returning in a rage, ready to destroy everything wasn't the solution. Gaia had fought for the power she wielded over mortals, taken it from the gods who'd *wanted* the responsibility, and imprisoned them.

For what?

It felt frustrating and wasteful. Unnecessarily dramatic, even. There was so much suffering, and for what?

"You okay, Grace?" Dare asked, reminding me that I'd been silent for a long time, lost in my thoughts.

"Sorry, yes. After you, um, passed out, Hygeia suggested we go to the home of the original agathos, that we would be safe there."

"You'd rather go there than Leonidio?" Dare's fingers burrowed through my hair, idly massaging the back of my neck, and I nearly groaned at the contact.

I wasn't sure he *meant* for it to be sexual, and it really wasn't the time, but there was an innate kind of sexuality to Dare that made my knees go weak. Maybe because he was a Philotes daimon?

"Yes and no. I don't want to put the others in danger, and ultimately the prophecy was for me, not them. There's going to come a point where I have to do this on my own."

"Never on your own," Dare replied, gripping my chin and guiding my face up to his. "I know we just met and this is all kind of weird and happening at warp speed, but if there's one thing I know, it's that you don't ever have to face the world alone, Grace. You're too loved for that."

"You're kind of a sweet talker, huh?" I whispered, my lips drawn toward his as though we were being magnetically pulled together. Dare's fingers were still massaging hypnotizing circles at the base of my neck, and somehow I felt that small amount of contact *everywhere*.

Dare smirked, lips brushing teasingly over mine, just a whisper of a kiss. A promise. I wanted the bond so bad that I could almost see the missing thread between us forming, reaching for him, eager to intertwine our souls.

The door opened and we broke apart with a start, finding Wild standing there with two bowls of food in his hands and a faintly amused look on his face.

"To be continued," Dare promised, shooting me a wink.

DARE

CHAPTER 6

Whatever healing magic that agathos goddess had used on me had really wiped me out. I scoffed down the delicious spinach and rice dish Wild had given me, fully intending to pick up where I'd left off with Grace, only to pass out immediately afterward, sleeping the day away then through the night. Her and Riot had both woken me a couple of times under the guise of giving me water, but I was pretty sure they were checking I was still alive.

I'd seen Wild standing in the doorway sometimes in those moments of wakefulness, watching over everything like a sentinel, but I got the distinct impression that Bullet was avoiding me.

Grace was asleep next to me as I pondered, Riot wrapped around her from behind, both of them breathing evenly. They looked so comfortable, so used to each other. I wasn't jealous, not quite, but I did feel a little unnecessary. A spare part that no one knew what to do with.

Get your shit together. You just got here, I told myself sternly, silently slipping out of the bed without disturbing either of them, desperately needing to wash. There was a stack of assorted guys' clothes on the dresser, all of which were sort of rest home-chic, but I guessed this was all they had on them. Finding a shirt and shorts that looked like they'd fit, I ducked into the ensuite, hoping the shower wouldn't wake Grace and Riot.

As physically draining as I'd found Hygeia's healing process, this was the best I'd felt in ages. Nothing hurt anymore, and that was a small miracle. I was free of open wounds and could finally have a proper shower and wash the remnants of the crash off my skin.

Unfortunately, my mind wouldn't be so easy to heal. Maybe the gods of the underworld would be kind enough to let us detour through their lands for the return trip, because I had zero intention of ever getting on an aircraft again. Fuck that. I'd rather swim home from Europe than get on a plane.

Home.

Was I ever going home? To Milton?

It wasn't that I felt super attached to it, really. Home was a concept rather than a fixed place, and without Mom around... I swallowed thickly, shaking off the thought. Almost everyone I gave a shit about was here, except for little Quinn.

Under the hot spray of the shower, on my own, small doubts about Grace arose that I recognized were partly motivated by fear. My experiences with agathos hadn't been good ones, and I didn't want to look into her and see *them*, but sometimes I couldn't help it. And then there was the almost overwhelming pull to Grace that I knew was supernatural, a side effect of the soul bond.

So how much was *me*? How much was *Grace*? Would we actually like each other without an external force shoving us together? If we'd met in the real world, would we be attracted to each other? She was objectively beautiful, in a polished, elegant sort of way that wasn't traditionally my type. And I was pretty fucking confident that she'd have never looked twice at a daimon if the Fates hadn't landed her with four of them.

I washed quickly, not wanting to use too much hot water when it sounded like there were a hundred people staying here, and hopped out of the shower, drying off and pulling on the dark linen shirt and shorts. I felt a bit like someone's rich golf-playing grandpa, but whatever.

More distressing were the jagged scars from the crash. I didn't care about scars in general—they made me look kind of badass—but they'd totally ruined the perfect symmetry of my tattoos, and I'd never get that back.

With a resigned sigh, I let myself out of the bathroom, peeking into the bedroom to find Grace and Riot still asleep, very much tangled up in each other. Not wanting to wake them, I tiptoed down the stairs into the living room where Wild and Bullet were crashed out on the L-shaped couch, the tops of their heads almost touching.

Interesting.

Instead of heading out the double doors where I assumed the rest of the rooms were, I went back through the kitchen and out the front door to the driveway so I could sit on the steps and enjoy a moment of quiet with the early morning sun on my face. I had no idea how people would respond to me as Grace's fourth soul bond, but I doubted there'd be a lot of moments of peace and solitude in my life going forward.

I did a double take, recognizing the slightly rusted white van sitting in the driveway. *Holy shit, Jack was still here?*

He was. Fast asleep in the front seat, head tipped back and mouth all the way open, shoulder-length dark hair sticking out in weird directions. I rapped my knuckles softly on the driver's side window, and he woke with a start, swearing up a storm as he scrambled toward the passenger side before realizing it was me.

"Fuck's sake," he panted, unlocking the door so I could open it. "You scared the goddamn life outta me, mate. What are you doing, creeping up on me like that? I've already been interrogated once."

"Right, well I do apologize for... walking up to the vehicle you have parked in the middle of the driveway in broad daylight. It was very sneaky of me."

I wasn't entirely sure he picked up on the sarcasm, given the seemingly quite genuine nod he gave me in return. "You alright? I wasn't sure if they were going to sacrifice you or something, but you actually look better than you did yesterday. Like way better. How'd you manage that?"

"No sacrifices yet," I replied drily. "I was healed by an agathos. By one of *the* agathos—as in one of the original spirits created by Gaia. She sort of came out of hibernation to help me? I don't really know how it works."

Jack blinked at me. "Rule one of magic: Don't fuck with things you don't understand. Come on, Dare, everyone knows that. That's like... finding a 2000-year-old holy artifact in a priestess' tomb and *touching* it. There are some things you just don't do."

"I wasn't exactly in the right state of mind to analyze it," I pointed out drily. I wasn't entirely sure I'd be alive if Hygeia hadn't intervened.

"Anyway, it all worked out fine. I'm fine. You can come inside, you know. From what I hear, there are plenty of other daimons staying here. You've met Vasileios, right?"

Jack made a grumbling noise of assent. If there was one thing I'd learned from staying with him, it was that he did a lot of drugs, spent too much time on the internet, and was incredibly paranoid about everything. Then again, the world was so fucked-up right now that he was probably feeling pretty justified in that paranoia these days.

"Your mates came out here yesterday. Billy Big Bollocks and his even bigger, silent bodyguard. Wanted to know who I was and where I'd come from, what my plans were. I don't go 'round just sharing my plans with every Tom, Dick, and Harry who asks, you know."

"Sure," I agreed, nodding along like I knew what he was talking about. "How about I get you some food and you can just come in when you're ready?"

Surely, at some point he'd need to use the bathroom and leave the safety of the van. It wasn't even his—from memory, he'd "borrowed" it from his neighbor.

"I found some crisps in the glove box. Not risking anything that might be contaminated. Oh, hold on a minute, I spotted something for you in the back when I was looking for water."

He rooted around in the packed van behind him, and I leaned in, trying to see what he was doing. I'd been too out of it when I'd gotten into the vehicle to realize he'd apparently hijacked a hoarder mobile.

"Here we are," Jack said, yanking out a heavy-looking silver case. Was that...? "My neighbor had actually mentioned this to me, a sort of traveling business idea thing they had, but now the world is going to shit so you might as well have it." He shoved the case out the door into my chest. If it was something weird, I could always dispose of it later and not hurt his feelings, I decided. "You sure you want to stay here? With the girl who grows people?"

"You mean Grace? My soul bond? Yes, I'm sure," I laughed. Whatever hesitations I had about our relationship and how much of it was *us* versus *the bond*, I didn't want to leave. "The growing people thing was a one-off."

"That's what they want you to think," Jack replied darkly. "She might be lulling you into a false sense of security before she sacrifices you and grows herself a new soul bond."

I blinked at him. "I'm going to go inside now."

"Suit yourself," Jack sighed, looking at me as though I was a lost cause. "If I'm not here when you next look, I'm out getting supplies. I really feel like I could use some explosives or something, you know? Always a good idea to be prepared. I should probably return the van too—bit shit of me to steal his means of transport in the middle of the apocalypse." He paused for a moment, looking thoughtful. "I'll try to find you some weapons too—something discreet, just in case your agathos turns on you. I'm sure I can swing by and drop 'em off before I go back to my place."

"I don't think that will be necessary, but, uh, thanks. I guess." I shook my head, slightly bewildered as I made my way back to the villa with the heavy case, ditching it inside the door to examine later. Intellectually, I knew that Jack had probably taken too much acid in his life to be considered a reliable source of critical thought, but on the other hand...

Was this really how people saw Grace? I thought she'd come across pretty well in that explainer video, but maybe we needed to do some social media PR work or something. I almost snorted at the idea. *Hey guys, welcome to A Day in the Life of the Prophêtis. Rise and grind, let's pour some coffee and start talking to deities you thought didn't exist!*

Grace didn't need PR, she needed miracles. Not in the figurative sense either. She needed literal miracles, enough to convince people that it wasn't a fluke or fancy visual effects. That she was real, and what she was saying was true. So far, out of agathos, daimons, and humans, the daimons were the only ones who overwhelmingly believed her. And yet Jack was a daimon, and he was still suspicious.

What a headache.

By the time I made it back inside, the place had woken up and honestly, the weird little commune-style setup that Grace and her bonded had going on in this villa was... bizarre, to say the least.

Efficient, but bizarre.

Humans, agathos, and daimons all mingled, preparing and eating meals side-by-side. Not to mention the Spartoi, who I had no idea how to classify. Human? Human-ish? I couldn't exactly ask them, since they only spoke Ancient Greek. Apparently, Bullet and a few of the Greek natives had a rudimentary understanding of it, but not enough to get into the philosophical question of what humans born from soil as fully grown men actually were.

"Welcome, Dare!" one of the humans said, approaching me with a beaming smile and a weirdly deferential pose, almost like they were bowing to me. "We're so honored to have the Prophêtis' fourth and final soul bond here with us."

Weird.

"Er, thanks. I guess. What's your name?"

"Oh! I'm Leonie, one of the Kakodaimonistai. Please, allow me to prepare your breakfast."

"That's really okay," I assured her. Grace had told me that the Kakodaimonistai were diehard daimon fans or whatever, who drank some kind of hallucinogenic so that they could see and know about us. I'd believed her, but actually seeing the fawning in action was *so* weird. "I don't really eat breakfast, I was just going to make some tea—"

"Right this way," she replied immediately, ushering me toward a corner of the kitchen they'd converted into a beverage station. Ignoring my protests, she shouldered past an agathos already waiting for their turn, and I watched, slightly bewildered, as she made me a cup of tea and honey exactly the way I liked it.

I vaguely remembered sipping tea at one point when Riot had woken me up, and I guessed he'd told them how I took it. Still, it was kind of surreal that these total strangers seemed to know so much about me. That sense of weirdness continued as I headed outside with my drink, through the covered porch area toward where Grace and her bonded were sitting in the shade. People shouted greetings at me like they'd known me my whole life, parting for me to create a path to Grace. Clearly, being one of her soul bonds came with some prestige, which was cool and all, but I definitely didn't feel as though I'd earned it.

If I thought it was weird coming from the Kakodaimonistai, it was even more bizarre when it came from agathos. Logically, I knew that the agathos here were the disenfranchised, cast-aside ones and that they had every reason to set themselves apart from the others, but it was still strange to have agathos look at me with something other than contempt.

They nodded to me like they respected me, when there was a very good chance I'd been beating up their teenage relatives back in Milton.

Riot immediately shifted over on the bench where he was sitting next to Grace to make room for me. Bullet was on her other side, with Wild next to him. Like, *right* next to him.

Riot had been my cuddle buddy for years when my Philotes instincts were acting up, I knew better than anyone that platonic friends could cuddle, but it seemed odd for *them*. Wild had a pretty notorious reputation in Milton as a loner, and Bullet had isolated himself at the Oneiroi property for years. Even when he'd shown up in my studio to get the tarot cards he'd dreamed about inked on his skin, he hadn't been overly keen on me actually touching him.

Was there something more to their relationship? Grace hadn't mentioned it when she was catching me up on their escapades yesterday, but maybe she felt like it wasn't her information to share. She seemed respectful that way.

"Hey, you doing okay?" Riot asked, clapping me on the back lightly so I didn't spill my tea. "It's unlike you to sleep for more than a few hours. I was worried you'd died."

I snorted. "These are pretty exceptional circumstances. I'm feeling a lot better, though."

A line of *Ancient Greek warriors*—cool, cool, just a normal day— filed in from the far corner of the property, equipped with spears and swords and shields, the feathers on the top of their helmets swaying as they walked.

51

"So, uh, what's going on?" I asked when no one offered any explanation for the sudden influx of armed soldiers, sipping my tea.

"Training time," Riot replied. "They usually come eat breakfast with everyone, then return to the barn to put on all their gear, then spar for a bit."

Wild stood, brushing his hand over Bullet's shoulder—interesting—before leaning down to kiss the top of Grace's head, signing something at her before he jogged down to join the merry band of warriors assembling next to the pool.

"Wild trains with them," Riot explained. "They seem to be picking up sign language faster than spoken English."

I watched as Wild and what may have been the leader of the Spartoi signed slowly at each other. Riot listed off the names of the Spartoi he'd learned, as well as pointing out the agathos, daimons, and humans milling around. I thought I had a decent memory but there must have been a hundred and twenty people here.

It felt like more than that. This place definitely wasn't equipped to house so many. Aside from the lack of accommodation, we were so exposed at the top of this cliff—a winding driveway on one side and a steep drop to the ocean on the other.

"That's Theras," Riot said, nodding at the guy opposite Wild as they both dropped into a fighting stance. "I guess he's like the Spartoi commander? He seemed like he wanted to take orders from Grace, but she directed him to Wild."

"And they eat and sleep and stuff? Like regular humans?" I asked, eyeing them warily. Wild was a big, shredded dude, and next to anyone else, he looked like an absolute unit. Next to the Spartoi, he appeared average-sized, at best. Each one of them had an unnatural level of cut muscle.

"They definitely eat and sleep," Riot confirmed while Grace nodded silently next to him. "How much they *feel*—emotion-wise—is up for debate."

"I don't feel the urge to make them horny, so I'm guessing they're not entirely human, but they don't have agathos or daimon eyes so who knows?" I shrugged.

Grace leaned past Riot, giving me a wide-eyed look. "Why didn't I think of that? Not making them, well, you know. But I haven't felt the urge to give any of them luck."

"He's not just a pretty face," Riot replied, clapping me on the back. I snorted, remembering him telling *me* that on the phone when he was stuck running errands for Viper not that long ago. Except I'd been a lot prettier in those days, before all the scars and the broken noses. I couldn't envision Riot saying that to me now.

"Oh, I meant to say that your friend is welcome to come inside," Grace said suddenly. "Jack, is it?"

"I did tell him that. He seemed a little skittish," Riot added with a smirk. I scoffed, doubting Riot had been particularly hospitable.

My lips twitched. "I don't know him very well. I'm guessing by what you guys have told me that the voice telling me where to go after the crash was Sophia the Wise, and she said Jack's was a safe place for me to stay, but that's about the extent of it. I did try to get him to come in, but he's content to hide out in the van for now," I replied, opting not to tell Grace he thought she was going to sacrifice me and grow a replacement.

I wasn't sure we were at that level in our relationship yet.

Before she could respond, two young agathos women appeared in front of us, one sheepish, the other determined.

"*Prophêtis*," the more confident one began. "Do you have a moment to talk to Evanthia about her daimon soul bond? She has a lot of questions about bonding and could use your guidance." And here was me thinking agathos were total prudes. Wasn't bonding a sex thing? "I have explained what it is like for me, maybe it would be helpful to hear your experiences."

"Oh, of course," Grace replied, giving Evanthia a soft smile. "Are you okay to translate, Xenia?"

She nodded curtly and Grace stood, looking between Riot and Bullet. "Maybe one of you should talk to Ovie? Daimon-to-daimon? I know patience isn't generally in a daimon's nature..."

"I'll go," Riot volunteered, taking me by surprise. "We all know Bullet is a hermit."

Bullet looked as surprised as I felt, watching Riot's back as he and Grace headed toward the enormous table that ran the length of the covered porch.

"I *am* a hermit, but I would have thought that would make Riot want me to go talk to Ovie more. Maybe he's forgiven me a little bit," Bullet said with a wry smile, pulling out his tarot cards and shuffling them aimlessly. The gold figures glinted in the sunshine against the inky black card, and I watched them, slightly mesmerized at the familiar sight of them. I'd spent a lot of time staring at those images, inking many of them onto Bullet's skin.

"He's mad at you?" I asked eventually. The spot that Riot and Grace had vacated remained empty, leaving an awkward-sized gap between Bullet and I that neither of us shifted to fill. I wanted to be fine with him, to get back to the easy if inconsistent friendship we'd shared for the past few years since he moved away. I wasn't sure we could, but I wanted to.

"Riot wanted me to do more to get you here. To tell you sooner, and he's not wrong to feel that way, to be pissed at me. I had my reasons, but some of them were selfish too."

There was a long pause, the quiet filled by the incessant sound of the cards shifting together. It was a heavy conversation for early on a beautiful morning—the blue water beyond the cliff glinted in the sunlight, the grape vines above where we sat providing a reprieve from the heat. Even the grunts and hits from the sparring Spartoi couldn't detract from the peacefulness of this place.

"I'm glad you're here," Bullet continued eventually, his voice pitched low enough not to carry. "I knew if you just got here, my Amazing Grace would fall head over heels in love with you."

I balked, twisting slightly to look at him. "Uh, I don't think we're quite there yet, man. We only met yesterday."

We *had* kissed, but then I promptly ruined that whole experience by nearly fainting all over her.

Bullet's lips twitched, his gaze fixed out on the makeshift training field. "But you'll get there. She'll get there. You're going to make her smile so hard." He shot me a sidelong glance, not quite able to hide the torture in his eyes. "Promise me you will."

Everything about this conversation was making me nervous.

"What is this about, Bullet?"

"You know what this is about, Dare," he singsonged, infuriatingly blasé. "My life is an hourglass, and the grains of sand are running thin," he added in a deliberately dramatic, ominous voice.

"No, that's bullshit. That's... That's something other Oneiroi have to deal with. You're bonded to an agathos, your souls were destined for one another, there's no way the gods would cut your life short."

They wouldn't be that cruel. I had to believe that, or what were we even fighting for?

"The length of our thread is determined when we come into this world. There's no altering it." He paused, giving me a sidelong look, and I got the feeling we weren't talking about his life expectancy anymore. "I would have told you if there was. If there'd been another way."

I nodded silently, my throat tight. "Grace said she got to meet... her. I'm grateful for that."

"A generous gift from the gods of the underworld," Bullet agreed quietly. "It's not so bad down there. The views are great," he joked weakly.

"Cool. I look forward to us all seeing them one day, after we've lived long, wonderful lives," I replied firmly, giving him a hard look. Yes, he did appear slightly worse for wear, but I was refusing to believe that this was the end for him. Bullet was strong. Fierce. *Constant*. I couldn't imagine a world without him in it.

"That's the dream. Still, there's no harm in you making a promise to make Grace smile every day. Wild is too serious and Riot is too moody, it's gotta be you."

"It's *going* to be *us*, but I'll do you one better. I'll strike a deal with you."

Bullet's eyebrows shot up. "You'd risk Nyx's wrath on the off-chance you can't make Grace smile? You must be really confident in your sense of humor."

I shrugged easily, sticking out my hand for him to take.

"I swear to make Grace smile every day or risk the goddess' wrath," I said solemnly. Bullet gave me a wary look, clapping his hand against mine.

"Deal—"

"And if you die before you're old and gray, I'll come to the underworld and fetch you myself," I added quickly, not entirely sure if Nyx would hold me to it or not since Bullet had already said the magic word, but I hoped she did. I meant it.

Nyx's magic rang out between our clasped hands while Bullet stared at me in wide-eyed horror, snatching his hand back. "Have you lost your fucking *mind*?!"

"You're the ones who keep saying that the underworld is a real place that you've visited—without any harm coming to you before—and the gods who rule it are nice enough to organize a meet-and-greet between Grace and my mom. But suddenly the idea of going there to bargain for your soul is impossible?" I shook my head, shoving my hair back from my face when it fell over my eyes. "Fuck that. I don't accept that."

Bullet gave me a shaky laugh, still staring at me like I'd lost my marbles. "You and Grace are kind of similar, you know? Both of you are hiding a strong stubborn streak underneath that friendly façade."

"Friendly," I scoffed. "Grace, for sure."

"Friendly for a daimon," Bullet amended with a grin. His eyebrows jumped as one of the Spartoi handed Wild his weapons, chattering away in Ancient Greek as he showed Wild how to slide his forearm through the straps of the enormous bronze shield.

"Badass," I laughed. "Do you think they'd let me play with the swords too?"

"It probably wouldn't be the worst idea," Bullet said quietly, immediately cutting my laughter short. "I'm a lover, not a fighter, but it makes sense for us to be prepared, ideally with our own weapons. Things that don't require reliance on anyone else."

"Have you seen a lot of fighting in our future?"

Bullet grimaced. "It's always been very unclear after you arrived. I've seen hazy visions further into the future, ones without me in them. We're flying even more blind than we have been recently now though."

Ah.

Suddenly all of Grace's apologies made a lot more sense. Was I some harbinger of Bullet's doom? Was that his selfish reason for keeping me away? I couldn't say I blamed him for that, I'd have kept me away too.

Doesn't matter, you've made a deal. Even if something does happen to Bullet, you're going to bring him back.

The gods owe us that much.

"Come on," Bullet said, standing shakily. "Let's join in. Crash shields, cross swords, if you will."

I snorted, pushing up from the bench. "Don't joke about that, I don't need a jealous Wild on my hands for flirting with his boyfriend. He's probably annoyed enough he has to share his girlfriend."

It had been a stab in the dark, but it landed. Bullet went as red as a tomato, stammering a few times before settling on an answer. "I wouldn't call him my *boyfriend*..."

"You're going to have to catch me up on all this," I laughed, heading down the steps. "Seems like you've all been even busier than I thought."

GRACE

CHAPTER 7

"Do you have any more questions?" I asked Evanthia, waiting for Xenia to translate.

Evanthia shook her head, giving me an unsteady smile. Honestly, the entire conversation hadn't gone how I'd thought it would. She'd been so immediately attracted to Ovie that I'd assumed they'd seal their bond right away, but apparently, once the shock of finding her first soul bond—a daimon no less—had worn off, she'd gotten cold feet.

The language barrier between them hadn't helped—she couldn't get to know him and get reassurance in the way that Riot and I had—but she was also just scared. Scared of what tying her soul to a daimon's would mean, scared of making a decision she could never take back, of losing her family permanently even though she'd already run away from them to be here.

"She says you have given her much to think about," Xenia translated, her concern written all over her face, her own agathos bonded hovering nearby.

"Okay, well, feel free to come back to me if you have any more questions."

Maybe I was naïve—almost certainly, in fact—but I hadn't expected that level of hesitation. I guessed when it came to bonding daimons, I was the odd one.

"Grace," Vasileios called from further down the long table, his two lovers draped on him from either side as he watched something on his phone. "You will want to see this."

"That doesn't bode well," I sighed. Before I could move, Foster appeared, setting up his phone on the table for me with a grim look on his face. There was a newscast already playing, and all of my soul bonds gathered at my back, drawn to my distress.

"I sat down earlier with Faith Bellamy, the mother of Grace Bellamy. Here is what she had to say," the human journalist said in a somber tone, drawing our attention back to the screen.

"Fuck," Riot muttered.

"Yup," I agreed faintly. "That about covers it."

The set changed, showing the interviewer and my mother sitting opposite each other against a plain, dark background. Mother was dressed in a black tweed skirt suit—a color that was an absolute no-go for agathos outside of mourning, and I had no doubt that was what she was doing. Very publicly mourning her not-dead daughter. Her hair was blown out perfectly, makeup glowing and perfect.

I could feel everyone's eyes on me, waiting to see how I'd respond, probably expecting me to burst into tears. Usually, I'd expect *myself* to burst into tears—I was a crier, and this was a high-emotion situation.

But when I looked at my mother, I felt *nothing*. It was a relief, in a way. My entire life, whenever I'd been around her I'd been edgy and anxious, trying constantly not to disappoint her and failing every time. There was a sense of peace in knowing now that I was so irredeemably disappointing to her that there was no point worrying about it anymore.

"Faith Bellamy, thank you so much for speaking with me today. I'll be frank—it's hard for me to even know where to begin with this, you're an agathos too? That's a very surreal thing for me to comprehend, the idea that there are non-human people living among us, let alone all the other statements your daughter made in her video, or the footage from Athens with the scorpions. The claims of a goddess…"

I felt a sliver of sympathy for the journalist, who seemed like she'd be very poised and articulate at any other time, but who was clearly out of her depth on this topic.

Mother nodded somberly, her face the picture of concern. "I am an agathos, a helper of humanity. The presence of my kind was meant to remain unknown; it is not for us to seek glory or recognition for the good deeds we do for humankind to protect you all from the evils of the daimons—" Someone made a dramatic retching sound, possibly Vasileios, "—and I understand it must be difficult for you to feel as though you have been pawns in a secret war all along. Rest assured that the agathos have always been here to shield humanity as best we can from the daimons' dark sway, and we will continue to do so for as long as we exist. Despite whatever claims my daughter made, agathos and daimons will *never* be united. The agathos stand with humanity. Daimons are a scourge, Anesidora herself wants to see them gone."

"Well, that's divisive," Bullet sighed. "The last thing anyone needs is humans feeling empowered to join the agathos attacks on daimons. It's not like it'd be good for the humans either—they're not immune to daimon gifts the way agathos are."

I nodded silently, my unease at my mother's words growing. There was absolutely no way that this interview was unsanctioned—whatever placating phrases she was spewing were pre-agreed with the Basilinna and the Elders.

"I can't lie, remember?" Mother said, leaning forward in her seat and giving the interviewer a conspiratorial smile before the woman could ask another question. "And while Grace can't either, much of what she claimed was untrue. That's not to say that she lied, but what she genuinely believes in her heart is untrue. It has been very difficult for me to come to terms with that, even though I've had twenty-five years to do so."

The interviewer frowned. "Are you saying that your daughter has always struggled with comprehending reality?"

Mother gave her a pitying smile. "I'm not entirely comfortable with the term 'daughter.' Not anymore. This is not how any child of mine should act."

"Wow, Grace, your mom is a stone-cold psycho," Dare murmured. Wild's hands came to rest on my shoulders, giving them a supportive squeeze.

"But yes, Grace struggles with reality, particularly the reality of her *own* life, her *own* situation. Agathos have a specific role in society, and we are primarily meant to carry out that role unseen. 'Live hidden' is a key tenet we ascribe to. Grace has always drawn too much attention to herself, never fully accepted the role she was meant to have, even when it was more than clear that she was being punished by the goddess for it."

"She actually believes all this shit," Riot said in disbelief.

"It's not that surprising," I replied quietly. "In her eyes, any attention on me was too much because I wasn't a *normal* agathos. It's not a lie to her, because it's her reality."

"What would you say to her now if you could?" the reporter asked.

Mother looked past the camera, the absolute picture of serene sadness and resignation. It was chilling. "I suppose I would tell her I forgive her." A surprised laugh escaped me before I could stop myself, and I felt Wild shaking with silent amusement behind me. "It's clear now—for the entire world to see—that she's being punished by having her soul forever tied to daimons. There could be no worse fate for an agathos."

Around us, people were translating my mother's words, and I glanced up in time to see Evanthia's face go pale.

"I can't be sure whether Grace is lashing out in response to being cursed with daimon soul bonds, or whether they have influenced her mind with their darkness." Mother sighed heavily. "I'm inclined to think that it's the former, since she's always shown rebellious tendencies. I should have been harder on her as a child. Many reputable members of the agathos community have spoken out, and many more will do so. I urge you all to listen to them, the voices of reason, not the voice of one delusional girl—"

Riot reached over, locking the phone and cutting off the stream. "Enough. The others are listening, they can tell us if your sociopathic egg donor says anything we actually need to know."

I nodded, a faint buzzing in my ears. I didn't feel angry or sad, I just felt *nothing*.

Well, perhaps a little humiliated, since everyone was staring at me in pity. But that was all.

"I think I'm going to take a shower," I said robotically, latching onto the first excuse for some alone time to process. "I'll be back down in a bit."

The sound of the chair scraping over the stone patio felt deafening as I stood, walking stiffly into the house without making eye contact with anyone.

Who would people believe? I'd been as raw and open as I could in the video I'd made, the total opposite of the calm, perfect restraint Faith had shown. I thought I'd done the right thing, approached it the right way, but now I wasn't sure.

Who would they believe?

I flopped back on the bed, staring up at the shadowy ceiling. I'd showered and changed, then pulled the curtains shut in the bedroom and laid down, too overwhelmed at the idea of facing everyone right then.

Just five more minutes, I told myself. I wanted to be a leader—sort of—the leader that those who'd followed me here deserved, but I also needed a second to pull myself together. To not be *Grace the Prophêtis,* whispered in reverent tones, or *Grace the Agathos,* usually a title delivered with dry cynicism. But worst of all was *Grace Bellamy.* Grace Bellamy was a disappointment of a daughter, a mentally unstable individual, a war criminal. It was a million things that weren't *me.* The name that I'd carried for twenty-five years no longer felt like my own.

So, who was I? Where did that leave me?

If I ever fulfilled the prophecy, brought forth the new age of heroes, created a world where all mortals were equally valued, where we didn't have to hide... Who would I be then? Would I still be Public Enemy Number One?

Riot and Bullet were both sending waves of love and reassurance at me through the bonds while fending off questions and concerns downstairs, and it helped a bit. Knowing that my bonded loved me and supported me unconditionally was always comforting, but it also wasn't quite what I needed at that moment.

I felt raw and a little angry, and I wasn't ready to let that anger go yet.

Though he could easily move silently when he wanted to, Wild gave me plenty of notice by stomping up the stairs to the bedroom. He'd been doing his best to contain his rage, blocking me from feeling the depth of his emotion, but it was there lurking beneath the surface.

My rage had called to his, drawing him to me.

He prowled into the room like a caged tiger, kicking the door shut behind him and pacing back and forth, crimson eyes filled with the need to avenge my honor. A need that couldn't be fulfilled. Killing my mother wasn't an option, my instincts would never allow it, even if a dark part of me wondered how much easier my life would be if she wasn't in it.

Wild tossed his burner phone on the bed next to me, and I picked it up, holding it above my face and scrolling through his message thread with Onyx.

Onyx: *Say the word and we'll burn Grace's mom's house down.*

Wild: *I'll get back to you. Grace has little brothers that live there.*

Onyx: *We'd get the kids out first. Maybe one or two of the dads— aren't a couple of them marginally less awful?*

I glanced up from the phone. "No burning the house down."

He had the gall to look disappointed, still pacing as I returned to scrolling through his messages.

Onyx: *Obviously, we all think her mom is full of shit, but you can tell Grace that plenty of humans do too. I've got eyes on the ground and the response to Faith was pretty mixed. Lots of people found her too rehearsed and kind of creepy.*

Wild: *She is rehearsed and creepy.*

Onyx: *Any update on the fire idea? I've got people in Auburn already, monitoring the agathos.*

Wild: *No retaliation until I specifically get the go-ahead from Grace.*

I laughed before I could help myself. "That's kind of sweet. Thank you for taking my wishes into consideration before kicking off Operation Revenge."

Wild raised a questioning eyebrow at me, clearly asking if I wanted him to issue the order or not. Even if I could, I didn't want to make more of a martyr out of my mother than she'd already done herself.

"No," I said firmly, typing my reply to Onyx, saying the same thing. "No retaliation. I have to believe that we're doing the right thing, that fulfilling the prophecy is adding *good* to the world, not evil. And if my mother is on the wrong side of that, well, I'm sure she'll learn soon enough with no interference from us."

Onyx: *Oh Good Girl, you're ruining all my fun. How are you holding up? Wild said Dare got there okay. Are you walking funny yet? I'm surprised you make it out of bed at all with four boyfriends.*

I surprised myself by nearly replying that I was, in fact, in bed right now. That I didn't feel the urge to blush and immediately downplay the sexual aspect of my relationships had to be a positive sign, didn't it? I'd wanted to get more comfortable with this side of myself, and I was.

The only reason I didn't send Onyx a teasing response is that I needed to give Wild my full attention. His arms were crossed over his chest, fingers drumming impatiently over his biceps in frustration. He wasn't used to feeling helpless, and my mother's targeted attack on my reputation had made him feel that way. At any moment, he'd disappear downstairs to spar with Riot to work off that excess aggression.

I liked that the two of them had something to connect over, but this time, I wanted to be the one to help him.

"Come here," I said softly, setting aside the phone and reaching for him with both arms. He paused his irritable fidgeting, raising an eyebrow at me. "Please?"

He nodded, lips tipping up slightly, the closest thing to a smile from Wild. Apparently only willing to let me call the shots to a certain point, he laid down next to me and snatched me up, dragging my body over his, trapping my leg between his while I propped myself up with my forearms on his chest, looking down at him.

"Don't go fight," I whispered. "Let me help you relax."

Wild was already shaking his head before I could finish speaking. He didn't trust himself with me, not all the way, and while I appreciated his concern, we'd never know until we tried.

"Stay," I insisted, smoothing my hands over his chest. He shook his head again, though his palms drifted down my back, giving my butt a distracted squeeze. "I know you won't hurt me. I trust you completely, and you should trust yourself. Besides, if I felt even a moment of fear or panic with you, Riot and Bullet would be at my side within seconds, making sure everything was okay."

Wild pursed his lips contemplatively, and I could feel his resolve weakening, an undercurrent of arousal stirring beneath all the rage and frustration that fed into my own desire. It was indulgent—there were a million other things I could be doing—*should* be doing—but...

But I wanted this. I wanted Wild. I wanted to be a little selfish for a bit longer.

His lips brushed against mine, hands sliding beneath my dress to pluck at the fabric of my panties, teasing me with a brief hint of amusement in his eyes before rolling me onto my back and carefully straddling my waist. The moment he bent down, I moved to cup his jaw, but Wild was faster than me, collecting both my wrists and pinning them above my head with one enormous hand. My heart rate spiked, but it was definitely from excitement rather than fear, and I knew that Wild would feel that through the bond.

I liked feeling a little helpless beneath him. Liked knowing that he'd take care of me, and that all I had to do was feel. Wild's eyes flashed with approval as he nipped my lower lip, his free hand sliding down my body to bunch my dress around my hips. He trailed kisses down my jaw, nudging my chin with his nose, encouraging me to let my head fall back onto the mattress, and I didn't argue. He kept moving down, teeth raking over one nipple through the fabric of my dress and thin bra, the movement in rough contrast to the soft ghosting touch of his fingers between my thighs.

My legs fell open, and I did my best to arch up into his hand despite his bulk pressing down on me. Wild tutted, stopping his ministrations completely.

"Do you want me to say 'please'?" I whispered, face flushing hot at the question. I felt his amusement as he shook his head. Wild pressed a soft kiss to my breast, glancing up the line of my body with a devastating look in his dark red eyes.

'*Stay still,*' he mouthed, all cocky confidence.

I made a sound of discontent, even though a small rush of excitement filled me at the idea. Then he took his fingers away, and I wanted to cry.

They pressed at my lower lip, the instruction silent but clear. *Suck.* I parted my lips, refusing to break eye contact, and Wild's flared with hunger as he pushed two fingers into my mouth.

I can't believe I'm doing this, I thought as I wet his digits with my tongue. But then again, why not? I wasn't doing anything *wrong*. So long as all of us were happy and comfortable, then why worry? Why question whether it was *okay* for me to feel good about something that *felt good*? If I was twisted and broken, then fine. I'd rather be twisted and broken with my soul bonds who made me feel like I was flying, than force myself into whatever prescribed mold agathos were meant to fit into.

'*Good girl*,' Wild mouthed, pulling his hand away. He roughly yanked my panties to the side, impaling me on his wet fingers. I let out a silent scream, surprised that I enjoyed the slight bite of pain that accompanied the pleasure.

Wild didn't miss a thing, tempering his movements less than usual because he clearly realized through the bond how much I liked it. The fabric of my panties dug into my hips where he was roughly pulling them out of the way, and he wasn't so much stroking me in a come hither motion as pressing against that magical spot inside me and *shaking* it. I gasped at the wave of pleasure threatening to rise and drown me, fingers grasping desperately at the sheets to anchor myself against the sensation trying to sweep me away.

It was too much and too good, and not enough, and so close—

Wild twisted my panties in his grip, a sharp bite of pain accompanied by a firm sense of *command* through the bond. A silent instruction to *come right now*, and I was helpless to do anything but follow. Happily, willingly, gratefully helpless. Under Wild's ministrations, the stress of the world went away. There were no obligations or prophecies, no overwhelming negative attention that made me want to hide and never see anyone again.

There was just pure bliss. His magic hands, the weight of his body against mine, his hot breath ghosting over my skin as he leaned down to press kisses everywhere he could reach.

His teeth scraped over my nipple and I bit my lip to stop myself crying out and letting everyone downstairs know what we were doing.

Though Riot and Bullet would be able to sense it clearly through the bonds, and I wasn't entirely confident in either of their poker faces.

Wild withdrew his fingers and my face flamed as he took his time licking them clean of my arousal, looking incredibly pleased with himself.

He freed his cock from his trousers, stroking it once while wrapping an enormous arm around both of my thighs and tugging me down to the edge of the mattress before grabbing my wrists and placing my hands on the backs of my knees, encouraging me to keep them pulled up.

Wild pushed my panties to the side again, sliding his cock through my wetness, bumping against my clit until I was a trembling mess.

Patience, I reminded myself, wanting to impress him with my self-control, trusting that he would get me there. *Be patient.*

Wild rewarded me with a slow, sinful smile that I somehow felt everywhere, before slowly pressing into me, my body stretching and pulling to accommodate him.

He watched me with his brow furrowed, like he couldn't decide if it was too much for me or not, and I gave him what I hoped was a reassuring smile.

Wild's movements were slow and measured, thrusting lazily while I kept my knees pinned to my chest, unable to do a thing to speed him up, and he knew it.

He pressed his body weight against the back of my legs, grinding his pelvis against my clit, and as delicious as the friction was, it was the way he firmly yet tenderly gripped my chin, encouraging me to keep my eyes on him, that sent me over the edge.

I twisted and writhed beneath him, but he didn't let up, dragging my orgasm out with every measured thrust. His self-control was slipping as I tightened around him, and I wrapped one arm under both my knees so I could grip the bed with the other hand as he picked up his pace, worried I was going to fly off.

His blood-red eyes were hazy with desire, and with him looming above me, trapping me in place, he looked dangerous in the best kind of way.

Wild.

He *looked* completely wild, and I loved every second of it.

I loved him.

I'd never told him that, and I wasn't sure now was exactly the right time, but I absolutely loved Wild.

He was too distracted to notice.

With a sharp exhale, his movements stuttered to a stop, and I fought to stop staring at him like a lovesick puppy, wrangling my emotions under control before he pulled out.

Ultimately, I wasn't confident that Wild loved me back. Or rather, loved me *yet*, because I had to have hope that it would happen one day. Aside from the aunt he'd lost, Wild hadn't experienced much love in his life for comparison. And there was his complicated feelings for Bullet to consider—sexually, Wild seemed pretty comfortable with his attraction to my other bonded, but emotionally, both of them were flailing a little.

We'd get there, I told myself.

Wild laid down next to me, hauling me into his embrace and giving me a questioning look, no doubt wondering what all the chaotic emotions I was feeling meant.

"I'm okay," I assured him, resting my palm over his beating heart. "Everything is a mess and I don't know what I'm doing with my life, but I'm okay."

Wild snorted.

"And I just want you to know..." I swallowed thickly, gathering my courage. I wasn't going to tell Wild I loved him, but I wanted to support us getting to that point in our own time. "If you and Bullet want to spend time alone together like... well, like *this*, I'm okay with that. More than okay. I want you two to be happy, whatever that looks like, and—"

Wild cut off my rambling with a kiss, shaking with silent laughter as he tangled his fingers in my hair. He pulled back after a moment, pressing his forehead against mine and searching my eyes as thoroughly as I was searching his.

'*Thank you,*' he mouthed.

"We haven't had a chance to talk since Dare arrived. Does it bother you, him being here?" I'd been so worried about Dare getting here, about Bullet and Riot's responses and the tension that still existed between them, that I hadn't really had a moment to make sure Wild was doing okay too.

Wild shook his head, squeezing my hips. Without any explanation, I knew that he was telling me that I was still his, that he was feeling a little possessive, but not in a jealous kind of way.

It eased some of the worry in my chest that I didn't know I'd been harboring. Our situation was unique, and I so wanted the guys to get along and find their rhythm, whether that looked like a regular group of soul bonds or something that was completely us.

I let out a long exhale, knowing I'd been hiding up here long enough. I could face anything with my bonded at my side.

RIOT

CHAPTER 8

"This is awesome," I told Dare as he examined the contents of the silver case his weirdo "friend" had given him.

"Right?" Dare agreed. Footsteps on the stairs cut him off before he could say more, his head shooting up like a meerkat to watch Grace emerge down the steps with a very satisfied-looking Wild, hot on her heels.

Through the bond, I already knew that Grace was a lot more *relaxed* after her brief interlude with Wild than she had been before she went upstairs, but Dare didn't have that insight into her yet. He was watching her like a hawk, trying to determine from her body language how she was feeling, though Grace didn't give much away. Not these days, with so many eyes on her.

Dare had missed the days when Grace had been even a little carefree. When she'd smiled easily and hadn't carried the weight of the world on her shoulders. Bullet shifted slightly in his spot on the further-most side of the L-shaped sectional from where Dare and I sat like he knew what I was thinking. With a soft smile and a hint of concern through the bond, Grace dropped down next to him, leaning her head against his shoulder.

Bullet murmured something in her ear that eased her worries, wrapping an arm around her shoulders. Dare bumped me softly, a silent encouragement to sort my shit out. I thought *he'd* be the one mad at Bullet, but Dare had always been better at letting go of grudges than I was.

"What is that?" Grace asked, tipping her chin at the case on the coffee table while Wild stalked behind us to look over our shoulders, glaring at it like it was a bomb threat.

"Tattoo kit," Dare replied with a laugh. "Apparently, Jack had it in the back of his van, which I honestly don't want to think too hard about, but it's brand new—everything is still all packaged up."

Dare held up his left arm, examining the scar that ran down the center of the beautiful koi fish tattoo sleeve. He'd always taken pride in the symmetry of his ink, and I knew it was bothering him.

"I vote you let me fix it," I suggested with a smirk, only half joking. "Blue did that one, right? I doubt you'll see her again any time soon."

Dare snorted. "I'm not against teaching you an employable skill, but you're not starting your tattooing career on my skin, that's for fucking sure."

The little shit. Bullet shook with quiet laughter and Dare shot him a grin that wasn't quite easy, but wasn't strained either. Nope, the problem was just me.

"I want a tattoo," Grace admitted a little wistfully, catching everyone's attention. "They're not very agathos, but I always thought they were so beautiful."

"Yeah?" Dare perked up instantly. It was maybe the most *himself* I'd seen him since he got here. "I'll give you one."

"How much does it hurt?" Grace asked with a nervous laugh.

"Depends where you get it," I answered. I'd napped through some of my arm tattoos, and made Dare swear not to tell anyone I'd cried for the hand ones.

'*Me too*,' Wild signed, shifting around the couch so we could all see him.

"You'll get one with me?" Grace confirmed, excitement flooding the bond almost instantly. "Like a matching one?"

Wild shrugged, mouthing, '*Sure, you choose.*'

"What? I want a matching tattoo with Grace," I said, sounding more affronted than I meant to.

"Me too," Dare added, shooting her a wink.

"But what should we get?" Grace mused, tipping her head back thoughtfully.

I looked at Bullet, surprised to see that he was staying quiet. It wasn't like Bullet had something against tattoos—he had a bunch of them.

All cards.

No, not just any cards.

All cards he'd been shown on his body in his visions. That was why he was being quiet—he hadn't seen any new ones to add. Maybe he was feeling some kind of way about it? I was guessing that if we decided on a simple matching design, he'd break tradition and get it too.

But maybe I could extend the olive branch. Maybe instead of asking Bullet to leave his comfort zone, we could meet him in it.

"The cards," I said in a low voice. "The ones on Bullet's wrist. There's one for each of us, right?"

He blinked at me before sliding his sleeve up and extending his arm to show us the five cards fanned out from wrist to elbow.

Grace smiled wistfully at the design, tracing the first card closest to his wrist—a skull wearing a jester's hat—with her finger. "You designed this, Dare?"

He shrugged, playing it cool. "Sort of? I mean, the cards are what they are, I copy the image on the deck. I just, uh, arranged them, I guess." Dare frowned at Bullet. "You never mentioned that design had anything to do with me."

"I didn't know at the time," Bullet replied with a slightly strained grin. "I saw the cards first. The faces came later."

Wild sauntered over, staring unabashedly, while Bullet hummed a tune I now recognized as *Wait For It*, because it was one of his favorites.

"That's you," Grace told Wild, pointing at the middle card as Dare and I moved closer. "The Chariot."

A leaping winged horse made for a pretty badass tattoo. Not that I was complaining about mine—a horned skull with bat wings and a floating crown. I could roll with that.

Wild tilted his head questioningly to the side.

"Control, willpower, determination," Bullet listed off. "All traits that are very you. Dare, this is you—The World. Completion, integration, accomplishment."

He tapped the card closest to his elbow that depicted a checkered globe with a sun on one side and a moon on the other.

"Completion," Dare repeated with a thoughtful nod. "And Riot is the bat devil thing, right? How come Grace is the clown?"

"The Fool," Grace corrected with a wry smile. "Which sounds worse."

"Beginnings, innocence, spontaneity," Bullet listed idly. "The Fool represents the start of a new journey into the unknown. An innocence of the challenges that lie ahead, the sometimes hard-won lessons that must be learned."

"That... That does sound like Grace," I replied, giving her an apologetic look since she clearly didn't love being referred to as The Fool. "Do you hate it? We can pick a different design—"

"I like it," she said softly, rubbing her thumb over Bullet's arm. "I like that it means something, that it's always meant something to Bullet. That it symbolized *us*."

"Then let's do it," Dare said enthusiastically, heading back to the case to get set up. "You guys decide who's going first."

Bullet and I exchanged a look, a silent agreement not to talk about what our cards symbolized. Mine because I already knew The Devil represented the worst parts of me, the internal battle I'd been waging until Grace came into my life and made putting my demons to rest feel more possible than impossible.

Bullet's because his card was Death.

"I'll go first," Grace announced. "I want it on my right wrist."

"It'll hurt a little there," Dare warned her. "And I don't have any numbing cream."

"I can handle it," she assured him. I doubt it had escaped anyone's notice that she wanted her tattoo in the same place as Bullet's. He pulled out his cards, flipping through them with impressive dexterity to find the ones Dare needed to reference.

"You suggested this for me," Bullet said quietly, coming to stand next to me after he'd reluctantly handed them over, his voice too low for anyone else to hear. "You knew I didn't want to get one I hadn't seen."

I shrugged, shoving my hands in my pockets. "No need to break with tradition when there was a perfectly good solution right there."

Bullet bumped me with his shoulder. "Yeah? That's all it was?"

I grunted noncommittally, but followed him to sit on the far side of the sofa, giving Dare plenty of room to work while Wild acted as his assistant.

"I don't love this pen," Dare muttered eventually. "But I suppose this is what you get when you're using equipment from the back of someone's van."

"Comforting," Grace replied with a grimace, unsuccessfully trying to hide her discomfort as Dare worked. "How are you guys so covered in tattoos? Maybe I have a low tolerance for pain."

"I did warn you the wrist was a sensitive spot," Dare teased. "Also daimons can pretty much go all out on, er, numbing agents without any negative side effects, so there's that."

Very true, there was only one or two I had done while completely sober.

"Is it too much, Gracie?" I asked, monitoring the bond to make sure she wasn't about to pass out or anything.

"It's not too much," she replied tightly, while I appreciated her inability to lie for a moment, even though I usually found it to be controlling bullshit. "It looks pretty."

"Dare is good at what he does," I assured her. "Besides, he's done this design before, and he's got a cheat sheet, so he can't fuck it up."

"I never fuck up," Dare scoffed. He cut me a look before hunching over Grace's wrist again, and I did my best not to laugh at his silent warning. Dare *didn't* fuck up really, but he was clearly trying to impress Grace and didn't want me to get in his way.

I got that. Dare felt like he was behind, like he had to *woo* Grace and get her to fall for him in the way she'd already fallen for the rest of us. There was something else there too—resentment maybe?—but I couldn't quite place what it was. As much as I hated to admit it, both Dare and I had been through so much since the last time we'd seen one another, we weren't the same people we were all of a few weeks ago. It bothered me that I couldn't read him the way I used to.

Dare and Grace started a quiet conversation about her brothers while Wild and Bullet sat shoulder-to-shoulder, watching them, and I slipped out onto the terrace, giving them all a moment.

Maybe I should have tried a little harder with Bullet. Maybe I should have *apologized*, which was basically the most undaimonic concept ever. He and Wild were so awkward with one another half the time that it seemed rude to interrupt them.

"Any news?" I asked Foster, taking the seat next to him while he watched a newscast, Estrella perched on his lap, disinterestedly examining her chipped nail polish.

"Nothing good," he replied with a grimace. "There's some kind of closed door meeting happening right now with a bunch of important people. Like, world leader-level important. They keep cutting to an empty podium, waiting for whoever is going to come out and speak."

"Great," I sighed, hoping it'd be good news for us and knowing that it almost certainly wasn't. We didn't have that kind of luck. Whatever the worst-case scenario was, that's what we'd get. "Any more of Grace's asshole relatives crawling out of the woodwork?"

Foster's lips twitched. "No, but there was a human from Milton who gave an impassioned speech about how amazing Grace is. Apparently, she was in and out of the shelter where Grace worked, and she said Grace was her angel and she'd always known it. I don't know if it'll sway anyone, but it was kind of... nice? You know, as an agathos. Usually everything we do is unacknowledged."

He shrugged, blushing at Estrella's derisive snort.

"How hard you agathos have it," she said drily, though she shot him an affectionate look that softened the blow. "There are no humans going on TV to talk about their gratitude for daimons. There's too much happening right now for people to focus, but when they really take in what we are, that we exist, we're going to get blamed for *everything*. Every bad decision some Joe Schmoe has ever made in his life is about to be a daimon's fault."

She was probably right, but in fairness, we *were* responsible for a lot of people's bad decisions.

I watched the newsfeed for as long as I could handle the hysteria and giant scorpion footage, before giving up and heading back inside. Grace immediately held out her arm with a beaming smile, showing me the design on her wrist wrapped with a clear tattoo adhesive. Dare had foregone the actual card the way Bullet had always wanted them on his skin, just inking The Fool—a skull in a three-pronged jester hat. It was surprisingly dainty and elegant, and suited Grace perfectly.

More than suited her. It was sexy as fuck.

She blushed, picking up my train of thought through the bond. "So, you like it?"

"I love it. I'd like it more if you were naked."

"I'm sure you would," Grace laughed.

Wild snorted, having taken Grace's spot in Dare's makeshift tattoo chair at the dining table while Dare worked on his forearm.

"Wild hasn't even flinched," Grace told me, giving him an indulgent smile. "You'd think he was just getting a haircut or something. The bond doesn't lie—he is feeling zero discomfort. Where are you going to get yours?"

I pulled the collar of my shirt to the side, showing Grace the empty spot on my collarbone.

"Nice," Dare said, glancing up at me before returning to his work. "I'm going to have to do my leg because I'm doing it myself—no offense, but I don't trust any of you to do it."

"So little faith," I sighed. "It's basically doodling with a needle. I could figure it out."

"Grace," Vasileios said, inclining his head as he sauntered into the room, Alesa trailing after him with the most obvious case of sex hair I'd ever seen. "I've organized a boat ride back to my home tomorrow with a friend, an uncle of sorts, who is docked at Piraeus. He can take ten people, five of them should be you and your soul bonds. It's too exposed here. We cannot stay. Not everyone, at least."

"There's over a hundred people here," Grace replied, her positive mood evaporating instantly. "How can I just leave most of them behind when they're looking to me for answers?"

"Gracie," I chided, wrapping an arm around her waist and pulling her against me. "We're all adults here, everyone knew what they were getting into. You can't babysit them all."

There was no way we could move as a group. Not now, after the video footage. We were way too obvious.

"The Spartoi..." Grace trailed off, probably wondering for the millionth time what to do with them. "We can't just abandon them. They don't know how to blend into society. They can't even communicate with the outside world."

Wild glanced up at us, frowning, and whatever Grace sensed from him through the bond, she didn't like.

"We're not splitting up," she told him fiercely. "I'm not risking it. If something happened to one of you..."

"Agreed," Bullet murmured, sliding past us to pour a glass of water from the kitchen.

"I don't know how to transport them without drawing everyone's attention, but I can find a way to house them if we just get them back to my hometown." Vasileios shrugged, indifferent. "Or maybe they stay here and use this home as a base? We can leave some Kakodaimonistai here to help them."

Grace nodded uneasily, worry for them warring with what would be the most practical solution. She wanted perfect comfort and perfect safety for all of us, and it wasn't possible. Something would have to give somewhere.

Vasileios sighed, noticing Grace's reluctance. "We can find more boats. I think we'll be safer traveling by sea than land."

She sent him a relieved smile, very deliberately not asking him to elaborate on 'find'.

Alesa was practically humping Vasileios' leg, ignoring the conversation completely. She was human, and susceptible to Vasileios' Philotes allure at the best of times, but having Dare around was probably making her too horny to think. They couldn't help it—to be a Philotes was to inspire lust.

"We'll decide in the morning, yes?" Vasileios asked, grabbing the back of Alesa's thighs and encouraging her to wrap her legs around his waist. "You keep doing... whatever it is you're doing. We'll talk tomorrow."

He was already heading back toward the terrace which led to the guest cabins, Alesa's lips suctioned onto his neck. Surprisingly, it wasn't Grace who was blushing this time, but Dare.

"Philotes daimons," he muttered under his breath.

"Don't be embarrassed," I laughed. "Grace is very accepting of all our daimon traits, and you've got one of the better ones. Wild is horny for violence, that's way worse."

Wild rolled his eyes.

"What are you thinking, Grace?" Bullet asked, leaning against the kitchen counter. "Do you want to head back to Vasileios' place tomorrow? Or is there somewhere else you had in mind?"

Bullet must have been paying closer attention than I was, because Grace immediately squirmed. "I keep remembering what Hygeia said. But maybe it's just agathos instincts talking. Maybe I'm swayed because of the connection I have to them."

"Maybe," Bullet agreed mildly. "Or maybe you have good intuition and it's the right choice. I'll make you some tea and we can plan an evacuation while these guys finish all getting tattoos just because you wanted a tattoo."

"This is my best work yet," Dare said, lifting the leg of his shorts to admire the depiction of The World on his thigh beneath the clear bandage. "Though I'm not in a rush to repeat tattooing *myself*. That was unpleasant."

"I did offer," I shot back with a grin, tracing the edge of the adhesive on my clavicle. "Aren't you going to repeat it on your other leg? Symmetry and all that?"

Dare shrugged, pulling the leg of his shorts down. "I was thinking I could teach Grace and then she could ink it on me. Eventually. You know?"

"I mean, I get why you'd rather have Grace touching your thighs than me, but I'm still a little offended," I laughed. Dare rolled his eyes,

bumping me with his shoulder as we made our way outside. Grace had pulled a few of the Spartoi aside for lunch—rice and canned beans—and between her English, Bullet's knowledge of Ancient Greek, and the sign language they'd been picking up from Wild, they were attempting to make a plan.

"Any luck?" I asked, flopping into the seat next to Wild and leaning my elbow on the table, propping my hand under my chin. Dare leaned his hip against the table, still holding himself slightly separate from the rest of our group. Apparently, matching tattoos wasn't enough to fully bring him into the fold, though the bond with Grace would definitely help with that, whenever they got to it.

Wild drummed his fingers irritably on the tabletop. Not good, then.

"They don't want to leave me," Grace explained, sounding slightly bemused.

"Theras even said 'no' in English," Bullet added cheerfully. "So at least the English lessons are going well. But they're never leaving Grace's side, ever, so there's that."

I laid my head down on the table with a groan. How were we supposed to do anything with a hundred soldiers following us around? There was no way to move discreetly with that many people, and the boat Vasileios had arranged definitely didn't have enough room.

"I know you guys said they nominally listen to Wild," Dare began hesitantly. "But have you considered, er, *commanding* them?"

I turned my head to the side, resting it on my forearms so I could watch Grace's expression. She chewed nervously on her lower lip. "I understand what it's like to be a slave to my instincts. I don't ever want to take away anyone's free will."

There was my Gracie again, wanting perfect safety and perfect comfort for everyone. No wonder the Fates hadn't made a daimon the Prophêtis. We didn't possess that kind of compassion.

"Hey," Foster panted, jogging up the steps and skidding a stop in front of us. "The big press conference kept getting pushed back, but it's happening now. You guys are going to want to see this."

He quickly turned up the volume on his phone, holding it out for us to watch the broadcast playing on the screen.

"There are no *gods*. This is nonsense."

"Is that the *President*?" I asked, squinting at the screen. Honestly, I didn't pay much attention to politics, but I was pretty sure that dude was the one in charge. Behind him were a bunch of other stoic, boring-looking people that I guessed were other politicians? World leaders?

"Sure is. We've really hit the big time," Bullet noted. "At least this one isn't an agathos, though I can spot a couple in the background."

Bullet was right—there were two pale-eyed agathos in suits in the crowd. While the humans may know about our existence, apparently the eyes, our biggest giveaway, were still hidden from them.

"There is clearly some kind of genuine threat, some elaborate hoax at play," the speaker continued, standing behind a podium. His suit was rumpled, and there were dark bags under his eyes. All of them looked terrible—like they'd been up for two days straight discussing the whole world-falling-apart issue.

Good.

"Perhaps some sort of *Satanic* magic involved—I'm not ruling that out. You heard her say herself that she wants you to do *rituals*. But the nonsense that this *woman*, Grace Bellamy, was spouting is just that—nonsense. There

are explanations for everything—the scorpions, the light effects at the ruins—all can be logically explained. *Will* be logically explained."

I didn't think I imagined the extra derision in his voice when he said 'woman'. Like Grace was some sort of hysterical, lesser being that only an idiot would listen to. Was that how people saw Grace? That was so unfair.

Where the fuck were Nyx and Gaia throughout the centuries of patriarchal oppression? They'd *chosen* to stay silent through all that bullshit.

"It is clear to all of us," he continued, "that Grace Bellamy is deliberately creating a divide between people who are already concerned about the very explainable rise in natural disasters. That she is exploiting their fear for her own gain. We have already seen evidence of the violence her words and actions have caused. Grace Bellamy must be found and detained. That is how we will get explanations. She is a threat, and while we don't currently know the full scope of what she's done or what she plans to do—"

"Joke's on them, we don't have a plan," I scoffed.

"—we know that it cannot continue. A notice has been issued by Interpol—this is with a view to locating and arresting Grace Bellamy with the intent of extradition back to the United States. We know that she was last seen in Athens, but she may have left Greece by now and her location is currently unknown. There will be a reward in place for anyone who helps in apprehending her, but we do urge you to be careful. This is an unstable individual with delusions of grandeur. Proceed with extreme caution."

He was wrong, and we all knew it, but Grace couldn't quite hide her shame through the bond at his words. She'd been told she was wrong and broken and unnatural her entire life, and now she was hearing it on a global scale.

"Why don't they know where I am?" Grace asked, her voice disconcertingly flat. "We weren't that secretive in getting here. There should have been witnesses."

"My guess is that they're either discrediting those accounts, or people here have been less than forthcoming with authorities who claim the very real threat they experienced was just *special effects*," Bullet replied, rolling his eyes. "They're trying to downplay it all. To keep everyone under control."

"They're suggesting Grace has a god complex as a way of undermining her," Dare agreed.

"Right, when what Grace actually has is a *Cassandra* complex, in that she gives people accurate warnings and no one fucking believes her," Bullet muttered. "Though those agathos in the background are looking a little nervous now."

He was right, they did look a little uncomfortable. Whatever they believed about Grace, they knew that what they'd seen hadn't been special effects. They knew Gaia was real, they knew she was mad and wanted the daimons wiped out. They fucking *worshipped* her. That they stood back now and said nothing just proved how cowardly they were, how even if they couldn't lie, they valued power and prestige over the truth.

"I'll take questions now—" the President began, immediately drowned out by reporters all clamoring at once to ask their follow-ups, their voices blending together into an indecipherable blur of angry sound. No, maybe not angry. Afraid, perhaps?

What we were facing *was* scary. Unfortunately, it seemed as though the human authorities were going to make that fear worse, not better. I doubted the two agathos in the back of the frame had helped keep things calm in whatever secret meetings had led up to this moment.

"I'm not entertaining this heresy!" the President shouted, evidently hearing a question that we couldn't. "This is all a *lie*. The elaborate speech she fed you was a *lie*. There is no Nyx, no *Gaia*. This is all—"

The stream cut out.

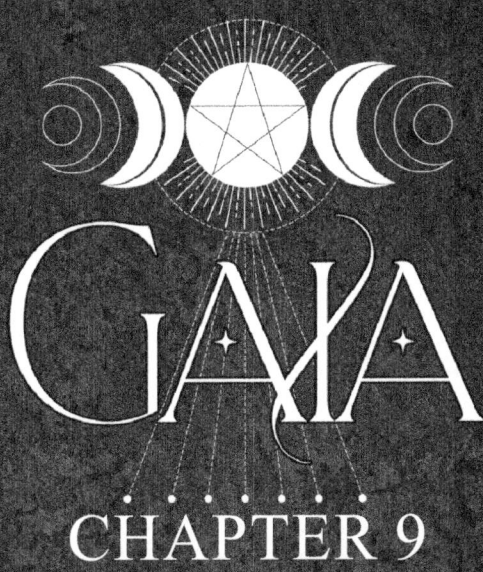

GAIA

CHAPTER 9

The noise was overwhelming.

Constant, *incessant* whining from ungrateful humans, who'd been more than happy to ignore my existence for centuries. Millenia, even.

Grace, Grace, Grace. It was all I heard all day long. Grace the Agathos. The *Prophêtis*. The enemy, or the savior, depending on who was speaking.

The last time I'd felt this level of irritation at a specific agathos, it was her selfish wretch of a mother, demanding an army of sons from her childbed. Muttering incoherently about her daughter learning someday that I didn't listen. Truly, Faith Bellamy was one of the Fates' biggest failures in their experiments to draw agathos and daimons together.

But in my rage at her offensively obnoxious request, I'd changed the course of my own fate forever. I'd intervened. Asked the Fates to give her no children until she learned some humility. Instructed them to keep the daughter's soul bonds from her until she was well into adulthood, to humiliate Faith.

Instructed them that Grace Bellamy's voice *should* be elevated above the rest, to spite her mother.

They had. They'd done everything I asked, and in doing so, Grace the Agathos became unique. Touched by the Fates. Destined for greatness. A *Prophêtis*.

Grace was a Prophêtis because of me.

She was the right combination of light and dark to bring together agathos and daimons, had suffered in her extended period of loneliness to make her even consider the idea of daimonic soul bonds, and I'd given her the ear of the gods in a moment of irritation with her mother.

She was the perfect storm. The exact combination the Fates had been waiting for, centuries in the making, ready to receive the prophecy.

The error had been mine. I hadn't believed a balance between agathos and daimons could be found. Nyx and I were too different, so our creations must be too. Dark and light warred for dominance, never able to comfortably coexist.

Until they did.

She was among a generation of balanced agathos and daimons, souls so stable they could be bound to one another. Perhaps that's all she would have been—an oddity among a sea of newfound oddities as agathos discovered daimon soul bonds—but *I* made her more. Grace's power, the risk she posed, all my mistakes.

She probably thought she deserved the mantle of power and prophecy the Fates had given her. That she'd done something to *earn* the glory bestowed on her. I already knew Nyx claimed credit, that she thought *she'd* made Grace important because Grace had prayed to her, but she was wrong.

Grace Bellamy was merely fortunate that her mother was a greedy wretch of an agathos. Nyx would have never heard Grace's prayer if I hadn't given her voice power. She was an agathos who spoke to gods because of *me*.

"There is no Nyx, no Gaia."

These infuriating creatures, little gnats who only existed because *I* allowed it.

How *dare* they?

They filled the rich soil I gave them with their horrid, intrusive pipes and wires, and I let them. The earth that was my very body, my home, my essence. They desecrated it, more and more each day—and I *let* them, because I thought they would love me for it. Love me and worship me the way the mortals had worshipped the Olympians so many years ago.

They'd forgotten me. They'd built monuments to their false idols and *forgotten* me.

They'd been confronted with proof of my existence, and still they denied me.

The earth shook, ripples of my power extending through every inch of land and sea.

No more.

I would tolerate the disrespect no more.

Above me, the sky turned dark as Nyx drew her veil of night across the world, hiding the sun from view and taking its warmth with it.

I could have laughed.

Was this sisterly affection? Nyx was a lazy, unambitious coward, but she would not tolerate being denied either. She especially would not tolerate seeing *my* retaliation without enforcing one of her own.

Loose earth fell into the place where man-made intrusions had once been, the land healing itself, renewing.

Finally, the incessant buzz of humanity and their horrid inventions went quiet. Mortals had managed just fine without such things for most of time.

Let them learn to manage again.

GRACE

CHAPTER 10

"Time to go," I translated, watching Wild's hands move without really taking in what he was saying. Someone had lit a candle, illuminating the suddenly pitch-black space. Pitch black, in the middle of the day.

There was no moon, no stars.

Just inky, cold, *unnatural* darkness. It was as though a veil had been pulled across the sky, trapping us in the dark.

Not only that, the lights didn't work. The faucet trickled dry. The phone signal had abruptly died. We'd gone from watching news coverage one minute to being plunged into the Stone Age the next. Or maybe the Ice Age. It was so cold.

Everyone was panicking.

"Pack your shit!" Vasileios yelled over the clinking sound of the Spartoi's armor as they shifted around restlessly, encircling the property.

"You're right," Bullet agreed, watching Wild's frantic signing. "People will be freaking out, it's a good time to move."

"Yeah, we're getting the fuck out of here," Riot muttered, hauling me out of the chair and into the house. My soul bonds were all gathered close behind me, Dare holding a tapered candle he'd snagged from a display.

It was so dark.

Riot immediately grabbed a duffel bag we'd brought with us, filling it with the few clothes we'd acquired before stripping the blankets off the bed. Wild moved to help, folding them tightly and stacking them inside pillowcases.

"So is Gaia's plan just to kill us all now?" Dare asked, moving closer to them with the light so they could see what they were doing. "We'll freeze without sunlight. Or starve. Or both."

"Whatever is happening with the electricity and the phones? That's Gaia," Bullet said, leaning against the doorjamb. He was so pale. Had he always been that pale? "The darkness? That's all Nyx."

"Nyx has never gotten involved before," I mumbled, pulling on the wool cardigan Wild handed me without paying much attention to it. We had very few clothes here—a few emergency items Orion's family kept on hand for guests, as well as a lost-and-found bin that had been thoroughly raided. I'd been wearing the same dress for days, washing it in the evenings and letting it dry overnight. "And I thought... I thought we'd reached some kind of truce with Gaia. After I offered those crocus seeds at the Temple of Zeus, she's been quiet."

Bullet accepted a sweater from Wild. "Maybe the truce still holds—Gaia wasn't responding to you, but the insult of being told she doesn't exist. And if she responded, then there was no question that Nyx would too. It's a pride thing."

"And now we're living in the fucking dark ages," Riot muttered, roughly zipping the bag shut and pulling on a black long-sleeved shirt over the t-shirt he was wearing. Out of the guys, only Bullet had a semi-decent sweater, and I didn't think it was an accident that the three of them gave us the warmest clothes.

"Where are we going?" Dare asked, as I slid my feet into my sandals and crouched down to buckle them. My toes were already starting to ache with cold.

"To the agathos," I said slowly. "To Sophia. If there's one thing we need right now, it's wisdom."

Sophia had whispered in my ear so many times recently, had watched over me and talked me through what needed to be done... I *trusted* her. I wasn't sure I could say the same about any other divinity.

"If Hygeia was telling the truth about us being safe with Sophia, an agathos stronghold is probably the last place anyone would look on the off-chance anyone still decides the bounty on your head is worth pursuing even while the world falls apart," Riot pointed out, sounding resigned. "Where is it?"

Riot was looking at Bullet for an answer, and while he knew more about the gods than me, this was *agathos* history. I'd grown up learning about the pilgrimage sites for agathos since I was old enough to begin Saturday morning lessons.

"Ephesus. The library at Ephesus is one of the few places where all agathos are to visit in our lifetimes to pay tribute to the original noble spirits. There are four statues there, and the agathos from their lines are heavily encouraged to go—Sophia, Arete, Episteme, and Ennoia. Wisdom, Virtue, Knowledge, and Thought."

I'd never considered going, too convinced that I was a damaged agathos and I'd either taint the sacred space with my presence, or spontaneously burst into flames the moment I set foot there.

"Ephesus is a popular spot for daimons too," Bullet volunteered quietly. "Not the library where those statues are, but centuries ago a daimon brought down a terrible plague on the city." He shrugged apologetically. "That's the kind of thing daimons are into."

"*Were* into," Riot amended. "Though I imagine this chaos is about to bring out every daimon's worst instincts. You're sure that's where you want to go, Gracie?"

Yes. No. Maybe?

I knew I wasn't thinking clearly, it was impossible to. But this is what my gut was saying, and maybe that was worth following.

"To have the *original* agathos on our side, that might be key in swaying the mortal agathos," Dare suggested hesitantly, glancing around like he wasn't sure if he should speak or not. "Surely, they'd have to take the founders of their lines seriously, if the goddess' rage hasn't already given them a much-needed scare."

He frowned, staring out the window at the dark sky. The shadows danced off his sharp jaw, the candlelight illuminating his daimonic eyes, making them glow. "It's not like this darkness is going to last forever, we need to think long-term. I have less than zero desire to work with the agathos, but there's only so many fronts we can fight a war on, you know? We need all the help we can get. Sophia guided me to Jack's place when she had no reason to, except that I was connected to Grace. To the prophecy and everything else that comes with it. That has to be a good sign."

Even without the bond I so desperately craved with Dare, I could see how much those words cost him. Of all of us, he might hate the agathos the most.

"What makes you think it won't last forever?" Riot asked doubtfully.

"Well, everyone and everything will die without sunlight, so..." Dare trailed off with a shrug. "Surely, that's not Nyx's goal?"

Bullet and I exchanged a wary look. Dare hadn't seen all the things we'd seen, maybe he wasn't quite as jaded as we were.

"Let's hope not," Bullet replied eventually. "But just in case, we should probably be prepared to beg for mercy on behalf of beings that Nyx does not give a fuck about, for zero gratitude from anyone."

The noise from downstairs grew louder and more insistent. We had to get down there, to *lead*.

Straightening my shoulders, I walked past my bonded with the most serene look on my face that I could manage, descending the stairs to where everyone was crowded around, panic thick in the air.

I should have stayed down here. I wasn't *just* Grace anymore—I didn't have the luxury of disappearing and taking time to come to terms with my feelings. Not right away, at least. People were relying on *me*, looking to me for guidance.

My soul bonds assembled behind me on the stairs, a steadying presence at my back.

The Spartoi were outside, I caught glimpses of them through the windows, lined up with their backs to the villa, weapons at the ready and pointed upwards, as though the sky itself would attack.

"You're leaving," Estrella said flatly, leaning on Foster. "Good."

"Good?" I repeated in surprise.

"It is essential that you are safe," Vasileios replied, his voice calm and steady, and unusually serious. "It always was, but now more than ever."

"Not to freak you out," Foster began hesitantly. "But literally everyone on earth will die without the sun. It won't even take that long. A couple of weeks? Maybe less? Prophêtis, we really need you to use that connection to the gods. To intercede."

"I know," I agreed, blowing out a long breath. "Nothing matters more."

Wild was scribbling furiously on his notepad, and he carefully edged around me to show Vasileios and a few of the other daimons what he'd written. There were glances at me and a few words of quiet agreement, and Wild sent a sense of apology through the bond to me, which meant he wouldn't tell me whatever it was he was doing. Something that my agathos instincts wouldn't like.

"Don't tell us where you're going," Foster said, coming to the same conclusion as he watched the daimons. "In case any of us are questioned."

"The Spartoi—" I began.

"Will have to come with us," Estrella cut in with a grimace, glancing out the window. "Whether they like it or not. Wherever they go, attention will follow."

Foster nodded. "An army of ancient soldiers is a great diversion."

Part of me balked at using them that way, but maybe I should have more faith in them? The Spartoi had turned the barn into a rudimentary war camp—they didn't need technology to get by. As much as they attracted attention, the others would benefit from having the Spartoi's guidance until we got things back to normal.

Because we *would* get things back to normal. We had to.

"I'll pack some food for you, *Prophêtis*," Leonie offered.

"Everyone, get your things," Vasileios called lazily. "We'll leave in groups, Grace and her soul bonds first. If you can get to Piraeus, my friend with the boat can transport you. He will be... sympathetic to your plight," he continued, pulling Riot aside to fill him in as I got swallowed up in the crowd, the Kakodaimonistai in particular crowding close to say goodbye. I felt the urge to give them some luck rising within me, rushing through my veins, but Dare's hand clamped down on my arm before I could. I couldn't bestow my Eutychia gift on daimons or fellow agathos, and it seemed to almost shy away within me in response to Dare's touch.

"Thank you," I breathed, eyes widening at how close we might have come to disaster if I'd doused all the humans around me in good luck. Whatever boat we went on would probably sink.

"Anytime," Dare murmured, sliding his hand down my wrist so as not to break the skin-to-skin contact, before linking our fingers firmly together.

He stayed as a silent sentinel at my back while the Kakodaimonistai assured me that they would continue making offerings to the Olympians, that they would pray for me, that they would do whatever they could to protect me. It was humbling and frightening all at once.

"Come on," Dare murmured, tugging me away from the crowd. "People either covered for us or they weren't taken seriously if they were asked where we were, but that might change if they blame you for the goddesses' actions. Best to get leave unseen if we can."

I held on tight to his hand, saying goodbye to as many people as I could as he dragged me out to the terrace, Riot joining me on my other side at some point, exchanging a loaded look with Dare over my head.

Wild and Bullet approached, both looking grim, while the Spartoi stood in their positions, watchful and stiff with tension.

"I have to go," I told Theras slowly, pointing at me then into the distance. "You have to stay." I gestured at the Spartoi, then pointed at the villa.

Theras narrowed his eyes. I was no expert in Ancient Greek, but I'd looked up a few phrases to try communicate with them a little better.

Shoot, what were we going to do without the internet?

One problem at a time.

"*Mē kheíron béltiston,*" I said slowly, not confident in the least about my pronunciation. *The least bad choice is best.* None of the options are good, this is the lesser evil. It wasn't exactly comforting, but Theras was practical, and this was the practical solution.

His lips twitched and he gave me a slightly exasperated nod. It was the most human gesture I'd ever seen from him.

"Listen to Vasileios, he will help you. I'll see you soon," I promised as he called out something to the other Spartoi, muscles flexing with the strain of staying in place. "We will meet again."

Wild was already dragging me away, through the shadows at the edge of the villa, towards the barn where the Spartoi had been staying.

It was harder to say goodbye than I thought. These people were here because of me, and whatever suffering they experienced because of it was on my conscience too.

This part of the property was less elegant and manicured, more filled with rough bushes and rocky dry dirt rather than lush lawn. We didn't light any of the candles we'd brought with us, clinging to each other's hands in the darkness as we stumbled our way... west? East? I had no idea.

The panicked sounds of frightened people grew louder as we approached the street, even though this wasn't a populous area. If the signs of panic were visible here, they'd be overwhelming in the cities.

"Want me to sing to you?" Bullet suggested as Wild helped us both over the fence. Cars sped past with headlights that seemed almost blinding in the oppressive darkness. Had they always been that bright? There was shouting, and Wild stiffened slightly behind me at the sounds of fighting and glass shattering.

It was already chaos, and it was only the beginning.

"Yes, please," I whispered to Bullet.

"Keep walking," Riot instructed us, draping a blanket over my shoulders and pulling it over my hair like a hood before slinking away into the darkness with Dare. Bullet linked our arms together, and we followed closely at Wild's back. I didn't know where we were going, but I trusted my soul bonds to get me there. I had to.

Bullet hummed for a while, before transitioning into a slower, low-pitched version of *Memory* from *Cats*. An ode to nighttime, the loss of memories past, and the hope of a new dawn on the horizon. I focused on the lyrics, keeping my head bowed, hidden beneath the blanket. Maybe it was cowardly to hide from the horror, but the soothing, almost lullaby-quality of Bullet's singing made the world a little less frightening, if only for a moment. It wouldn't last. I'd need to look up eventually, and I knew what I saw would terrify me.

He finished on a haunting note, and I clung on tighter, feeling Wild's gentle appreciation for the both of us through the bond.

"What are we going to do?" I whispered, staring at the ground. "People will die. So many people…"

It wasn't just the dark and cold. If it was Gaia that had somehow turned off the power, would she turn it back on again? Could those actions be undone? Nausea churned in my gut at the thought of hospital patients, reliant on machines to keep them alive. Even now, babies would be born into this new, bleak, terrifying world. People were giving *birth* in this nightmare. And the temperature—it was cold here, and this was by no means a cold part of the planet. What about the people farther north? They'd freeze within the hour…

"What are we going to *do*?" I reiterated, my voice catching.

"We can't save them all," Bullet said quietly. "*You* can't. I'll visit Nyx in the dreamscape, I'll beg her to lift the darkness. But even if I do, there are no guarantees. It's not me Nyx wants repentance from."

No, it wasn't. Her pride had been hurt by the human assertion that the goddesses didn't exist. Would they make that connection? Would they admit they were wrong? The last thing I wanted was for Bullet to go to Nyx in the dreamscape. He already looked so exhausted, and he'd collapsed the last time he'd used his cards—

"I have to try," Bullet said, squeezing my arm. "At least to lift the darkness and the cold. No one else has a direct line to Nyx, I can't ignore that responsibility. As for what Gaia's done... Well, we don't know the full extent, I guess. We don't know if it *can* be undone." He snorted. "If Gaia wanted to fuck with humanity, she should have tried this earlier. Sure, natural disasters are bad, but mortals will lose their shit without power and internet. Plus, you know, all the plants and animals will die, and we'll starve to death. There's that too."

I made a strangled sound of agreement, not sure I was ready to come to terms with the ramifications of all that yet. To confront what the world would look like now.

For me, life had changed dramatically from the second I'd said a prayer to La Nuit and that candle had gone out. For those mortals who'd managed to avoid the worst of Gaia's wrath—the natural disasters and plane crashes and giant scorpions—*this* was their defining moment. Their time before and time after. Nothing would ever be the same again.

Wild grabbed our shoulders, pulling us to a stop as a car stopped at the curb. There was a group of people on the street, approaching us, and Wild all but threw Bullet and I into the backseat before climbing in behind us, smacking the back of Riot's seat to get him moving.

"Let's hope it's got a full tank because I imagine gas is about to become a very hot commodity," Bullet pointed out, his hand trembling slightly in mine. He was doing such a good job of locking down his fear through the bond—they all were—that the slight shake was the only giveaway that he was as terrified as I was.

"How long is the drive?" I asked, blinking at the fuel gauge. Between the headlights and the lights on the dash, it was almost blinding after absolute darkness.

Riot glanced at me in the rearview. Was that... was that blood on his face? "According to Vasileios, it would normally be an hour but we need to avoid any crowds or stops, so I guess it takes as long as it takes. I know that's not a very satisfying answer."

I nodded. "You, um, you have a little something on your cheek."

Riot glanced at himself in the rearview and muttered a curse under his breath, lifting the bottom of his shirt to rub at the splatter. "Pretend you didn't see that, Gracie."

"The other guy is fine," Dare added hastily. "Sans car, but fine."

"Right," I replied weakly, my guilt colliding with the vaguely sheepish ambivalence I was getting from Riot through the bond. "He's fine."

"Probably best you don't ask," Bullet murmured apologetically, linking our fingers. I gripped his hand, grabbing Wild's with my other. They were daimons, and their moral compass didn't always align with mine. It was hard to reconcile with the fact that I trusted them implicitly.

Wild cupped my jaw gently, turning my face to his and resting his forehead against mine, a wealth of apology in the gesture.

"It's okay," I assured him quietly. *Mè kheíron béltiston.* It was the least bad choice.

CHAPTER 11

To think we'd been worried about being seen by someone who might report our whereabouts. For one, nobody's phones appeared to be working, so reporting us wasn't exactly easy; what had been a three-second task roughly a few hours ago was now impossible as the world turned to shit.

Aside from that, absolutely no one cared who we were as we ditched the car and walked to the waterfront, because everybody was way too busy panicking about the end of the earth to care about what we were up to.

Every shop window we'd passed was broken. The streets in and around the city were packed with angry, terrified people. Riot had done a good job at steering us away from the crowds, but every time we'd gotten close, we'd had to speed up because even the shit box we were driving attracted the wrong kind of attention.

Perhaps I'd been naïve to think the darkness was a temporary blip. Grace and the others hadn't shared that optimism, and the general population was *definitely* acting like it was the end of the world.

It was a disaster. I'd always hated Gaia, but Nyx was making it very fucking difficult to be on her team right now.

"Can you watch over Grace and Bullet?" Riot asked, looking solemnly at me. "Between me and Wild, we should be able to acquire a small boat that we can row out to where Vasileios' friend is anchored in the harbor."

"Of course, but how confident are we that he's still here?" I replied uneasily. It had seemed like a sound plan when we left the villa, but the port was mayhem, violence breaking out in every direction. Wild's fingers flexed incessantly at his side, his breathing forcibly even. I didn't feel the call to bloodshed like he did, but I knew what he was going through. When I was surrounded by lust, it seemed to beat like a second pulse inside me, urging me to act, to submerge myself in desire and spread it to everyone. I imagined Wild was experiencing the same thing.

"Vasileios said he'd been in touch with the guy earlier today, so hopefully he hasn't left." Riot grimaced, glancing out at the water. There were still waves lapping against the shore, and that had to be a good thing, right? Weren't tides connected to the moon? It felt like Nyx had just drawn a black curtain over the sky, and I hoped everything was still functional *behind* that curtain, even though the temperature seemed to drop by the minute.

"I don't know if he cares about us," Riot continued. "But Vasileios said they were really close—more like an uncle and nephew? So hopefully the guy wouldn't leave without him. The sooner we go, the better. Wait down on the rocks, we'll get as close as we can."

I didn't like the sound of that at all, but the rocky area of coastline we were standing above was a lot less chaotic than the port proper a little further down. Despite the darkness, the number of fires burning did a good job illuminating the carnage.

"Wait, there's something in the water," Bullet said, grabbing Grace's hand as she moved to climb onto the rocks. We all held still, watching the surface ripple outwards from a spot not too far from the coastline.

"What now?" Riot muttered, sounding surprisingly exasperated rather than *fucking terrified*. I guessed that for them, the weirdness was a little more routine than it was for me.

"It's a boat," Grace murmured, squinting at the water. "It's *the* boat. The one that carried us through the cave when we left the underworld."

Well, better that than a sea monster.

"Is it watertight?" I asked, trying to sound less nervous than I felt. It looked older than dirt, bobbing in place near the rocks as though it was anchored there even though nothing tethered it.

"It is," Grace replied with confidence, tugging on my arm slightly. "It's a gift from the underworld."

Because they want us to join them there sooner? But everyone else seemed happy enough, so I kept my thoughts about accepting gifts from the gods of the dead to myself.

The five of us carefully picked our way over the boulders down to the sea line. With the sudden disappearance of *the sun*, the breeze coming off the water was freezing. It felt more like we were standing on the coast of Antarctica than Greece.

111

A crowd of angry humans moved closer, running along the street just above us, and I crouched down, grabbing the most jagged rock I could comfortably hold as a weapon.

"We're definitely going to have to wade, it's too rocky," Bullet whispered as the group passed us. "I think we might need to strip. It's way too cold to be sitting in wet clothes."

Wild went first, yanking off his clothes and shoving them into the bag Riot was holding before wading into the water. Of course he didn't make a sound and made it look easy. Next up was Riot—naked and carrying the bag above his head to keep it dry—who let out a string of curses as soon as he went in, letting us know just how cold it was.

Grace's nerves were potent and definitely not all nudity-related as we stripped off. She clearly didn't like the water. The three of us held hands as we climbed down the rocks, clothes shoved safely in the pillowcase of stuff I was balancing on my head, and I sucked in a breath at the frigid temperature.

Fuck me. My balls are going to fall off.

Thank you to all the divinities for watertight tattoo adhesives.

"Cold, cold, cold," Grace whimpered, gripping my arm tightly with icy fingers.

"Nearly there," Riot encouraged, hauling himself into the boat while Wild held onto the other side, keeping the vessel steady. "Come here, Gracie."

"Bullet first," she insisted through chattering teeth.

Before Bullet could object, Riot leaned over, hooking his arms under Bullet's armpits and yanking him out of the water. Riot carefully deposited Bullet in the boat before reaching for Grace, lifting her even more gently.

"Get the blankets out," I instructed Bullet, tossing the sack I was holding into his lap.

"You next," Riot ordered, grabbing my hand and pulling me up with a grunt of exertion. Grace, already bundled in a blanket with Bullet, handed me and Riot one to share, while Wild climbed into the boat with a slightly aggravating amount of ease even though he'd been standing in the water the longest.

"We have the coordinates," Riot said, rattling off a bunch of numbers that meant nothing to me. "But since none of us know shit about sailing, I guess we're going to have to try read the names of the boats in the dark and hope for the—"

The rowboat lurched suddenly, making each of us grab onto it for purchase as it started weaving through the water with no help from us.

"Nifty," Bullet said with forced cheer. "Built-in GPS."

"Yes, nifty," I deadpanned, heart pounding out of my chest. We dried off with the blankets as best we could, teeth chattering loudly, before pulling our clothes back on. Even that felt like a monumental effort. My limbs just weren't cooperating.

We swerved closer to the shoreline where an enormous bonfire was growing out of control. Someone threw a punch, but their opponent dodged it, knocking them into the water where they quickly emerged, shouting furiously. None of it was in English, but I felt like I got the gist without understanding the words. Wild's breathing was labored, his teeth gritted together as he forced his eyes away from the violence on the shore.

Everyone wanted to get the fuck out of Athens where Gaia had unleashed her scorpions, and without an organized evacuation, they'd fight their way out to protect their loved ones. I doubted these people agreed with Mr. President's statement that the goddesses didn't exist. They'd experienced Gaia's magic firsthand.

"What are we going to do?" Grace asked, her quiet voice difficult to hear over the crashing of the waves and the yelling and fighting of the people. "It wasn't meant to be this way. Not just the darkness and everything, but the *fighting*. I didn't mean for that to happen."

"It was probably always going to be this way," Bullet sighed, his face so pallid he was almost glowing in the darkness. "Change is hard—you told them that yourself in your speech. It doesn't come easily, and it doesn't happen overnight."

Grace's guilt brushed faintly at my psyche, a slightly unnerving but welcome sensation.

"Don't feel bad," I said firmly, huddling up to Riot in the hopes we'd both avoid hypothermia. "You didn't ask for this. You couldn't have controlled what two ancient, powerful goddesses decided to do. You can't control the violent responses either. Fear makes people do irrational things."

"Exactly," Bullet agreed. "And once we're somewhere a little less volatile, we can pray and I'll try to visit Nyx in the dreamscape. I don't love the idea of risking a goddess' wrath when we're in the middle of the ocean; drowning is not how I want to go."

It was a weak attempt at a joke that may have landed better if Bullet didn't appear to be actively dying right in front of our eyes.

The rowboat slowed as we approached a white sailboat that looked to be about thirty feet long. A light moved back and forth, and as we got closer I realized it was a daimon holding a torch in one hand and a gun in the other.

Great.

Riot, Wild, and I all tensed, shifting to hide Grace and Bullet from view.

"Please don't shoot us," Grace called out before any of us could speak, her voice far softer and more non-confrontational than any of us daimons could have managed.

"You're Arsène, right?" Riot added. "Vasileios sent us to you."

"You are her. The agathos," Arsène replied, his accented voice carrying over the waves. It was a different accent from the mostly Greek ones I'd heard recently. French, perhaps? The rowboat brought us up to the very side of his vessel, and he peered over the railing at us. It was hard to see him from where we were, but he looked to be older, with chin-length hair that occasionally glinted silver in the torchlight, and deep wrinkles around his face, although he appeared bulky and strong. I had no idea what kind of daimon he was. "You are Grace."

"I am. And I'm wanted by the authorities, so if you don't feel comfortable helping us, I completely understand."

"What did you say that for?!" Riot hissed.

Arsène set the gun down, holding up his empty hand. "You should board before anyone sees you, Grace the Agathos."

The mysterious rowboat disappeared into the sea the moment we boarded, Arsène fussing with sails and muttering under his breath when we told him we needed to get to Ephesus.

The minute Arsène had the sails unfurled, the wind picked up, and he looked at us with narrowed eyes. "You have powerful friends."

"The wind gods are descendents of Gaia," Bullet replied, sounding confused in a way that was deeply unsettling. Bullet was supposed to know all the god stuff. "I'd like to think that this is a good sign, but I'm not confident."

"Well, they are taking us in the right direction," Arsène acknowledged gruffly, scratching his thick, gray beard. "But a good wind means everyone is moving too," he added, gesturing at the other ships in the harbor.

"What sort of daimon are you?" I asked, trying to get a read on him. It wasn't always obvious, but generally we could pick up a vibe of some kind that gave us a clue. Arsène was a total mystery, though.

He gave me a look so resentful that I regretted asking. "Pothos."

"No shit?" Bullet replied, all curiosity. "I've never met one of those."

Arsène grunted, squinting out over the water as lights drew closer. "Perhaps you should go in the cabin, agathos. If someone questions us, you are the only one here who can't lie."

"Right," Grace agreed, throwing another uncertain glance at the dark water. She clearly didn't feel great about being out at sea in general, let alone stuck in a room below deck.

"I could join you?" I offered before I could stop myself. It felt so instinctive to soothe her, but was that just the bond pushing us together? "I have a *lot* of embarrassing stories about Riot that would make excellent distractions."

Riot narrowed his eyes at me. "You might want to think about some of the more embarrassing *dares* you took on before you start telling stories."

"I'll keep it in mind," I laughed, reaching out my hand and hoping Grace took it. I felt like a blushing schoolboy, trying to hold my crush's hand, but I had to start somewhere, right? Whenever I felt like I was getting closer to Grace, life had spectacularly gotten in the way.

"I will show you your room," Arsène said, gesturing to follow as he led us down past the steering area—captain's wheel? Whatever, I didn't know shit about boats—into the surprisingly wide space below deck. He grabbed a smaller flashlight as he went, chucking it to me, while shining his ahead so we could see where we were stepping, all of us ducking down slightly to avoid the low ceiling.

"Bathroom," he grunted, illuminating a closed door on the right. "Kitchen. You can cook here. I have some canned items, and we will fish," he added, waving at the small cooking area with a tiny gas stove and sink. There were long bench seats down each side with a fold down table in the middle, and two more doors beyond.

"There are two cabins. This is mine," Arsène said, showing us the smaller one, packed to the brim with stuff. "This will be yours. No one has used it in many years. Once, other daimon friends lived on board with me, but they are... gone now. Make yourselves comfortable."

He shrugged, stomping back through the dining area, shoulders hunched over to avoid hitting his head on the ceiling.

"Daimons living together?" I muttered. "That's weird."

Arsène looked to be in his sixties. Daimons in his day weren't exactly out there making buddies.

"I think it helps to remember that we're the first generation of successful experiments after a string of failed ones," Grace replied wryly, giving my hand a quick squeeze. "The Fates have wanted to bring agathos and daimons together for a long time. What is a Pothos daimon?"

"I've never met one before, but they're sort of the dark side of love," I admitted, feeling bad for the guy. "Longing, yearning, that kind of thing."

"Oh," Grace breathed. "That's so sad."

We both ducked our head to enter the cabin, which was basically just an odd-shaped sleep space. I shone the flashlight around, getting the feel of the wood-paneled room. Thin mattresses were arranged on a wooden platform like a puzzle to form an almost W-shaped bed, built into the curved shape of the room. It was definitely too small for all five of us, but we could probably fit three quite comfortably. There was a hatch in the center of the roof, which was the only space with slightly more headroom, and I assumed could be opened to the deck above. A couple of narrow shelves overhead was the only storage space. I couldn't imagine someone actually *living* here.

"Hold the flashlight up and I'll put the sheets on the bed," Grace instructed, kneeling in the doorway beneath the hutch, the only floor space in the cabin, and unfolding a pile of off-white flat sheets. She worked quickly, tucking them in around the odd angles, and setting out the thicker blankets for us to lie under. All of our own blankets were wet, and unlikely to dry any time soon with how dark and cold it was.

"Done," Grace breathed, climbing onto the bed and pulling a blanket over her bare legs before patting the spot next to her.

"Is this okay?" I asked her as I shut the door behind me, suddenly aware of how small this space was. "I can get one of the others—"

"No, it's okay," Grace assured me quickly. "I want to spend time with you, Dare. And you mentioned a distraction, and I could really do with one."

I nodded, able to sit upright under the hutch, perched at the edge of the mattress.

"You're not claustrophobic, are you?" I asked, propping my thigh up on the bed. Grace slid her blanket-covered feet under my knee, tucking them underneath for warmth.

Cute. She was so fucking cute.

That wasn't the bond, surely. I found her cute because she was cute, didn't I? I hated not being able to trust my own judgment.

"I don't know if I'm claustrophobic. This is my first real test," Grace replied, glancing warily around the cabin. "I'm pretty confident I hate sailing, though."

I laughed unexpectedly at the completely flat way she'd delivered the words. Grace was almost always sweet, polite to everyone, constantly battling to see the bright side in all the darkness that had been thrown her way.

But apparently she drew the line at sailing.

"All my past boat trips involved me being drunk in the sun. I don't know how I feel about this," I admitted, absently resting my hand on her shin and rubbing circles into her leg with my thumb. "Obviously, it's not the worst thing that's happened today, but we don't have to talk about that," I added quickly as Grace's face fell.

Smooth as silk, Dare, you fucking moron.

"It's not as though I can avoid it," Grace replied, twisting the blanket nervously between her fingers. "I have to fix this, Dare. People will die."

119

"*We*," I corrected. "You're not in this alone. Though for what it's worth, *you* didn't provoke the goddesses into responding, and said goddesses might not care too much about what you have to say on the matter." I thought about it for a moment, assessing the likelihood of humans groveling enough to appease both goddesses. "Though if you *could* convince the goddesses to drop it, or it at least looked that way, it'd probably do wonders for your reputation. Optics, and all that."

"Except we can't broadcast it," Grace pointed out. "Though I'm not sure I'm that upset about that part. After watching my mother talk about me like I was deranged on international television, I was pretty ready to never watch TV again." She shot me a strained smile. "Though now it'll be so much harder to keep in touch with people. Impossible, basically. I know Wild is feeling the pressure already. He has so many daimons back in Milton who rely on him and now he has no way of contacting them."

"Onyx will hold down the fort," I replied confidently. "Milton was falling apart around us when I was there, but Onyx was cool as a cucumber. She even took time to check in on me and encouraged me to get my ass over here, despite all her other responsibilities. She's got this."

"I've been wondering why you didn't stay at Underworld," Grace said cautiously, evidently worried she was wading into dangerous territory. "I mean, you knew Onyx, right? That's why she was sending those pictures of me. And you weren't banned from the club like Riot was."

I let out a surprised laugh. Riot and Wild were so clearly comfortable around each other that I'd forgotten how thoroughly Wild had fucked Riot up for selling drugs in his club. "I mostly avoided Underworld establishments in an act of solidarity even though Riot had one hundred percent been in the wrong. I was staying at Rogue's place—I woke up there, and she called in Dr. Martinez to patch me up."

I swallowed thickly, thinking of baby Quinn. I missed my little Quinbee like crazy, honestly. When I'd made the decision to leave, my focus had been totally single-minded, a need to get to Grace. But once I'd boarded the plane, I'd been filled with regret at leaving Quinn behind without saying goodbye. For leaving her behind at *all*. Rogue wasn't a bad person—well, no worse than other daimons—but she clearly struggled with motherhood. Resented it, even.

Dice wasn't around to help out because he was too busy chasing Mercy's ghost, and I just wanted little Quinn to be okay.

"Rogue was nice to both me and my cousin," Grace murmured, a sad look crossing her face. "She let Mercy spend time at her house to get to know Dice, even though it was apparently awkward." Grace shook her head slightly, bewildered. "My feelings about Mercy are complicated. She would have been under a huge amount of pressure from the agathos, but I struggle to wrap my head around what she did. I could never betray any of you the way she did to Dice. He, Riot and Bullet could have all been killed that day because of Mercy's actions. I know it haunts her, I've seen her dreams and they're... Well, they're horrible. Traumatic. I wouldn't wish them on anybody."

I reached across the bed, giving Grace's hand a squeeze. "I don't know if this helps, but from what I hear of Dice, he's not *struggling*, per se. He's just really fucking angry."

Grace gave me a resigned smile. "What about you?"

"Me?"

Her fingers flexed against mine. "Any anger? Even among, um, *normal* soul bonds it's pretty common for there to be some jealousy or resentment, especially for whoever joins last. It's very unusual for an agathos woman to meet all of her soul bonds at once—sometimes there's years between the first and last." Grace swallowed thickly. "It's something we were warned about, things we're supposed to do to make sure everyone feels equally appreciated—"

"Hey, I promise if I need extra attention, I'll ask," I cut in, a faint sense of nervousness skittering over my skin that wasn't mine. "I always need extra cuddles, but I blame my Philotes heritage for that."

Was I angry? It didn't feel that straightforward. I decided to offer Grace as much of the truth as I could, while still trying to keep a little to myself while I worked out how I felt.

"I think I'll always have guilt. I feel bad that I wasn't here with you guys when you could have used me, but if I was, I'd have struggled forever with the guilt of not spending time with my mom before she died. Either way, I was going to lose."

Shit, I hadn't meant to make Grace cry. A steady stream of silent tears were streaking her cheeks, and she shoved them away roughly with the heel of her hand like she was frustrated they were there to begin with.

"And I'll always feel guilty—" Grace began.

"I know why you did it." It was the elephant in the room, and it had to be addressed. "I know now that Bullet's future became less certain the moment our paths crossed. Honestly, if he'd told me that was the case, I'd like to think I'd have been selfless enough to stay away, though I don't know if that's true or not. I'm still a daimon."

I shrugged, unease sitting heavily in my chest at the thought of condemning Bullet to death by just existing in the same space as my soul bond.

"I'm not going to let anything happen to Bullet," Grace said firmly.

I reflected back on the deal we'd struck, which suddenly felt like it had been years ago rather than yesterday. "Me neither. Want me to go get him?"

"He'll come down soon," Grace replied easily, rubbing her chest where I guessed she felt the bond with him. My own jealousy tasted bitter in my mouth. "I think he's enjoying the darkness, just a little, but he feels bad admitting it. For an Oneiroi daimon close to the Goddess of Night, he wasted his nights sleeping so he could be in the dreamscape with me."

"I guarantee you, he didn't see that as a waste," I assured her. She yawned, and even though I didn't think it was night yet, going to bed early didn't really matter now that the whole world was in perma-darkness.

"You, Bullet, and Wild should sleep in here," I suggested, reluctantly taking my hand off her leg. "Riot and I can take shifts helping out Arsène. I don't know what Vasileios told him, but if he was expecting ten of us, maybe he thought he'd be getting more help."

"Right," Grace agreed, scrunching her nose slightly. "Maybe you and Riot can nap in here later to make sure you get enough sleep too? We'll be on the boat at least a few hours, won't we?"

"I'll ask." I could hear movement in the cabin, probably Bullet making his way down here, and shifted to the edge of the bed to leave.

"Hey," Grace said softly, scooting up behind me and lightly touching my elbow. "You know that serene smile doesn't work on me, I can sense what you're feeling. At least a little."

"How am I feeling?" I asked playfully, hoping to trick my brain into a less sensitive mood. We had too much going on for me to get up in my feelings right now.

"Like you need a hug," Grace replied, wrapping her arms around my middle and pressing her cheek between my shoulder blades. I rested my hands over her arms, my thumb brushing the edge of the adhesive on her wrist. I'd shoved some spare bandages in the bag, and made a mental note to change it. "I know it's a lot of change, and that you've been through a lot to get to this point, and even now you're here, everything has been hard. But please don't doubt you belong here just as much as the others, okay? You do. You're where you're meant to be too."

I nodded silently. I was where I was meant to be, but was it just fate that put me here? *The* Fates? Did it matter?

"Get some sleep," I told her, giving her arms a quick squeeze and twisting back to press a kiss to her temple. Grace pulled back, but instead of moving away completely, her hands came up to cup my face, holding me in place. For a long, quiet moment we looked at each other, and I tried to memorize the unique mix of colors that made up her strange, pale agathos eyes, barely illuminated by the flashlight on the bed.

"I think you feel like you need a kiss too," Grace whispered. "Am I wrong?"

"Not even a little."

I could have done with more. It wasn't the time, and neither of us was really in the mood, but despite my reservations, I *wanted* the bond with Grace more than I'd ever wanted anything in my life.

But for now, I'd take a kiss and be grateful for it.

The fact that I wanted it so much was probably the biggest warning sign of all.

Grace leaned forward, her lips brushing softly over mine, tentatively exploring me, learning me the way I was learning her. I swiped my tongue over her lower lip, teasing her and tasting the salt of her tears all at once.

Kissing Grace was an entirely different experience—one that wasn't primarily motivated by arousal. I wanted to kiss Grace because she was Grace, not because I wanted to stick my dick inside her.

Since Grace was feeling more emotionally raw than aroused too, my Philotes instincts were quiet. I was just kissing her as a man, not a daimon, and it was *good*.

Grace's tongue slid against mine, her movements curious, like she wanted to be playful but didn't have it in her right now and I totally got that. Nothing about our surroundings lent itself to the idea of 'playful'.

She pulled back with a soft smile, her gaze dipping to my lips before meeting mine, the longing in her eyes clear.

Longing for me, for more of this, but also for *time*. For a moment of peace where we could truly enjoy one another without the weight of the dark, rapidly freezing world pressing in on us.

"Bullet is waiting outside the door," Grace whispered. "Showing an impressive level of patience and restraint. For him."

I snorted, brushing one more kiss over her lips. "Come in, Bullet," I called, reluctantly letting Grace go.

He opened the door quietly, poking his head into the cabin with a bright grin on his face that almost detracted from the dark shadows under his eyes. Eyes that seemed duller than usual, though maybe it was just our shadowy surroundings?

"Hey, B, come lie down. Grace needs a nap buddy."

Bullet chuckled, climbing onto an angled section of the bed and sliding around me to lie next to Grace. "Cute of you to pretend you're not worried about me, Dare."

"Alright, I'll be blunt about it. You look like shit," I deadpanned. "Like, really fucking terrible."

"Stop flattering me, my ego can't take it." Bullet swooned into Grace's lap, pressing the back of his hand to his forehead. "How do you cope being surrounded by all these charmers, Grace? Dare over here with his sweet talk, Riot with the absolute filth he spouts, and Wild... who definitely is thinking less than pure thoughts that you can probably sense through the bond."

"I have no complaints," Grace laughed softly, sifting her fingers through Bullet's blonde hair.

"I'll let you two rest." I awkwardly crouch-walked to the door. "I'll let Wild know to come down and join you. Riot and I can take the first shift. I have a lot of questions about this apparent filthy mouth of his."

CHAPTER 12

If we ever had a home of our own, which seemed unlikely at this stage, I was going to insist on the biggest bed possible. Not that I minded sleeping with Grace sprawled over me the way she was, but it didn't make for the most restful night. Maybe that was just the incessant rocking of the boat, which I hadn't found soothing in the slightest. Give me solid ground any day.

I shifted slightly, my head brushing against the top of Bullet's head on the odd-shaped bed. I wished we could lie next to each other, but there was no way we could fit side-by-side on the narrow mattress, and Bullet had insisted he be the one to sleep by himself since he was so uncuddly at night anyway. When he was in the dreamscape, his body was stiff as a board.

Be grateful, I reminded myself. That the three of us got any time at all together when the world was falling apart was something to be grateful for. As much as I didn't want to accept defeat, the constant niggling feeling that the darkness would never lift persisted. The idea that these moments where it was just us might be numbered...

I swallowed thickly. It was too terrible to contemplate. The kind of negative thinking that could stop you from getting out of bed in the morning because what was the point?

These moments where Bullet was healthy and Grace wasn't fighting not to break under the pressure that had been put on her... These moments were precious.

Careful not to wake her, I slid my palm up to cradle Grace's skull, the roof of the cabin brushing against the back of my hand in the process.

Precious as this moment of peace was, it was suffocating in here.

The oppressive darkness didn't help, but we had to conserve the battery light on the torch, so we'd turned it off when I'd arrived. Besides, we didn't want to draw any unwanted attention to ourselves by lighting up the boat. I thought my eyes had semi-adjusted to the blackness, but I couldn't see anything in here, and the ceiling was too low for even Grace to stand in the cabin, let alone the rest of us.

I needed to get up, to go check on Dare and Riot, and make sure they were getting some rest too. Getting some rest *and* keeping an eye on Arsène. He seemed like a decent enough daimon—and being a Pothos was a fucking curse—but out at sea in his boat, we were completely reliant on him with nothing but Vasileios' word to reassure us.

While I distrusted Vasileios marginally less than other people, I'd rather depend on myself. Before both the sky and all forms of communication had gone dark, I'd been able to get in touch with a few Keres daimons I knew from my travels through Europe, and I'd been confident we were on the way to having a decent network of our own, rather than just Vasileios' empire built on sex and favors. None of the Keres I knew had turned me away—they'd all seen me on the livestream where Grace approached the temple. Even at the peak of my fighting career, I hadn't been this popular.

And now I had no way of contacting them, even to confirm they were alright. That was an even harder pill to swallow when it came to my Milton daimons. I knew Onyx would do her best to look out for them, but Underworld really wasn't set up to provide emergency housing. A mistake on my part. I should have equipped them better for disaster relief.

I should have done a lot of things differently. Prepared for a far worse scenario. I, more than anyone, appreciated how capricious the gods could be.

There would be time, I told myself. We'd fix all this, con some rich fuck into letting us use their private island indefinitely, and we'd take some time, just the five of us. I'd get to know Dare better, and Riot and Bullet would get their friendship back to where it had been. I'd do whatever I had to do to bind Grace and Bullet so closely together to me that they couldn't imagine us being apart.

That was what I wanted.

However, I had to trick Grace and Bullet into being as obsessed with me as I was with them, I'd do it. If only it was as simple as sex. Fucking, I could do. I could make them both feel great without a second thought, but Bullet and Grace wanted more than that from me. They deserved more than that.

My beautiful bonded shifted in my arms, her hip pressing painfully against my morning wood—or at least I thought it was morning—distracting me from my musings. Grace nuzzled into my chest as she slowly woke up, and I stroked her back, telling my dick to stand down.

"Good morning," Grace mumbled, attempting to lift her head, but melting underneath my hand as I pushed her down before she cracked it on the ceiling. "Or good afternoon. Good evening? Did you sleep okay?"

I nodded, a total lie, before remembering she couldn't see me. With some effort, I focused my intent through the bond, pushing some sort of vaguely content emotion toward her.

Grace made a frustrated sound, wriggling around as she reached for the torch—*flashlight*, as they all called it—in a way that was definitely not helping my dick situation.

"Sorry," Grace whispered, flicking on the light and angling it away from us, filling the small cabin with an almost blinding glow. She blinked down at me as our eyes adjusted, her dark hair a tangled mess obscuring half her face. Despite the long sleep, Grace still looked exhausted. The bone-deep kind of exhaustion that not even the best rest could fix.

I smoothed her hair back before disentangling my hands enough to sign.

'*Happy dreams?*' I asked, never entirely confident where Bullet was taking Grace in the dreamscape, and it was frustrating that I never knew if I'd seen them or not, or what we'd discussed if I had. She frowned, glancing over at a still-sleeping Bullet.

I heard the murmur of quiet voices in the main cabin next to us, a small sliver of light shining through the cracks in the door, so it appeared that Riot and Dare were still awake.

"No dreamscape last night. Bullet didn't visit me at all." Grace leaned over, still mostly sprawled over my body, grabbing Bullet's forearm and giving it a light shake. "Hey, wake up, sleepyhead. You know if I don't get dreamscape assurance that you're okay, I freak out."

130

Bullet continued to sleep deeply, and Grace's panic spiked almost instantly. I sent her waves of calm through the bond as Riot ripped the door open, Dare standing over his shoulder and shining the flashlight in Bullet's direction.

"He's not waking up," Grace said frantically, shaking Bullet's arm again. I rolled Grace off me so she could get closer to him, laying on my side next to them both. "Bullet *always* wakes up. He knows in the dreamscape when we wake up."

He does?

I was trying to stay calm for Grace's sake, but I wasn't calm. I didn't feel calm. My vision was going hazy at the edges, bloodlust rising up to meet whatever the threat facing me was. Except this wasn't a threat I could rip apart with hands and weapons, it wasn't a threat I could beat into submission. I couldn't do *anything*. I was completely helpless.

Come on, Bullet. Come back to us.

"Bullet!" Grace army crawled onto his part of the mattress, carefully straddling Bullet's still form with her upper body bent low to avoid the ceiling, and cupping his face in her hands. "Wake. Up. Wake up! Why aren't you waking up?"

Her voice cracked, and even if I could speak, I wouldn't be able to around the sudden tight pain in my throat.

"I'll get a wet cloth, see if the cold wakes him," Dare suggested, handing Riot the torch before dashing out of the room.

It had to. He had to wake up. This couldn't be the end. But Grace had said that Bullet couldn't see his future after Dare showed up…

131

No, no, I refused to accept that. Bullet was young and full of life. His Oneiroi gifts had weighed him down his entire life, but now he'd been cut off from them, surely he'd heal? I hadn't heard of any other Oneiroi being forcibly weaned off their ability to see the paths of the future by the Fates or La Nuit before. They favored him, they wanted to help him.

He was going to be *fine*.

"Wild," Grace whispered hoarsely, looking up at me over Bullet's head, tears streaming down her cheeks. "He's not waking up."

"He's still breathing," Riot cut in stubbornly, crossing his arms over his chest. "What can you feel through the bond, Gracie?"

"Nothing, but I never can when he's in the dreamscape."

Dare returned, handing Grace a cold cloth which she used to dab at his forehead, alternating between pleas, encouragement, and prayers to every deity she could think of except Gaia for Bullet to wake up.

Behind her, I caught the wary look Dare and Riot shot each other, and I gave them both a hard glare. Whatever pessimism they were feeling better not fucking seep through the bond, Grace didn't need that shit.

She sucked in a horrified breath, and I snapped my gaze back to Bullet's face, where a thin line of dark blood trickled from his nose.

My chest felt like it was caving in on itself, Grace's pain and mine combining to create something too heavy for either of us to bear. I couldn't live with this agony. It was already morphing into something dark and dangerous. My Keres instincts meant I wasn't someone safe to be around when I was suffering. I focused as hard as I could on Grace's grief, letting that anchor me before I started ripping the cabin apart.

We hadn't even gotten a chance to say goodbye. Bullet knew Grace loved him, but did he know how much I cared about him? That I couldn't imagine a future without him in it? Without the three of us together?

Why hadn't I told him that?

I should have written it down.

I should have written it down every single *day*.

Somewhere in the back of my mind, I registered that someone was yelling something from outside the cabin, the threat of violence in the air coating my tongue with the metallic warning signs of the bloodlust.

"I could use a little help here!" Arsène yelled. "Ideally, before I start shooting!"

"Shit," Dare muttered, stumbling out of the cabin. With a pained look at Bullet, Riot followed, a strangled noise escaping him as he dragged himself away.

Grace sobbed harder, dabbing at the blood tricking down Bullet's face, and I wasn't sure she was even aware of what was happening above deck. I tapped her arm to get her attention, my silence feeling more suffocating than ever.

'Sleep? Look for him.'

It was a stupid suggestion, borne of desperation. There was no way Grace would be able to quiet her mind enough to sleep when Bullet was dying right in front of us.

She shook her head, tears splashing over Bullet's chest, soaking through the fabric of his shirt. Every drop felt like a dagger in my heart. I needed to *do* something.

"Bullet controls the dreamscape, not me."

Right. And he probably wasn't in the dreamscape right now, necessarily. Not if he was unconscious.

I swallowed thickly, reaching for the bond with Grace by instinct, trying to smother her terror with calm and reassurance that I wasn't even feeling myself.

The bond.

Maybe I was being overly optimistic, but for me, the bond was a beacon of sorts, lighting the way to Grace. To her soul, to the very core of her being.

If it was possible...

'*Use the bond?*' I signed hesitantly, wishing I could communicate more easily, that I could explain to Grace the way she felt to me.

"How?" Grace replied, cutting me a frustrated look that quickly turned apologetic. She paused, frowning down at herself. "Maybe... I can't *feel* him through the bond now, or whenever he's in the dreamscape, but maybe I can draw him to me somehow. Or maybe I could follow it and use it as a guide rope? I don't... I don't know if it would do anything, if it would help. But if I concentrate, I can visualize the bond—it's like strands of moonbeam between each of us."

That almost made me smile in spite of the overwhelming crush of desperation threatening to pull me under. We looked like moonbeam to Grace, like Nyx's night. The bond to Grace on *my* end looked like a thread of pure golden sunshine—brilliant, yet gentle at the same time. I gently took the wet cloth from Grace's hand, encouraging her to focus while I dabbed at the steady trickle of blood.

If there was a chance, I knew without a fraction of a doubt that we'd both take it. And if anyone could track Bullet via a metaphysical thread and bring him back from the cusp of death, it'd be Grace.

She rested her palms on Bullet's chest, exhaling heavily and closing her eyes. Tears clung to her dark lashes, leaving wet tracks down her reddened cheeks. Heartbreakingly beautiful, and beautiful in heartbreak.

For a long moment there was only the sound of her breathing, deep and unnaturally even, forcing herself to calm. Maybe I'd asked too much of her—Grace may be the Prophêtis, but she wasn't a goddess herself, and I'd never been much of a believer in the supposed power of love to save all.

The shouting from overhead grew louder, more urgent. They needed me up there—if it came to a fight, I was the best hope we had. As much as I wanted to stay, protecting the boat meant protecting Bullet and Grace as well.

With an ache of regret pressing heavily on my lungs, making it hard to breathe, I tapped Grace's arm, hating to distract her but needing to sign to her that I was going so she wouldn't panic.

I waited a moment.

Her eyes didn't open.

A shot rang out overhead. More shouting. Grace's eyes didn't open.

I went to reach for her again, to shake her arm with a little more urgency, but a strange, flickering sensation in my chest froze me in place. An unnatural, *uncomfortable* feeling where my own bond with Grace sat.

There was a pained shout of agony from directly above me that I knew without a doubt came from Riot.

And then Grace collapsed over Bullet's body with a quiet thud.

GRACE

CHAPTER 13

"Amazing Grace?" Bullet asked. "Oh no. Oh no, no, no, you are definitely not supposed to be here."

Where was *here*?

Somehow, seeing a light sky again was jarring, even though it couldn't have been more than hours since Nyx blocked out the sun. The field around us was a lush green, a wide, rushing river not too far away, and the sky above a dusky purple streaked with gold. What was this place? The underworld? That didn't seem right—I'd seen the underworld, and it didn't look like this.

But there *were* rivers in the underworld. Rivers that *led* to the underworld...

Surely, such a place would be busy, but I couldn't see anyone else around.

I couldn't see Bullet.

Where was Bullet?

"You're not meant to be here either." My voice sounded strange and hollow, and when I went to reach for Bullet, I realized I had no body. Whatever this place was, it was nothing like the usual dreamscape we visited. "I've come to take you back."

"Are you... are you dying?" Bullet asked, horrified. "It shouldn't be possible for you to be on the banks of the Styx, otherwise. No, no, this can't be happening. You're not meant to die, Grace—"

"I'm not dying." I paused. "Well, I don't think I'm dying. I followed the bond here to you, and I have no idea how it works or why it's possible, but I'm going to use it to drag you back with me." I said the words with more certainty than I felt. I'd never *heard* of anyone using the bond this way, but then again, we were an agathos and daimon pairing. There was nothing normal about us.

"This shouldn't be possible," Bullet muttered. "None of this was meant to happen. I thought I'd just go visit Nyx, to plead with her to stop the darkness. I didn't think it was going to be too much for me. I should have been able to handle it."

He'd tried to visit Nyx? That was what had caused all of this? The guilt threatened to swallow me whole. He'd already told us he would, and I hadn't protested. I should have told him not to, that we could have found another way.

Bullet had looked exhausted and frail for days. He'd pushed himself beyond his limits, and I'd *let this happen*. How could I have let this happen?

I'd been in denial. Hoping for the best, hoping there was another way, that the Oneiroi curse was something that affected *other* Oneiroi, not *my* Oneiroi.

"This isn't possible. I must be imagining you. I'm in the denial stage." The distress in Bullet's voice had me trying to reach for him again before remembering there was nothing to reach *with*.

"I wish I could see you, but at least I can hear you," I whispered.

I could imagine the crease between his brows as he puzzled something over, the way he'd shove his hand back through his blonde hair, or drum the rhythm of some broadway song on his thigh while he thought.

I would see him again, just as soon as we got out of here.

Somehow, without hands, I gripped the bond that had brought me here tightly, feeling the essence of Bullet more acutely than I ever had. For a favored son of the Goddess of Night, he felt surprisingly bright and vibrant, full of love and music and laughter, of excitement for new possibilities, and a steady hum of fear that he wouldn't live up to expectations.

"I love you so much," I sighed, heady with the emotion of being surrounded by him. "You've always been my guiding light."

Had I always known that? I wasn't sure. Riot had always felt like home and safety. Wild was a pillar of strength and protection. Dare was still to be determined, but he definitely brought a side of me that I hadn't experienced before. He made me feel confident, *sexy* even.

Bullet had always been my teacher, but it was more than that I realized now. He was my guide, my compass, my North Star. And now I wanted to be that for him.

I wanted to be his way home.

"Let's get out of here."

"Grace, wait. I'm scared this will hurt you somehow," Bullet whispered, sounding more truly terrified than I'd ever heard him sound before. "But I'm too selfish to let you go, and I'm cowardly enough to ask you to do it for me. I'll never be ready to say goodbye, even though I know it's inevitable. I need you to do it for me. To let me go. Don't drown yourself to save me."

"There's nothing inevitable about losing you," I shot back fiercely, gripping the silvery bond closer to me, tugging it into me. "I'm not drowning. We're swimming *together*."

I gave the bond another fierce yank. It didn't feel as though it was pulling and coiling like a length of string, but rather *shrinking*, lessening the distance between us until our bond was an immediate, tight, tangible tie, rather than a long expanse of rope.

The silvery threads that connected me to Wild and Riot looked thinner than I expected them to, and I forced down the rising panic, latching onto them and dragging the weight of Bullet's soul along with me.

It was frightening, but a wise Oneiroi had once told me to do what scared me, and I'd never regretted following his advice. If I hadn't, I'd still be lonely and unhappy in Milton, watching the world slowly fall apart around me and having no idea why.

"We're going home," I rasped, somehow aching with exertion despite not having a physical form. The missing bond with Dare felt like a hole in my heart, and maybe it was selfish, but I was going to get back to the real world and heal it. I finally had all four of my soul bonds with me, and I wouldn't let any of them go.

Dark red eyes rimmed with purple stared down at me as I blinked awake, my head throbbing and throat painfully dry. Terrified eyes.

"Don't you *ever*," Riot rasped, his arms tightening around me where I was cradled in his lap. "*Ever* fucking do that again."

"Bullet—"

"Is waking up," Dare said quietly, kneeling at the edge of the mattress, staring at me in alarm, angling the flashlight to illuminate the cabin.

Riot moved me gently so I could see the opposite side of the bed. Bullet was in a similar position to me, Wild's large form hunched over him to avoid banging his head on the ceiling.

The fear coming from both Riot and Wild was overwhelming, but I could just make out the stirring of Bullet's bond flaring awake, filled with a mixture of confusion and relief.

He was back. He was okay. Everything was going to be okay.

"It's okay," I told Riot tentatively, reaching up to stroke his cheek. Was that a bruise forming over his cheekbone or just a trick of the light? "We're okay. Everyone is okay."

"Nothing is okay," Riot gritted out while Wild nodded, a slightly shellshocked look on his face. "You were... fading, somehow. Like the bond was fraying, and then somehow it wasn't." He shook his head, swallowing thickly. "We threw the humans trying to board into the water, but by the time I got down here, you were unconscious."

Okay, I could see how that would have looked. How it would have *felt*. I snuggled into Riot's arms, sending as much apology as I could through the bond.

"Wait, what humans?" I asked.

"Don't worry about that," Riot replied instantly, which didn't ease my mind whatsoever. "What happened?"

Bullet groaned loudly, shifting in Wild's arms. "Grace saved my life, that's what happened. I don't know how, I'm pretty sure it shouldn't be possible. She used the bond like a bungee cord and swooped in to my rescue."

Wild gathered Bullet up carefully, pressing a gentle kiss to his forehead that had my throat growing tight with emotion. I knew Wild cared for us, but showing it was hard for him, harder still with Bullet than it was with me.

I was so glad they had each other, too. Their lives had been so lonely before, they deserved all the love in the world. I wanted that for them, wanted them to *know* they deserved that. To believe it.

Bullet tipped his head back, surprising Wild by brushing a faint kiss over his lips. I couldn't quite suppress my dreamy sigh as Wild captured Bullet's jaw, stopping him from moving away and deepening the kiss into something far less sweet. Something more raw, desperate, and possessive. There was a roughness they had with each other that they didn't have with me, and I *loved* it, loved seeing the hidden sides we all brought out in one another.

"I'm trying to be angry that you put yourself in danger and you keep feeling all mushy and loved up. It's very distracting," Riot grumbled into my hair, pressing grumpy kisses all over my head.

"I should go check on Arsène," Dare said with a brittle smile, leaning forward to place the sweetest, most tender kiss on the tip of my nose. He clearly wasn't sure where he fit in among our little group, but not for long. Dare was mine, and I was going to claim him. "We, uh, sort of left him with cleanup duty—"

Riot cleared his throat loudly, a thread of panic coming through the bond.

"—I mean, just, you know. General tidying up," Dare amended lamely. "So, I'll just go... Help. With that. Glad you're okay, B," he added, backing out of the cabin and leaving the four of us alone.

Bullet and Wild broke apart, both of them turning to me, but Riot clung on tighter, not ready to let me go just yet.

"I'm grateful, don't get me wrong," Bullet began, frowning slightly to himself. "But Riot is right. Don't you ever do that again, Amazing Grace. You probably defied some kind of natural law of the universe. Defied the *Fates*. Those kinds of actions tend to have consequences."

"If I can save you, I will. Every time," I replied, attempting to sit up as my head swam and my muscles burned as though I'd run a marathon. Despite being a determined rule-follower my whole life, there was something incredibly satisfying about hearing that. I'd break the rules a million times over when it came to my soul bonds. "Besides, all I did was use the bond to guide you back, it was already there, waiting for me to grab on to. What could possibly be unnatural about that?"

Bullet met my eyes from across the mattress, his emotions so deeply embedded in me as though they were my own now he'd fully woken up and I could fully appreciate the new depth of the bond between us.

Truthfully, I wasn't sure I'd be able to repeat what I'd done, not with Bullet. Where before it had felt like there was some slack for me to use as a guide, now our bond felt like two sides of a magnet.

If Bullet returned to that place, that in-between by the river—the Styx—my soul would go with him.

But that wasn't going to happen.

I'd saved him. There was no Oneiroi curse for him, not anymore.

"You're hurting, Gracie," Riot said roughly, the displeasure in his voice clear. I knew he was happy to have Bullet back, despite the distance between them lately, but his fear tended to manifest as anger. He guided my head back so he could look at my face again, and I stared up at him with all the love and adoration I felt, not holding anything back.

Reassuring him that I'd walk through fire for him too.

"I'm okay, I'm just a little hungry and I need water," I assured him. Both true. My head hurt, but the water would probably fix that too.

Wild's fear morphed into guilt as he watched me, absently stroking Bullet's sweat-soaked hair off his forehead. I sent him an exasperated look. "Stop that. You would have done the same thing in my shoes. It was a good idea, and I'm glad you suggested it."

Wild nodded once, his guilt not abating in the slightest, while Riot made a grumbling sound of discontent.

"Go on, go snuggle with them," Riot sighed, shifting me gently off him. "I'll go warm up some canned stuff. Dare and I were talking last night about heating up water so we could all wash a bit too."

He shot me a wry smile, picking up the excitement I wasn't quite able to stifle at the idea of getting even a little bit clean. The salt from our freezing ocean excursion to get here clung to my skin and some of Bullet's blood had dried on my hands, and I wanted nothing more than to wash both off.

I all but army crawled along the mattress to get to Bullet and Wild, attempting to snuggle in next to them without crowding them. Neither of them were having that—Bullet grabbed me under my arms and hauled me over his body until we were both lying in Wild's lap.

"You saved me, Amazing Grace," Bullet murmured. "You've saved me every single day just be existing and giving me hope when I felt like there was none, but this time, you literally saved my life. How can I repay—"

"Don't even finish that sentence," I cut in, affronted. Carefully, I propped myself up with my forearms on his chest, glaring down at him. "I *love* you."

"I love you too."

I twisted to glance up at Wild, who was watching us with unguarded affection on his face, though his emotions were a lot more chaotic.

"I love you too, Wild," I said softly, smiling at his jolt of surprise. "You don't need to say it back, I know that's a lot for you and maybe you're not there yet. I just wanted you to know."

Our strong, silent protector nodded, swallowing thickly before gently turning my head back to face Bullet. I didn't take it personally—I could feel through the bond loud and clear that Wild needed a moment to compose himself, and I wanted to respect the wishes he couldn't vocalize.

Bullet stroked the side of my face, tucking a stray lock of hair behind my ear, his purple eyes contemplative. Even in the shadowy lighting of the cabin, it was clear how much brighter his eyes were than they had been recently. His complexion had lost the grayish tinge it'd had, though he still looked a little gaunt in the cheeks. *I'll make sure he eats more*, I promised myself.

I'd feed him and love him and encourage him, and Bullet would be just fine. He'd grow old and gray with the rest of us.

"No more trying to visit Nyx in the dreamscape," I instructed him, doing my best stern voice. "I should have told you that when you suggested it—that it had a slim chance of success and a huge chance of causing you harm. I got too caught up in trying to fix the world that I didn't think of what the consequences might be at home. I'm sorry, Bullet. You deserve better than that."

He gave me a bemused smile, but I felt his flutter of panicked confusion like it was my own.

"Right. No visiting Nyx in the dreamscape," he repeated solemnly. There was only a faint sense of relief from Wild at Bullet's words—he hadn't picked up the brief panic Bullet had hidden so well.

"Promise?" I pressed. What was he worried about? Was the idea of not visiting Nyx any longer that concerning? Surely not, when it had almost killed him.

"Promise. Can I have a kiss now?" Bullet asked, shooting me his most charming smile. His eyes twinkled with mischief, and he looked so like the Bullet of my dream memories, the Bullet I'd met back at his home before the weight of the world had come crashing down on us, that I couldn't answer with words. I immediately dipped my head, fusing our lips together, sinking into the incredible sensation of his desire and love and relief combining with mine, our emotions too close to separate.

It was heady and addictive, the most potent arousal, ramped up several notches. *Dangerously good.*

Wild fidgeted beneath us, not so discreetly adjusting himself, and I acted on the impulse of Bullet's mischief as it flashed through me, breaking the kiss and twisting to press my lips against Wild's instead, while Bullet teasingly ran his fingers over Wild's chest, playfully biting his bicep through the fabric of Wild's shirt.

There was a lack of inhibition between them that hadn't been there before, a gratitude that we were all still here, an appreciation that no day was promised to us.

It was a terrible and beautiful lesson to learn.

Wild's surprise at the two of us pouncing on him morphed into pleasure, tinged with an indulgent kind of amusement. As though we were two fluffy bunnies trying to take down a giant grizzly bear, and he was just humoring us by letting us even think we stood a chance.

He pulled back with an arrogant smirk that had butterflies launching into flight in my stomach.

'*You two need to eat, clean up*,' he signed, plucking at the bloodstain on Bullet's shirt.

"You're no fun," Bullet replied, almost pouting for a moment before shooting me a dazzling smile. "He's right, though. I can feel how hungry you are, Amazing Grace. And as much as I'd love to hole up in here and try all the things I thought I might never have the chance to do..."

Wild exhaled heavily, his desire a heavy, syrupy sort of sensation, snaking through the bond.

"As much as I want that," Bullet continued. "I think Riot might need a little extra reassurance right now, and I know Grace wants to make things official with a certain soul bond."

I blushed, reluctantly disentangling myself from the two of them. I did want to cement the bond with Dare, I never wanted him to wonder whether or not he belonged, and how I felt about him. And while it wasn't perhaps the most romantic reason, not sealing the bond weakened both of us, and we couldn't afford to be weak right now.

"Are you two coming out?"

"We'll be right behind you," Bullet said, flopping an arm across his eyes and reclining in Wild's lap. "I need five more minutes before I try standing up. I don't think I have sea legs."

I could relate to that. I gripped the cabin door as I climbed out of the sleeping area, into the main living area where Riot was moving around the small kitchen, body taut with tension.

"Here," Riot said, guiding me to sit at the bench seat. "I heated some water for you to wash with. The shower is functional but we should really save the gas for cooking, so it's all sponge bathes from here on out, unfortunately. I'm heating up a second pot for you now."

"I'm not complaining, I'm grateful we have anything. Thank you for heating it up for me," I replied sincerely as he set a basin and cloth down in front of me. We were probably better off than most to be on a boat right now, relatively self-sufficient compared to what we'd be dealing with on land after Gaia's tantrum. There was a small bathroom, and I planned on taking the second pot in there to try to scrub the salt off the rest of my body.

"Where's Dare?" My hands shook from hunger and exhaustion as I picked up the cloth, and Riot quickly plucked it from my fingers, sitting on the bench next to me and dipping it in the water.

"Helping Arsène. Some people tried to board the boat. Desperate times, desperate measures, that sort of thing. We managed to shake them, but there'll be more." Riot grimaced. "I need to get back out there, but I can't bring myself to leave you alone just yet."

He was angry about it too. Not *at* me, but at the whole situation, at how out of his control it all felt.

"Don't be mad," I whispered, hating the tight set of his jaw and turbulent emotions I sensed through the bond. "Riot, look at me."

Despite how stormy his gaze was, his hands were gentle as he gripped my chin and dragged the damp cloth over my skin. "I can't even explain to you what that moment felt like, Gracie. I *felt* the bond stretch tight like it was going to snap. I've never been so afraid in my fucking *life*."

I swallowed thickly, my throat dry and aching. "I didn't mean to scare you. I knew I could get back; you and Wild guided me home."

Riot grunted, suddenly very interested in working the cloth over my neck. I could sense he needed the distraction, so I didn't protest, tipping my head back to give him more room.

"The worst part is I know you'd do it again," Riot grumbled. "You'd follow Bullet into the depths of the underworld if you thought there was even a slim chance you could bring him back."

"Don't for one second think I wouldn't do the same for you, Riot," I replied instantly, my voice harsher and not as comforting as I'd intended it to be. Now that I knew I could use the bond that way, I wouldn't hesitate to do it again.

"That doesn't make me feel any better," Riot sighed, patting me dry with a clean towel before moving down my body, leaving my bloodstained hands for last. "But I guess I'd be a hypocrite to argue, because there's nothing I wouldn't do to keep you. The Fates themselves couldn't keep me away, Gracie. Just don't leave us behind, okay? We can't function without you. If you follow Bullet into the underworld, you can expect to have the three of us right on your heels."

I leaned forward, stealing a kiss from his lips, hoping it never came to that. Hoping that when it was our time, we all went together.

BULLET

CHAPTER 14

It felt shitty to be grateful for silence when Wild physically couldn't speak, but I'd nearly died, so I figured I could be a shitty person for a few minutes at least.

Without Grace right in front of me to act happy for, it was easier to let the intrusive thoughts take over. The privacy was an illusion, of course. Grace could feel whatever I was feeling through the bond with even more clarity than before, if the sensations in my chest were anything to go by. Where there had been a thread between us, there was just... each other. Like a second heartbeat, right next to my own.

I'd love it if I wasn't fucking *panicking* about what it meant for Grace.

Wild stroked my hair, his head tipped back against the wall, eyes closed. He was very obviously giving me time to work through my feelings about not dying in peace, and I appreciated him immensely for it. I was low key impressed he wasn't full-on Keres hulking out, which was why I *definitely* wasn't about to tell him that Thanatos had shown up to carry my soul to the banks of the River Styx. That might stress him out a little when he was doing so well. When the God of Death shows up, you know shit is getting real.

The problem was, I'd been ready for him.

I'd tried to go to Nyx in the dreamscape, to reason with her, and realized almost instantly that I'd expended too much energy, drawn on too much of a gift that had been rapidly trickling dry. I'd *known*. I'd checked in on Wild and Grace, feeling them both settled in sleep, and then I'd waited for Thanatos to come.

Was I happy to die? No, of course not. But I also knew that there would *never* be enough time, and at the same time, we'd all be reunited in the underworld for eternity. I'd accepted that fate, and I didn't know how to cope with this new one.

Wild tugged at the roots of my hair softly, apparently growing impatient with my silent brooding. Fair enough, that was usually his thing.

"I'm good," I lied, pulling off an impressively casual voice. Annoyingly, there was a song right on the tip of my tongue that totally captured my general mood, but I couldn't quite grasp it.

Why couldn't I grasp it?

This...

This had never happened to me before.

Don't freak out. Grace will know, and then she'll come rushing back in to check on me and then Riot will hate me even more than he already does because they're having a moment right now.

She was already feeding me love and comfort through the bond, so I wasn't doing as good of a job at hiding it as I'd hoped.

151

Wild sighed loudly, shifting so that both his hands were free before softly cuffing my wrist with one and running a finger over my palm. It took several attempts before I realized he wasn't just doodling random shapes on my skin.

T-A-L-K.

"Bossy," I muttered affectionately, grateful I still got to experience his subtle brand of dominance. Craving *more* of it. I'd always been attracted to Wild—obviously, he was the hottest man I'd ever seen—but there was a sense of freedom in that desire that hadn't been there before.

Maybe it was just a lack of inhibition. I'd come so close to never getting to experience this again...

I leaned up to kiss him again, but before my lips could brush against his, he'd caught me gently by the throat, giving me a smirk that promised trouble.

This was going to be a total redo of that time I came in my pants with Grace. An arrogant smile and a soft chokehold? I could only get so hard.

Wild shook his head slightly, using his free hand to trace letters on my palm again. *T-A-L-K.*

"Ugh, fine. I'll talk." I flopped back onto his lap, dislodging his grip in the process. He ran his thumb over my stubbled jawline instead, and I couldn't decide which felt better. "It's a real boner killer, though. Just FYI."

I glanced up at him through my eyelashes to see if that had changed his mind. Nope, nada. Apparently, I was getting out of it that easily.

"You suggested Grace use the bond to follow me," I stated, only somewhat successfully keeping the note of accusation out of my tone. Wild nodded, more sheepish than I'd ever seen him.

Shit, he was potent when he was being kind of cute too.

152

"I want to be mad at you," I said eventually, huffing a quiet laugh. "I am, a little, actually. I'm grateful, and I was selfish enough to let Grace carry me back even though I had concerns about what it would mean for her. I still have those concerns. I'd rather be waiting for you all in the underworld than weakening Grace with my presence here. I should have said no, should have sent her away."

That was easy to say in hindsight, though. In reality, I hated denying Grace anything, and I'd never seen her so determined.

"I'm selfishly glad to be here, but in the symphony of my life, this feels like *tempo rubato*." I swallowed thickly, staring up at the low ceiling rather than making eye contact with Wild. "*Stolen time*. Time that has to be caught up somehow. Given back."

Out of the corner of my eye, I could see Wild shaking his head, but we both knew that to be an agathos was to sacrifice, and to be an Oneiroi was to suffer. That there was a very real chance that saving me might have condemned us to something even worse as the Fates tried to fix the scales we'd thrown out of balance.

If it were anyone else, I'd scoff and dismiss that kind of talk as hubris. I'd tell them that no one had that much power to change their own fate, that things had worked out the way they were meant to.

But Grace wasn't just anyone. She was a Prophêtis. When she spoke, the gods listened.

"I want more time with Grace, with you," I said quietly, the potential ramifications of what Grace had done hanging over the back of my neck like a guillotine, ready to drop at any moment. "More time with Riot and Dare. I want to help Grace fulfill her destiny and see her free of this incredible burden. But next time, Wild, you have to let me go."

153

DARE

CHAPTER 15

"Dare," Riot called, crossing the deck to where I was standing watch, huddled inside one of Arsène's oversized jackets. "Switch. Head on in."

"What? No, I'm fine. You need to be in there." I'd never been a big sleeper anyway. Of the two of us, Riot needed a nap more, plus his bonded had almost... died? I wasn't even entirely sure. They all talked about the bond stretching and fading and whatever else, but it was all kind of meaningless to me.

I didn't *have* a bond with Grace. I didn't know what it felt like to have it, let alone to almost lose it.

And I wasn't jealous about that at all, no siree.

"Dare," Riot said, in an offensively exasperated tone. "Go inside. Talk to Grace. She needs you as much as she needs the rest of us, and *you* need *her*."

"No, I don't," I replied, sounding a smidge more petulant than I'd intended to. I didn't *need* Grace. I barely knew her. I wasn't even sure what I did know, what I did feel, was real.

But when Riot had raced below deck shouting for her and we'd found her passed out on Bullet's chest...

I'd never been so scared in my life. Not even when I'd found my mom's body. Maybe because I'd known I couldn't save Mom, but with Grace it had felt... It had felt like there was still sand in the hourglass. Like if I just knew *what* to do, I could save her.

In the end, she'd saved herself and brought Bullet back with her. She'd used the bonds to find her way home, and not having one with me didn't seem to impede her in any way.

Whenever I was away from Grace, from her magnetic presence, I wondered why the fuck I was here and if she'd notice if I was gone. When I *was* in her presence, I was as drawn to her as ever, jealous and resentful that the others shared something with her that I didn't.

Something that I *wanted*. Whatever it was, whatever the consequences were, I still wanted Grace to be *mine*.

"For fuck's sake," Riot snorted. "You have it so bad, and you are so in denial. Go. Talk to her. There's a bowl of lukewarm beans sitting on the table for you. Everyone's eaten. I think Bullet was going to lie down again."

"Ugh, fine," I sighed, not about to waste food in our precarious circumstances. "What about Arsène?"

"I brought him a bowl of food while you were staring broodily at the pitch-black ocean, wishing for a flower so you could pull off the petals. Grace loves me, she loves me not—"

155

"I'm going to throw you overboard," I muttered, slipping past him to head back inside. There was a faint amount of light emanating from the interior of the cabin, and in the absolute darkness of outside, it was enough to act as a beacon to get me inside.

Arsène was inside, looking at navigation equipment I didn't understand at all. Grace was there too, sitting at the table, sipping a cup of water.

"A few more hours until we reach shore," Arsène told us, eyeing Grace warily where she sat at the table. Arsène didn't seem to despise Grace in the way that many daimons did with agathos, which was comforting. If anything, he seemed a little frightened of her. "I have never seen so many vessels on the water at once in my life, or so many frightened, angry people."

"I'll head back up—" I began, but Wild materialized out of the shadows like a fucking ghost despite being the size of a tank. He still didn't look one hundred percent himself, but I guessed that was to be expected after this morning. He'd nearly lost both his lovers, and it had been his idea to send Grace after Bullet in the first place.

I had some feelings about that.

Wild gave me and then the bowl of lukewarm beans on the table a pointed look.

"Yes, sir," I muttered, throwing him a mock salute before sitting down next to a smiling Grace. Wild kissed the top of her head before following Arsène back outside, leaving Grace and me in awkward silence. Or at least it felt awkward to me; surprisingly, Grace looked rather determined.

"What's on your mind?" I asked, wondering what it was that had put that look in her eye. I spooned a mouthful of the least tasty thing I'd ever eaten into my mouth. *Food is fuel, food is fuel.*

"I'm going to bond you, Dare... What's your last name?"

I almost spat out my beans, coughing and spluttering for a moment, until I regained some semblance of dignity. "Abe."

"I'm going to bond you, Dare Abe," Grace repeated with a firm nod of her head, as though that was that. Decision made. "If you're amenable to the idea, that is."

Amenable to the idea? I shoveled some more food into my mouth, giving myself a moment to formulate a reply.

"Are you sure that's what you want?" I asked eventually, my dick already stirring in my shorts. A regular response for a *regular* Philotes daimon, but an unusual one for me. I wasn't normally so easy. "Is this because of the near-death experience? I don't want you to have any regrets by rushing into this—Riot mentioned that it took you guys a little while before you took the leap to fully bonding."

"*That*, I regret," Grace replied easily, no hint of hesitation. "It seemed like the right decision at the time when no one knew what was going on, why Riot and I were drawn together, or what it meant. Hindsight being 20/20, knowing now that we were always destined for one another, I can't help but feel sort of foolish looking back. Denying the bond is physically painful, and I hate that I put Riot and Bullet through that. I didn't let it get so bad with Wild, and I don't intend to with you either. As long as that's what you want."

Grace folded her hands in her lap, watching me expectantly as I made myself finish the bowl of beans in case it was days before we got to eat again.

Was this what I wanted? It had been *everything* I wanted, and in some ways, it still was. But was it *real*?

157

"Would it help to talk about it?" Grace suggested quietly, shrinking in on herself a little. God, I was such a piece of shit. Even if it *was* the bond creating this false sense of obsession, or whatever it was, that wasn't Grace's doing. She wasn't some evil mastermind, trying to seduce me for her own ends.

If anything, she'd demonstrated earlier that she used the bonds to help us, to her own detriment. If I could offer her another way back when she went chasing into the void after Bullet, then I wanted to do that.

"I don't need to talk about it," I replied, standing up and grabbing her hand. "It's not the most romantic of locations, and I really hope Arsène doesn't know what we're about to do to his boat."

"Oh my gosh, you're right. This is so inappropriate—"

"Just so we're clear, I don't really care about that at all," I laughed, pushing open the door to the cabin. "If he does realize, I'll just have Riot run interference so you don't have to deal with the awkwardness."

Bullet was awake, watching us closely from the bed, dimly lit by the flashlight. He caught my eye and grinned. "Is it time? Is it happening? Want me to close my eyes? I can be real quiet."

I snorted, letting Grace decide. I didn't really care if Bullet was in the room or not. As a Philotes, albeit a bad one, I was basically built for fucking—with or without an audience.

I sat on the very edge of the mattress, kicking the door shut and pulling Grace down to straddle me. She scanned my face, bracing her hands against my chest, searching for some kind of reaction. "I'm used to having my bonded in the room."

The admission made her blush so pretty, and I tugged her further up my lap so she could hide her face in the crook of my neck. The move put her directly over my dick, and she sucked in a tiny breath at the contact, but didn't move away.

"I don't mind putting on a show, Grace," I teased, trailing my fingers up and down the notches of her spine. "Maybe I can teach him a thing or two."

Bullet laughed, more carefree than I'd heard him since I arrived here. Had Grace really saved him from the Oneiroi curse? Was that why he was so relaxed? It seemed too good to be true.

What did that mean for our deal?

I was still going to stick to the terms. If Bullet went to the underworld before we were old and gray, I was going to drag him back.

"If you think that's going to hurt my ego, you couldn't be more wrong," Bullet told me. "When it comes to pleasing my Amazing Grace, I'm a dedicated student."

There was the faintest brush of Grace's pleasure at that pronouncement, and it only urged me to reach harder for the bond. I wanted to know every little thing that went through her head, to know when she was feeling anything less than perfectly happy so I could make her smile, to know when she felt even the slightest bit needy so I could satisfy her.

I'd promised Bullet I'd make her laugh every day, and I was going to be good to my word, no matter how hard things got.

"Are you sure, Dare? I know we haven't known each other very long," Grace whispered. "And maybe I'm a little bit motivated by fear, which isn't the best reasoning—"

"It's okay, Grace," I assured her, sliding my hands over her hips to grip her thighs. "Life is scary right now. Maybe we do things that we wouldn't normally do, rush decisions we wouldn't normally rush." Bullet's pale, still form this morning flashed through my mind, the image burned in my memory forever. "You have no idea how much I want this, how *long* I've wanted this. I swear, Onyx used to send me those photos of your pretty smiles at Underworld just to torture me."

Shit, I totally lost that bet with Onyx. She'd been so adamant Grace was mine that she'd made me wager a free giant back tattoo on it.

"That's why she was always taking pictures of me?" Grace laughed, blinking in surprise. "Honestly, I should have questioned it more, but Riot seemed comfortable with it so I trusted she wasn't doing anything nefarious."

"Just tormenting me," I replied drily, absently massaging her thighs for a moment before I realized how handsy I was being and resting my palms more respectably on her knees. I needed to remember that Grace was an agathos, and even with the whole multi-partner setup, I was pretty sure sex had been a whole new concept when she met Riot, not all that long ago.

"You can touch me," Grace encouraged with a shy smile, gently gripping my wrists and encouraging my hands higher again. "I'm yours, and you're mine, Dare. You can touch me whenever you want."

"Mm, and *wherever* I want?" I teased, pushing the fabric of her dress up so I could rub circles into the silky skin of her inner thighs with my thumbs.

"That too," Grace whispered, leaning forward to unbutton the old-man linen shirt I was wearing, eyes tracing the ink on my chest as she exposed it. Bullet kept quiet in the corner, giving us this moment that felt like it was just us, and I appreciated him for it. "You know, when I'm around you, I feel so..."

She bit her lip, deliberating.

"Horny?" I suggested, lightly tracing Grace's waist over her dress, my thumbs brushing against the undersides of her breasts. "Philotes tend to have that effect on people."

She shuddered slightly, arching into my touch. Between my desire and Grace's, as well as the not-insignificant amount coming from Bullet, my inner daimon was definitely coming out to play. My dick was harder than steel, and would stay hard for as long as Grace needed me, no matter how many times I came. I shifted my hips restlessly, offering her a little friction while trying to keep myself under control.

"It's more than that," Grace rasped, taking us both by surprise as she ground down hard on my cock. "You make me feel *sensual*, confident. Like some kind of sex goddess that I definitely am not."

"We can agree to disagree on that. Are you on birth control?"

"Yes. You can... you know."

"Come in this sweet pussy?" I teased, all but dry humping her, my control rapidly slipping. "I don't know if I'd be able to stop myself, Grace. If you take this cock bare, you're getting all my cum with it."

She made a delightfully strangled noise that went straight to my dick, and I patted her softly on the ass. "Panties off. Let me see what's mine."

Bullet exhaled heavily from the corner, reminding me he was there. It didn't seem to bother Grace though; she braced her hands on my shoulders to stand beneath the roof hatch, clumsily shoving her panties down her legs and kicking them off, her dress hiding everything as she stood above me.

Not for long.

"Oh," she said suddenly, flushing. "I, um, haven't shaved my legs. For obvious reasons."

"Okay." I blinked. "Is that... a problem?"

"I don't know, is it?" Grace chewed on her lower lip, looking genuinely concerned, as though her personal grooming standards shouldn't have slipped in the middle of the apocalypse.

"It's not, Amazing Grace," Bullet interjected, his voice soothing. "Trust me, I know how much appearances have been drilled into you from birth—your mother really did a number on you there. But I promise, we all just want you to be happy and comfortable, whatever that looks like. Shave, don't shave. Cut your hair off, leave it long. Wear what you want, experiment, get more tattoos. Whatever makes you feel good."

"It's not like we've been shaving either," I pointed out with what I hoped was a reassuring smile, scratching the scruff on my jawline. It didn't suit me at all, but the world was possibly ending, so whatever.

"Right, you're right." Grace shook her head slightly. "I'm sorry. I get stuck in my own head sometimes."

A pang of sympathy hit me square in the chest. It was clear that in leaving the agathos community, Grace was doing some pretty hefty deconstructing, and she was doing it in the middle of a divine war that she'd been given a central role in.

"Let me help you get *out* of your head for a little bit," I suggested. "To just feel and not think..."

"Yes, please," Grace replied breathily, without a second's hesitation.

"Bend over, brace your hands on the bed," I instructed as I shifted out of the way so she could set her palms on the mattress, looking at her with a lazy smirk. Letting her know that it wasn't that serious, that while I was more than happy to issue her orders, there'd never be any repercussions for her not following them.

She wouldn't be getting any spankings from me, though I imagined that was the kind of thing Wild was into.

"Good girl," I murmured as my brave Grace flattened her palms where I'd been sitting, bending forward and watching me out of the corner of her eye with a bashful kind of curiosity.

I shot her a quick wink before sitting on the floor behind her, lifting her dress and scooting between her legs, slightly underestimating how wide my shoulders were. Grace laughed lightly, letting me lift one thigh so I could get in position, her dress falling into place over top of me.

Then I buried my face in her naked cunt where it belonged.

"Dare!" she gasped in surprise. I ate at her pussy like I was starving, like I'd die if her cunt didn't nourish me. She tasted like heaven and hell and home, and I was going to make it my goddamn mission to lick her pussy every single day.

I should have made *that* deal with Bullet, though her laughs were good too.

"I can't, I can't, it's too good," Grace whimpered, fingers scrambling for purchase on the mattress, boat rocking incessantly beneath us. I gripped her ass tightly, pinning her in place while I tongue-fucked her to completion.

I paused for a second, rubbing the coarse hair of my mini beard over her sensitive inner thigh. "See? Not so bad going without razors."

A breathy laugh turned into a moan as I resumed lavishing attention on her clit until she came with a soft cry, thighs trembling on either side of my head.

Make Grace smile: Check.

As much as I wanted to draw this moment out, my dick felt like it was going to explode. I pulled my cock out of my shorts, fisting it roughly as I captured every drop of Grace's orgasm on my tongue, my own desire so potent that my muscles shook.

This must be how regular Philotes daimons felt. I'd always been a defective one—needing to at least give some semblance of a shit about a person before my dick would come to the party, and even then, I lost interest pretty quickly.

That would never happen with Grace.

"I need you," Grace panted, scrambling away from my tongue and dropping to my lap, eyeing my dick with a flattering level of appreciation.

We were on the small triangular patch of floor with Bullet watching from a foot away—it was probably the least romantic setting ever—but it didn't matter in that moment, and I vowed to myself to make it up to Grace later.

"You have me," I assured her, shoving her dress out of the way and lining my cock up at her entrance. Grace didn't hesitate, eyes fluttering closed as she lowered herself down my length, letting out a breathy moan that I resolved to hear at least once a day for the rest of our lives.

I'd never *not* used condoms before, and my eyes rolled back in my head at the feel of her. Shit, it was lucky I could come multiple times because the base of my spine was already tingling, balls drawing tight in anticipation.

It felt so good that it took me a moment to realize that something was happening in my chest. Something warm and intense and all-encompassing, threading my soul at one end and Grace's at the other, tying us together.

I came with a violent shudder. I couldn't help myself.

I'd wanted this for so long, even if I didn't entirely trust it. Grace was irrevocably mine and I was irrevocably hers, and I had to hope that those feelings were real. God, I wanted them so much to be real.

"Oh," Grace whispered as I stilled beneath her for a moment, flooding her pussy. It felt raw and primal, like I was marking her as mine. I *felt* her surprise through the bond, a tangible thread between us that felt like pure sunshine, allowing our emotions to pass back and forth.

"Don't worry," I gritted out. "I can keep going for as long as you need me."

"You can— *oh*."

I bounced Grace on my cock like I'd die if I didn't, her nails digging roughly into my shoulders, gouging bloody crescents into the skin. *Mine, mine, mine.* The word repeated like a mantra in my head with each rough thrust, each bounce of her breasts in my face, each muffled moan. Grace was mine, and now we were bound in a way that could never be undone.

"Dare," she gasped, cunt clenching tightly around me, her pupils dilating as she found her release. I followed again right after her, not bothering to hold back, dick still painfully hard.

Grace collapsed against my chest, breathing heavily, hands moving over every part of me that she could reach like she was memorizing me. "That was so good. So freaking good."

"Oh, you're definitely not done yet," I teased, rolling my hips slightly. My desire was feeding off hers, and Grace wanted more.

Grace's eyes widened. "Didn't you... twice? How are you still hard?"

Bullet laughed from his spot on the bed. "Perks of being a Philotes, for sure."

"A perk I've never been able to use until you, Grace. Only you make me feel this way."

I unashamedly spied on her reaction through the bond, glad to feel how much that idea pleased her. It made me a little uneasy that the connection went both ways, having never opened my soul to another person before. I guessed I'd get used to it?

"As much as I've enjoyed keeping you all to myself, don't you think Bullet could use a little loving?" I asked, grinning up at Grace to disguise the more vulnerable emotions I was hiding underneath. She absolutely knew how I was feeling, but I didn't want to remind Bullet of how terrifying this morning had been for us. How we'd nearly lost him, and how grateful I was that we hadn't. "You up for it, B?"

"My dick is definitely up for it," he replied with a laugh. "Nothing gets me in the mood faster than experiencing Grace's arousal through the bond."

"What did you have in mind?" Grace asked, curiosity mixed with something else I couldn't quite identify coming through the bond.

"I'm suggesting that I bend you over the bed so you can suck Bullet's dick while I fuck you from behind." I shrugged. "But if you'd rather me spread you out on the bed and ride you until you forget he's in the room, I'm down with that plan too."

"Oh. Bend me over, please," Grace whispered, all prim and proper. It only made me want to see her come undone that much more.

"Well, since you asked so nicely..."

She climbed off me without any prompting, bracing herself on the bed on her forearms, head level with Bullet's crotch as she pressed a kiss to his hip. He tangled his fingers in her hair, stroking it softly while I moved behind her, flipping her dress up and admiring the trickle of cum leaking down her thighs.

My Grace was so pretty and put together all the time, and I just wanted to make an absolute mess of her.

Bullet shuffled down the bed for a moment, capturing Grace's lips in a soft kiss. To my surprise, she was the one who broke it, bracing herself on the bed and breaking out a stern teacher voice that I'd for sure never heard her use before.

"Move up," she commanded. "Pants off. I want to make you feel good."

Well, well, well. Did Grace break out a secret bossy side just for Bullet? He clearly had no objections, scrambling back up the bed. I shamelessly kneaded the globes of her ass while she helped free him from his shorts, confidently pumping his shaft before taking him into her mouth.

Sexy as fuck.

Agathos may have had all kinds of hangups about sex, but apparently group sex among their bonded was not one of them. She moaned around his length as I slid my still-hard cock back into her dripping pussy, pinning her hips in place with my hands as I picked up my pace, the three of us falling into a rhythm together.

167

I drew the bond close, immersing myself in Grace's feelings, adjusting my angle to give her what she craved but hadn't asked for. That was a convenient perk for sure.

Grace let out a muffled moan, and with just a few circles of my finger around her clit, she was coming again, her movements growing shaky and uneven.

"Oh fuck," Bullet groaned, fisting the sheets as he came. I followed not long after, stilling behind Grace and wrapping my arms around her waist, pulling her back against me. Grace was sated, and finally my cock began to deflate.

I clumsily pulled her back to my chest before sitting down on the edge of the bed next to Bullet's hip with Grace on my lap. He politely tucked his dick away before grabbing her hand, stroking the back of it with his thumb.

She hummed contentedly, leaning her head against my shoulder, occasionally nuzzling me like a happy kitten. Whatever fears I had about the bond, justified or not, it was still the best moment of my life.

"Does it feel different to have all four of your bonded, Amazing Grace?" Bullet asked, his voice pleased, if not a little slurred.

"It feels nice. Right, perfect. Not necessarily *different*," Grace explained. "More like this was the way it was always meant to be, and now it's here."

She stiffened for a moment before letting out a heavy sigh.

"What is it?" I asked, rubbing her back and trying to work out what her sudden inner turmoil meant.

"I think Wild needs some... reassurance, or something." Grace frowned. "There's a lot of jealousy coming through the bond, which is weird."

Bullet looked equally puzzled and I couldn't quite suppress my chuckle that they hadn't worked it out yet. "Bullet, you're involved with Wild, right?"

"Right," Bullet agreed, his red cheeks obvious even underneath the shadowy overhang that half covered his face.

"And I'm in here with both of you..."

"But he's never responded badly to Riot being around us, and it's the same, right?" Grace asked, glancing at me. Ah, that's what that weird emotion had been when she wanted to know what I was suggesting with Bullet. She wanted to know if *I* was going to touch him.

"It's the same in that my interest in Bullet is purely platonic. It's different because Riot isn't a Philotes daimon."

Bullet glanced away, looking slightly ashamed, while the furrow between Grace's brow grew deeper. "So? What does that have to do with it?"

"Daimons can be judgmental assholes, even of each other," Bullet mumbled.

"Basically, I'm a Slutty McSlutterson Philotes daimon, and Wild probably thinks I had my hands all over his man because I wouldn't be able to control myself," I scoffed. "Which wouldn't be true even if I was a *regular* Philotes daimon who didn't need to feel some baseline emotional connection to people to be interested in them. Every other Philotes I know has self-control. We're not just mindless fuck puppets."

"I'm sure Wild doesn't think of you like *that*," Grace assured me quickly, looking horrified. I shrugged—maybe, maybe not. He was a Keres daimon, after all; I had no doubt he'd experienced his fair share of bullshit assumptions over the years because of his line too. "We've been staying with Vasileios for a month—we *know* Philotes daimons don't just throw themselves at the nearest person. That's *ridiculous*," she added vehemently.

"That's probably too polite of a term," Bullet sighed.

"Don't worry about it. I've been a Philotes my whole life. I promise you I'm used to people making assumptions about me," I snorted. Did it sting a little that it was coming from Wild? Yeah, a little. Not that we'd spent much time together for him to get to know me, but I guessed I wanted him to give me the benefit of the doubt the way I'd done for him.

He'd beat the crap out of Riot, and I'd still come here with an open mind, with no intention of holding it against him if Riot himself wasn't going to.

"I'll send Wild in, take over above deck for a bit," I said, shifting Grace gently off my lap.

"No, we just bonded, we need to spend some time together—"

"We will," I promised, pressing a firm kiss to her temple, trying not to let my annoyance with Wild show. Aside from the fact that his insecurities were cutting into my time with Grace, I just really wanted a fucking lie down—I hadn't slept since we left the villa, and the cold was extra draining. "But it's going to bother you that he's out there thinking the worst, when a quick conversation can easily clear it up. I'll let him know that I'll be back to steal more time with you shortly, so he better get over himself fast."

"We'll make sure of it," Bullet said firmly.

170

WILD

CHAPTER 16

Riot cut me a warning look as I cracked my knuckles for the thousandth time, rolling my neck back and forth to release some of the tension that had been building up as Grace's arousal had poured steadily through the bond. Grace, who was shut in a tiny, enclosed space with Bullet and a Philotes daimon she'd been eager to bond with since the moment she laid eyes on him.

I didn't *want* to be jealous. I wasn't of Grace's relationship with Dare—I always knew she'd have four soul bonds and this came with the territory. But there was a possessiveness over Bullet that I hadn't expected. I didn't want to share him with anyone but Grace.

I never had, but after almost losing him this morning... Even this small amount of distance between us felt like too much. I needed to be close, to know he was okay, sandwiched safely between me and Grace.

Dare emerged from the cabin with a flashlight, sauntering out on the deck with all the swagger of a well-fucked daimon, and I briefly contemplated tossing him overboard.

He said a quick hello as he passed Arsène before stopping in front of me, leaning against the side of the boat with one hand on the railing to keep him steady, the sea breeze blowing his hair back out of his face. He was a pretty little bastard, I'd give him that.

Riot approached cautiously, eyeing the two of us like he wasn't sure if he was going to have to break up a fight or not.

"You're being a fucking idiot, did you know that?" Dare asked me casually. Riot's jaw dropped, gaze bouncing between us as though he was watching a volleyball match. "Tell me, Wild, do you go around punching everything that moves because you're a Keres daimon? Do you beat the shit out of every person who irritates you because you have no leash on your anger?"

What?

"No, of course you don't. If you did, you'd have decked me in the face already, but you have self-control. Just because I'm a Philotes daimon doesn't mean I stick my dick in everything with a pulse. I'll tell you this *once*: I only have eyes for Grace. It's your call whether you listen to me or your own insecurities—ones that stem from some bullshit ideas about Philotes in the first place. I'm not going to try to convince you."

My face felt strangely hot, and for once I was glad I couldn't speak because I'd have probably spouted something idiotic to try to defend myself. Had I needed some reassurance that Dare wasn't interested in Bullet? Yes. But he was right in that I'd made some unfair assumptions based on nothing more than his line, and I knew exactly how frustrating it felt to be on the receiving end of that sort of thing.

"They're waiting for you," he said, tipping his chin at the cabin. "But you should know I'm not going to give you long. Grace and I just bonded, and your stupid jealousy is eating into our moment, so get in there and sort it out."

I nodded stiffly, turning back to the cabin. Dare was right, I was fucking up what should have been a moment of joy for him and Grace, and I needed to get in there and reassure her. Grace was too compassionate on the best of days, but especially with her soul bonds. She wouldn't be able to truly relax until I sorted this out, too worried about managing *my* emotions instead.

"You have the biggest balls of anyone I've ever met," I heard Riot mutter to Dare as I left, the comment making my lips twitch. I had to agree. Not many daimons had the stones to go toe-to-toe with me.

I nodded at Arsène as I went past, hunching over as much as possible to fit below deck. *Never again.* I'd never felt so claustrophobic in my life.

Grace immediately stood beneath the hutch when I entered the sleeping cabin, ushering me to the edge of the bed where she'd been sitting.

"Sit, you're way too tall to stand in here," she fussed. I let her drag me down next to Bullet, who was reclining on the bed with his fingers interlinked over his stomach, staring at me with one unimpressed eyebrow raised. The last time I'd felt so cowed by just a look, I'd been ten years old and I'd just kicked a football through Auntie Samira's kitchen window.

Grace remained standing, wrapping her arms around her waist, and I hated that she looked so vulnerable in a moment that should have been celebratory. She had a new bonded, her *last* bonded, and I was ruining it with my moodiness.

'*I'm sorry,*' I signed immediately, before pulling a pen and notepad out of my pocket so I could give them more detailed explanations.

"It's okay—" Grace began.

"Good, you should be fucking sorry," Bullet said at the same time, huffing irritably. "You shouldn't have assumed anything about Dare based on his line, for one. You definitely shouldn't have assumed that anything would happen between me and Dare—we've known each other since grade school, we're *friends*, always have been. Aside from that, you should trust that both Grace and I would talk to you if either of us intended to change the dynamics among the group."

I nodded, thoroughly humbled by Bullet's telling-off.

'*I was wrong,*' I scribbled on the notepad. '*I made offensive and incorrect assumptions about Dare, and I will apologize to him for that. I'm sorry that I let my feelings get in the way of what should be a special moment with Dare right now, and for diminishing the connection the three of us share.*'

Grace read the note first, giving me a sympathetic smile before handing it to Bullet and stepping into my space. She wrapped her arms around my neck while I rested my head against her breasts, and I guessed I was forgiven if she was going to let me touch her like this. I could *feel* through the bond that I was forgiven, though she'd never really been mad in the first place, just worried about everyone else, and maybe a little disappointed.

Bullet crumpled up the paper, sighing dramatically enough that I knew he wasn't really upset. "I suppose I forgive you. There's no need to be so..."

He trailed off, and I twisted back to look at his face, his brows drawn down. Grace's concern spiked, and I could admit that it wasn't like Bullet to be lost for words.

"Never mind," Bullet said eventually, plastering an easy smile on his face that didn't quite meet his eyes. "You should probably get Dare back now. He and Grace are due for some snuggles now, don't you think?"

I nodded with a wry smile, gently cupping Grace's jaw and pulling her towards me, intending to give her a proper goodbye kiss before I left. To my surprise, she pulled away, the bond flooding with embarrassment. I frowned, cocking my head to the side.

"I, um," Grace stuttered. "*GaveBulletablowjob.*"

I snorted. Did they think *that* would bother me?

I yanked Grace back onto my lap, pulling her face to mine and licking at the seam of her lips, encouraging her to open for me. Tasting Bullet's cum on Grace's tongue only made her sweeter to me.

Her arousal reignited like a low simmer in the bond as I ravaged her mouth, but I wasn't going to let it go any further. I'd intruded on Dare's moment for long enough.

'*Later*,' I signed, pulling away and giving Grace a heated look. Bullet cleared his throat, raising an eyebrow at me expectantly, though a playful grin played around his mouth.

Bullet was always handsome, but in that moment, reclining on the bed, he invoked the image of a youthful Greek god. He wouldn't look out of place in a toga, a bunch of grapes in one hand and a goblet of wine in the other, ideally lounging in the sunshine with the light reflecting off his golden hair.

"What?" Bullet asked, tilting his head to the side. "Why are you looking at me like that?"

'*No reason*,' I mouthed, giving Grace's hips a quick squeeze before lifting her off me and leaning across the mattress to reach Bullet. I pushed his hair back from his face, tangling a hand in it and angling his head back to capture his lips, teasing him with tongue and teeth before drawing back, letting him chase me.

There was an edge of desperation to our kisses that hadn't been there before. A sense of urgency, even though the immediate risk had passed. Grace had saved Bullet. We'd visit the agathos of wisdom and find out how to lift the darkness, and things would go back to how they were. We had time.

Didn't we?

Why did it still feel as though we were balancing on a knife's edge?

Reluctantly, I pulled away, searching Bullet's eyes for a long moment, verifying he was okay. He was fine and he was here, and we were all going to be okay.

We had time. There was still time.

"This is where I leave you," Arsène said a couple of hours later, giving us an apologetic look as we stood on the shore, getting used to the feeling of steady ground beneath our feet again. Grace had draped herself in a blanket that covered her head, something we'd seen both men and women doing along the way, so she didn't look too out of place. "You'll be okay traveling on foot from here?"

I nodded curtly while Grace shot him a grateful smile. "It's only a few hours. I'm sure we'll be fine."

Her optimism was probably misplaced. Dare and Riot hadn't slept at all since we'd gotten on the boat, and Bullet had almost died a few hours ago. Walking for miles in the freezing darkness was the last thing we needed.

Arsène didn't look as confident, but like any normal daimon, he was disturbed by the idea that we were going to the home of the agathos.

"Where will you go?" Riot asked, sounding faintly curious.

Arsène looked back at the boat. "The cabin you were staying in once belonged to *my* daimon lovers, decades ago." He swallowed, shaking his head. "They are both gone from this world now. One was Vasileios' father. We all wanted to be more than what we are, and we tried. We lived at sea to resist the temptation." He snorted. "But we couldn't. There was no hope for us, but there seems to be for you. I will go to Leonidio, to see what I can do for Vasileios."

Grace nodded, silent tears streaming down her face. "I'm sure it wasn't easy for you to bring us here when it meant leaving Vasileios behind. I'm more grateful than I can say."

Arsène smirked. "Vasileios will be fine. He was always a smart boy— even when he's thinking with his dick. You should go, Grace the Agathos. It doesn't matter how smart any of us are. We will all die if the darkness doesn't lift."

"I'll do everything I can," Grace promised. I gave Arsène a warning look over her shoulder when he looked like he was going to respond with something I wouldn't like. Something that would put even more on Grace's shoulders than the impossible weight she was already carrying. He wisely kept his mouth shut, handing Dare a bag of emergency supplies from the boat he'd put together for us before disappearing back to his vessel.

He'd avoided the port, rowing us to a quiet beach in what was probably a bustling resort town under regular circumstances. It was bustling now too—but not in a good way. The blazing flames of buildings on fire had been easily visible well before we got to the shore. The temperature was growing colder each day, and I wouldn't be surprised if the inferno had been caused by a well-meaning attempt to stay warm that had quickly gotten out of control. Though we were a few miles away from the flames, the stench of smoke was overwhelming. Beneath it was the faint, stomach-turning smell of sewerage, and I guessed whatever Gaia had done to kill technology was impacting that too.

Just fucking delightful. And Gaia wondered why no one ever worshipped her, the fucking sociopath.

We watched Arsène go before trudging up the sand to the road, keeping our flashlights off to avoid drawing any unwanted attention.

Not that anyone was paying us any attention. People were burning furniture, books—everything short of each other.

They'd get to that point too, I realized uneasily. If there was one thing mortals would do in dire circumstances, it was *anything to survive.* The smell of violence in the air called to my Keres senses, a faint metallic taste coating my mouth. I wanted it. I craved it, even knowing it was wrong. These people would destroy each other, and my inner Keres reveled in it.

"Wild?" Grace whispered, looking back at me as she walked arm-in-arm with Bullet. "Everything okay?"

"He's probably also wondering if they've resorted to cannibalism yet or not," Riot muttered, his head moving as though it was on a swivel. Without technology to communicate with, I felt even more useless than usual. Luckily, Riot and I were more in-sync than I'd expected. Often, when Arsène had asked me a question, Riot had predicted exactly what I'd wanted to say.

"They wouldn't do that," Grace murmured. I gently grabbed her arm to slow her down for a moment, pulling the blanket more securely over her head so she would only see the ground in front of her and not the litany of corpses nearby.

"I wouldn't be so sure," Dare replied absently, his focus also on the bodies as we started moving again. "Half of these people have no idea what's going on or why. Those who do know probably assume that nothing can be done, and this is truly the end. Veer left, Grace. There's, um, broken glass over here."

"This is not the end," Grace said stubbornly. "I'm going to ask Sophia for guidance, and we're going to make it right."

We walked for hours, leaving the chaotic seaside town and finding ourselves on a quiet tree-lined street with overgrown grass on either side, using the flashlights sporadically to see where we were going. Grace's nerves grew more pronounced with each step we took away from the city, which I hadn't expected. Maybe because she'd always been surrounded by people, but the quiet of the countryside didn't bring her particular comfort. After a few miles, Dare stole her away to walk with him, a fairly miserable way to celebrate their new bond, but it was the best we could do under the circumstances. In spite of that, he did manage to make her laugh quietly at least twice.

He was good for her. A good final addition.

My heart hurt at the discomfort I picked up from Grace through the bond as she leaned increasingly heavily on Dare. The rest of us had raided Arsène's supplies for more functional clothing, and while Grace now had a heavy jacket and knit beanie, none of the shoes had come anywhere close to fitting her. She'd put on thick woolen socks, but the sandals were still causing her pain.

Avoiding humans was easy enough—all of us were tuned in enough to their presence because of our gifts that we could direct ourselves away from them. We didn't have that same internal warning system for agathos or daimons though, and the idea of us walking into an agathos stronghold blind had me on edge.

We were either strolling quietly into a trap or allying ourselves with a formidable force. One that could maybe turn the tide of agathos support to our side, to make them realize they were just pawns in Gaia's war, and that she'd never actually cared about them.

Bullet stumbled, and I rushed forward, my hand shooting out to grab his elbow. Riot looked back at us and I waved him on, trusting him to keep watch for both of us while I steadied Bullet.

"Thanks," Bullet muttered, leaning into my side while I linked our arms together. It wasn't a show of affection, I didn't think. He didn't want the others to see how much he was struggling. Bullet shot me a sidelong look, his purple eyes taking on a silvery sheen from the flashlight. "I shouldn't feel this shit, I had more sleep than any of you. Riot and Dare haven't rested at all."

I huffed in irritation, lightly pinching his elbow. "Right, right, they didn't almost die, I know. But I *didn't* die. That's my whole point."

Even if I could have spoken, I wasn't sure I'd know what to say. It may not have been the most comforting of advice, but I wanted to gently point out to Bullet that the weakness might not just be from lack of sleep. That he may need to come to terms with having less strength and energy, but that it was worth it because he was alive.

"I have a good song for this," Bullet mumbled. I glanced at him, waiting for him to continue and surprised to find him looking almost... frustrated? It was a very un-Bullet-like action. Why would he be frustrated about singing? He loved to sing. "A *great* song," he reiterated.

I grabbed his hand, clumsily tracing the letters *S-I-N-G* on his palm.

"I will," Bullet replied petulantly. "Soon. I just need to think about it a little more. I need to... just make sure I have the right lyrics."

I forced my muscles not to tense, frantically shutting down my rising concern before Grace could pick up on it, while the same three words looped around my brain on repeat.

This isn't normal.

Bullet wasn't acting normally. Then again, he'd come back from the brink of death. Grace had dragged him back from the brink of death.

What did that mean for both of them? What had I really been asking of her when she'd followed the bond to him?

My muscles burned with a frustrated rage I had nowhere to direct. I protected people; that was what I did; that was who I was. Whole networks and systems existed in Milton to look after Keres daimons I barely even knew, and yet when it came to the two people I cared about the most, I may very well have failed more spectacularly than I'd ever failed at anything.

181

Bullet stayed silent, shoulder leaning heavily on my bicep as we trudged on, Grace now sandwiched between Riot and Dare in front of us. Occasionally, a vehicle would race past, and we'd turn off our flashlights and hide under the cover of the trees, but it wasn't frequent. Had people already gotten to where they wanted to go in the past few days? Did they not have access to gas to travel? For the millionth time, I wondered how this was all going to end. Even if we convinced Nyx to lift the darkness, I wasn't sure Gaia could undo whatever it was she'd done. By the way everything had shut off, we assumed she'd destroyed all the cables and pipes in the earth, and I doubted she could undo that destruction even if she wanted to.

Was this our permanent new reality?

I swallowed down the panic that arose every time I contemplated that idea. I relied heavily on technology just to *communicate*. Life without it was a more frightening prospect than I wanted to acknowledge.

The sealed road eventually turned to orange dirt, the grass lining the road becoming coarse brush as we headed further inland, closer to the temple site.

Bullet shuddered, his grip on my arm tightening. "That is… potent. Can you feel it in the air? There is a lot of power here."

Grace glanced back at him over her shoulder, too far ahead to hear his words, but giving him a knowing look as though she could sense it too.

"I don't think we'll be alone," Bullet added under his breath. "It's a pilgrimage site. There's a very good chance that agathos will be traveling here to ask for guidance or hoping they can find some kind of sanctuary on ancient soil."

I nodded, hearing the unspoken warning. Keep your guard up.

Hopefully, if there were any agathos, they were of the Foster and Orion variety, rather than the Bellamy family variety.

We passed through an empty parking lot, the silence of this place deafeningly loud. Riot, Grace, and Dare slowed down, allowing Bullet and I to catch up so we could enter the ancient site as a group.

"It's too quiet," Dare murmured, looking around anxiously as we walked through a dark, tree-lined path to get to the archaeological remains.

"It'd be convenient for us if everyone was just avoiding temples after Grace's light show," Bullet chuckled, the sound unusually loud in the stifling quiet. "But historically, we have not been that lucky."

Grace hummed quietly. "The perils of being bonded to a Eutychian agathos, I'm afraid."

I was pretty sure all four of us were thinking that Grace being a luck-bearing agathos was the smallest burden she had to bear, but none of us said anything.

The murmur of voices reached us as we continued on the avenue and we all stiffened. I dragged Bullet forward to stand with the others, gesturing at them to turn off the flashlights before pointing at myself and then the direction the sounds were coming from.

"You can't go alone!" Grace hissed.

"You can't fight an agathos and Bullet is in no shape to fight at all," Dare said placatingly. "None of us want to leave you undefended for even a moment, and Wild knows what he's doing."

I gave Grace's arm a quick squeeze, sending reassurance at her through the bond as I stalked into the darkness, following the noise while keeping my eyes out for any signs of trouble. The site was bigger than I thought, the hum of conversation coming from the remnants of a theater. Pressing my body behind a column, I stood there for a few minutes, assessing what I was seeing and trying to decide whether or not they were a threat.

They were definitely agathos. They had a few torches and candles burning, and the unnaturally pale eyes were obvious even from here. The stage area of the theater had been set up with makeshift housing—a few tents, but also a lot of rudimentary shelters made of blankets. They spoke in hushed tones, bustling around, making food and boiling water on a camp stove, working as a community unlike everyone else we'd seen so far since the world went dark.

That didn't necessarily bode well for us. Not if they were the kind of agathos community Grace had been raised in. As tempting as it was to storm in there and beg, borrow or steal hot food and a place to rest, if we could get past them without attracting attention, that would be the better option.

I snuck back, finding the others where I'd left them.

"Agathos?" Dare asked. I turned my flashlight back on, nodding. "Friendly or unfriendly?"

I shrugged my shoulders, pressing my finger to my lips and pointing past the theater to the library we were supposed to be going to.

"Right, avoid them, got it," Riot said with a curt nod, and I was grateful that they all seemed to understand me despite the communication barriers. "Did you see any lookouts?"

I shook my head before flicking the flashlight back off, not wanting to risk attracting attention, just in case. We all moved forward with even greater care than before, creeping through the expansive site until we got to the reconstructed façade of the library. Riot, Dare, and I turned our lights on, illuminating the two-storey-high façade, eight columns at the front framing the archways that would have once been the entry points to the building. In between each set of columns was an enclave built into the wall—four pedestals, housing four statues.

We were on the threshold of the courtyard space in front of it, none of us moving. None of us able to go any further. There was an insistent sort of pressure, not quite pushing us back, but not letting us in either. More like it was testing us, deciding whether or not we were worthy to enter.

My heart dropped to my stomach. There was no way four daimons were going to be able to enter an agathos sanctuary, and I wasn't sure I had it in me to let Grace walk in alone and unprotected. Had we come all this way for nothing?

"Go with your gut," Bullet encouraged her.

"You know, when I don't know what to do, I remember you telling me to do what scares me," Grace whispered, staring in awe at the statues. "And what scares me is to come here not as a Prophêtis with some grand task I'm supposed to be carrying out, but to come here as a regular agathos. To humbly ask for help, knowing that I've always resented what I am, and they may not forgive me for it."

It was a conclusion I'd never have reached, possibly no daimon would have. It wasn't in our nature to humble ourselves in the face of judgment—I certainly didn't give a fuck if anyone assessed my character and found me wanting. For all the ways the mortal agathos descendants had drifted from their founders' ways and ideals, apparently their judgmental nature was timeless.

"Sophia," Grace whispered. "Please, forgive me. Help me. Guide me. I cannot do what needs to be done without you."

185

There was no response, but the bubble of pressure pushing us back seemed to soften, and Grace wasted no time pushing forwards, confidently approaching the statue on the farthest left. The four of us immediately rushed to follow, stumbling over the uneven stone ground.

With an alarming look of serenity on her face, she fished out the small pocket knife she was carrying, slicing the pad of her thumb and holding it out to drip blood over the base of the statue where the name 'Sophia' was engraved in Ancient Greek.

Flashes of gold immediately shot up the statue, lighting up the library façade like some kind of pyrotechnic show. There was no way that the agathos in the theater wouldn't see it, though hopefully, that shield of judgment would keep them out. The cool white marble of Sophia's statue transformed in front of our eyes. The missing nose regrew, the chipped marble smoothing into an elegant face. The arm that had been lost somewhere to time seemed to shoot out of the shoulder like a rapidly growing vine, the grinding sound of stone against stone filling the air, all while Grace stared up in a state of complete, unnatural calm.

The white stone eyes shone gold—there was no iris, no pupil, just the kind of almost robotic glow that seemed like it would precede laser beams shooting directly at us. And then a soft, feminine voice spoke, though the mouth of the monument didn't move.

"Welcome, Grace the Agathodaimon."

GRACE

CHAPTER 17

I blinked up at the talking statue above me, feeling as though I was coming out of a trance, finally recognizing the faint throb in my thumb. I'd been aware of what I was doing all along, but felt separate from it somehow, as though I was watching my actions from afar.

It was a deeply unsettling sensation.

"What did you call her, goddess?" Dare asked, hastily tacking on the term of respect.

"*Agathodaimon*," Sophia replied, her voice a strange combination of booming and serene, coming from the center of her chest somehow. "Over the centuries, agathodaimon became known as agathos, and *kakodaimon* became known as daimon. Perhaps, had the language not changed, our kinds would not have grown so very far apart. Perhaps we would have remembered that we are sides of the same coin, equally as essential as one another. We are nothing without balance."

I didn't necessarily think she was wrong, but it hardly seemed like the most pressing issue right at that second. We were freezing to death. What we needed was sunshine, not philosophical quandaries.

"I can see you wondering what the relevance of this is, but it is all connected. The imbalance has been left too long. Mortals think they are gods. Gods think they are untouchable. Greed begets greed, hearts fill with hatred. This world is a sad, lonely place. Only once the balance is corrected, when the ground is even enough for everyone to find their footing, can we grow beyond this and become who we are meant to be."

"Right," Riot drawled, his flat, unimpressed tone making me startle. "But in the meantime, what do we do about the fact that we're rapidly freezing to death? That soon there will be nothing to eat, even if the temperature doesn't drop any lower?"

"Unless killing off humanity is the solution," Bullet added warily.

"The darkness is a symptom of the imbalance, not the solution. The hatred between Nyx and Gaia was too extreme, creating one kind of imbalance, but they are unified in their spite, and it has created another. Two beings as powerful as they are must keep each other in check. United, they're a danger to us all."

"So we want them to hate each other, but not all the way hate each other?" Dare muttered under his breath.

"Balance," Sophia replied simply.

Right. Balance.

The golden glow of Sophia's eyes shifted somehow, casting light towards Bullet. It sent a shiver of unease down my spine, and I decided I didn't want her looking at him. "For the Moros who bring doom, there are the Elpis who bring hope. For the violent death of the Keres is the peaceful death of Thanatos. For the sex and affection of the Philotes, there is the quarrel and strife of the Neikea. For the luck and good fortune of the Eutychia, there is the retribution of Nemesis."

"What are you saying?" I asked sharply, not liking where this conversation was leading at all.

"That there is no balancing force for the Oneiroi," Bullet replied, his voice quiet and even. "That's why I'm the last one."

"As a spirit of wisdom, I must tell you that you aren't meant to be here, Oneiroi. That this new world is not meant for your kind. The gods must be freed, new heroes will arise, old orders will fall. Nothing strong can be built on crumbling foundations."

"Bullet isn't a crumbling foundation," I rasped, stepping back towards my bonded, finding Bullet's hand. We shouldn't have come here, we didn't need to hear this. The agathos were heartless, and apparently that had always been the case. "He's a pillar of strength. Nothing about this world would be better without him in it."

"Thanks, Amazing Grace," Bullet replied, attempting to keep his tone light and teasing.

Sophia stared—or at least I thought she did—and I fought to keep my spine straight and my shoulders squared. I'd go to war with Sophia for Bullet, just like I would with anyone else.

"As you say," Sophia said eventually. "I can only offer you my wisdom—how you choose to use it is up to you. I can grant you access to the realm of the gods for a short while through these doors. You cannot stray far, however. If there is, say, a primordial goddess you'd like to speak to, I will need to invite her to come to you."

189

Hint, hint, I thought wryly. Sophia was making no bones about what she wanted me to do. What she thought was *wise.*

We couldn't get to Nyx in the dreamscape—I would *never* let Bullet try again, not after last time. And we could pray, but it was a one-sided conversation.

I'd always felt pretty powerless, even with all the titles and expectations heaped on me, because what could I *do*, really? Being a Prophêtis seemed sort of lame in terms of god-gifted abilities.

But it was a gift of speech. It was words that carried weight. It was time for me to learn how to use it.

It wasn't the lesson of wisdom I thought I'd learn from Sophia, but it was what I was coming away with.

"What do you want to do, Grace?" Dare asked softly.

"I'd like to call a meeting with Nyx and Gaia. A meeting of the goddesses." I swallowed thickly, tilting my chin up. "It's time to finish what they started. We can't go on like this."

My teeth chattered as I made my request, the relentless cold growing worse by the hour.

"Then I will call for them, though you should know neither are likely to respond right away. They will not want to appear weak by being the first to agree."

"Politics," Riot grumbled, sounding as thoroughly exhausted by this whole thing as I was.

"Quite. In the meantime, you should rest and stay warm—no meeting will occur if you're dead." Wasn't that a comforting thought? "The temple custodian will come and fetch you. Her family has guarded these lands for generations. You will be safe with her."

"An agathos?" Dare clarified flatly.

"Did I steer you wrong before, kakodaimon?" Sophia asked mildly, a hint of censure in her voice. "If I wanted harm to come to you, it would have. But I am a spirit of wisdom, and I do not feel that is wise."

"But Bullet can kick rocks, right?" Dare shot back, unimpressed.

"My hero," Bullet teased, his light tone masking the tired resignation he'd been feeling since Sophia addressed him.

"All five of you will be safe with the custodian," Sophia said evenly. "Wait here for her. When I have heard from the goddesses, I will be in touch. Rest, Grace the Agathodaimon."

The gold faded, leaving smooth, *perfect* white marble in its place. There were three other statues here, should I heal them too? I swayed slightly on my feet, leaning into Bullet, who was himself half-collapsed against Wild. *Maybe later.*

Wild righted Bullet before stalking to the edge of a stack of broken marble before gesturing at us to come closer, glancing nervously out toward the avenue.

"Nothing is ever straightforward. Whenever I think someone is on our side, it's more that one or two of our interests align and we can go fuck ourselves other than that," Riot grumbled, pulling blankets out of the bag while Bullet and I dragged ourselves to the obscured spot Wild pointed out. It wasn't exactly secure, but hopefully it meant that no one would see us if they were just casually walking past. The custodian might take minutes or hours to get here, and in the meantime we were freezing.

"Ultimately, nobody has our back except us," Bullet replied mildly. "Gods, mortals, it doesn't matter. Everyone has an agenda, and we just have to hope we come across the people whose agenda lines up at least most of the way with ours."

"Depressingly true," Dare sighed. "I'll stay out here and keep watch. There's no way that light show didn't attract attention, but at least no one will recognize me. I wasn't in the videos."

There wasn't any resentment in his voice, but I shoved my apology through the bond at him anyway, and he shot me a soft half-smile before shutting off his flashlight and standing in the darkness.

Wild helped Bullet and I to the ground, and we leaned against a stack of marble, my head resting on his shoulder, gazing up at the sky. The endlessly dark sky.

Nyx's doing. We couldn't live like this. Plants weren't growing, and people were panicking. Within days, at best, we'd get to freezing level, and we were in one of the warmer parts of the world.

No, this couldn't continue. They *had* to agree to meet.

Ultimately, the anger between the agathos and daimons, which had then overflowed into the human world, had started because of the enmity between two sisters. An enmity that had spiraled out of control, because no one wielded the knife quite like family when it came to cutting you down.

But there had to be an end point, and ideally that end point came before the end of the world. The prophecy had sidetracked me—no matter what I was meant to do on that front, nothing could happen until Gaia and Nyx came to some sort of truce, or in a moment of anger, either one of them could undo everything we'd worked towards anyway.

There *had* to be peace between them. But at what cost?

I blinked in confusion, looking around the inky black garden I'd found myself in, wondering how I'd ended up here.

This wasn't a dream. It was too neat, too detailed, too perfect.

No, this was a dreamscape. Except that shouldn't have been possible anymore. If Bullet was messing around with the dreamscape again, we were going to have serious words about him putting his health at risk.

It didn't feel like Bullet, though. This place was too moody, too dark. Not that Bullet couldn't be those things at times, but the dreamscapes he concocted were light and beautiful, designed for me.

"Bullet?" I called hesitantly, picking a direction on the stone path and committing, my fingers lightly brushing over silken petals as I went. My subconscious must have been feeling dramatic today—I was wearing a sweeping black gown with sheer beaded sleeves and a scandalously plunging neckline. The flagstones felt cool beneath my feet, and I idly wondered why I'd foregone shoes.

"Bullet, where are you? I'm getting a little nervous now..."

He'd never left me alone in a dreamscape before. We'd played hide and seek sometimes when we were kids, but this felt different. Ominous.

"Oh my, little agathos. You are very lost."

I shrieked in surprise at the sound of the cool feminine voice, spinning clumsily on the spot to try to find the source. The dark flowers seemed to reach for me, leaning in as though they were sniffing me, and I shrank in on myself, wrapping my arms around my waist.

Wake up, *I ordered in vain.* I don't want to be here. I want to wake up.

A woman—a goddess—veiled in black with a magnificent silver crescent moon crown on her head materialized in front of me, and I knew in

my bones it was Nyx. I dropped to my knees instantly, grateful that the motion of bowing gave me a second to hide the terror on my face.

How on earth had I ended up here? Where was Bullet?

Nothing about this signaled anything good.

"*Usually, I don't reveal myself to mortals in their dreams—except for the Oneiroi who are meant to bear the weight of my presence—but you shouldn't be here, so clearly you can handle more than the average mortal.*"

Could the Oneiroi really handle more? The fact that they didn't live beyond thirty suggested otherwise.

Either way, it just made me more eager than ever to get away from here. To get back to Bullet and make sure he was safe because the last time he'd tried to visit Nyx, it had nearly killed him.

Then again, while I was here...

"*You are quite the puzzle, little Prophêtis,*" *Nyx remarked, sounding bemused.* "*I summoned the Spirit of Dreams. Did you choose to come in his place? This is my personal domain; it is not the sort of place one stumbles into by accident.*"

"*I don't know,*" *I whispered, still prostrated on the ground, hesitating for a moment before deciding to say more.* "*It wasn't a conscious decision, but if I had a choice to come in his place, I'd take it. Bullet nearly died the last time he tried to speak to you.*"

Nyx hummed thoughtfully, the train of her long gown sweeping along the ground in front of me as she wandered between flowers, my gaze still trained on the ground.

"That is why I summoned him, of course—you snatched his mortal thread from the scissors of the Fates, something that shouldn't have been possible. You used the bond the Fates gifted you to forge a stronger connection between you, a different kind of connection. Perhaps one that is symbiotic."

Symbiotic? That was good, wasn't it? We were helping each other. Then again, Bullet looked so exhausted...

"Am I draining him?"

"You're sustaining him," Nyx corrected softly. "And it's clear you rely on him heavily in return, but you won't be able to do it forever."

I swallowed thickly, pushing the thought aside as best I could and cautiously glancing up at her. "It won't matter if we all freeze to death on a lightless planet."

Nothing about the goddess' body language was apologetic. "If the earth freezes over, there will be no more awful mortals to ruin it. Once they're all gone, I can simply allow the sun to shine again. A paradise free of you polluting, ungrateful creatures."

Terror gripped me by the throat. "Please don't do that. There's a lot of good in humanity. And we can change, adapt. And you like the animals, right? That's why the daimons are vegetarians. They'll all die too."

"At some point, I have to consider the greater good, little agathos. If I'd tried to wipe out humanity in one fell swoop at any other point in time, Gaia would have fought me. It is too convenient of an opportunity for me to overlook that she's too enraged at the mortals to defend them."

My hands shook and I clasped them in front of me, trying to hide it. Her words were chilling, a perfect encapsulation of what Sophia had told us. Balance. We needed balance.

Here I'd been, thinking I was some kind of peacekeeper, when what I needed to do was get these two terrifyingly powerful goddesses to hate each other again. At least enough to always be on the opposite team, but not enough for outright war.

"I'm sure once she realizes that, she'll be furious," I said slowly, dropping my eyes to the ground and shaking my head lightly. "She would have offered you anything, but by that stage, it will be too late."

Nyx froze, and I got the impression that I was the full focus of her attention. It was an incredibly unsettling sensation.

"Unlikely. She's punishing the humans, too, for daring to deny us."

"Not quite to the point of wiping them out, but yes, you're right," I agreed, blood rushing loudly in my ears. This was a dangerous game, one that Nyx had been playing for longer than mortals had even existed. I was outmatched in every single way and we both knew it, but that was my secret advantage.

I had nothing to lose. No immortal being could ever truly know what that was like, how it could make us do and say things that we'd have never done or said otherwise.

Nothing encouraged innovation like desperation.

"I wonder what she would offer..." Nyx mused. "Sophia requested a meeting between us, and I was going to decline, but perhaps out of curiosity..."

If Nyx agreed, then surely Gaia would have to agree also, if only not to appear afraid. While I wasn't confident that Gaia would fight to save us, I did think she'd offer Nyx a worthwhile concession, if only because Gaia would want to pull the plug on humanity herself rather than let anyone else do it.

I was walking a knife edge between two psychopaths, and this was why the prophecy existed in the first place. This was why we needed the Olympians back.

We needed a buffer between us and the all-powerful Primordials. Divine middle management, so to speak.

"I have not seen Gaia in centuries, after all. It might even be fun to watch her beg."

I doubted Gaia wanted to save us enough to beg, but I managed to keep that thought to myself. The world around me rippled, a sure sign that I was about to wake up.

"What a strange agathos you are," Nyx murmured. "Though I suppose it no longer matters. Once you're in the underworld, it's no longer relevant. But if you'd like to go to your pyre knowing, then perhaps that is a question for you to decide before you meet the goddess who gave you your agathos gifts. Who do you want to be? What would you be, if you could choose for yourself?"

I woke up with a gasp, jackknifing upright, Bullet's fear pouring through the tight bond between us, washing back and forth as it mixed with waves of my own terror.

"Amazing Grace..." he whispered, his voice barely audible over my loud, rasping pants for air.

"What is it?" Riot asked, grabbing clumsily at my arm in the dark. "What's going on?"

The marble ground beneath was so cold it was soaking into my bones, and my teeth chattered with the effort of answering. How long had we been sitting here?

"Nyx tried to summon me to her," Bullet replied, grabbing my hand with his shaking ones. "But Grace answered the call in my place. I tried to get into the garden, tried to get to you, but I couldn't."

"Good," I rasped, ignoring his sound of protest. It hadn't been a *decision* I'd made to go in his place, rather an *instinct*. One I wasn't going to fight.

"How?" Riot demanded in a hoarse whisper. "How is that possible? You're an agathos..."

Wild's guilt and sense of responsibility was suffocating, and I pushed as much love and warmth down the bond as I could. Whatever the cost was for saving Bullet, I'd pay it. I was grateful every day that Wild had seen past my panic and encouraged me to use the bond to bring Bullet back.

"Someone's approaching." Dare's voice from behind the ruin where we were sitting made me jump.

"We're not done talking about this," Riot grumbled, patting my arm like he was verifying I was still whole and present.

"It's a good thing," I reassured him. "I think Nyx is going to agree to the meeting so she can gloat. It's our opportunity to get them back on opposing sides."

"Clever," Bullet replied. I could hear the smile in his voice, despite his shaky nerves. "Gaia has to show up now, though it may take some time for her to agree. She won't want to look like she's coming running because of Nyx."

"How many people are going to die while we wait for them to make up their minds?" Riot asked. "We don't have the luxury of just waiting around for them. Maybe we need to take another look at the prophecy—"

"Quiet," Dare instructed. "They're here."

DARE

CHAPTER 18

I crossed my arms over my chest, attempting to look like I was casually studying the ruins in front of me as shuffling footsteps and clicking claws approached the library.

Sophia could make all the claims she liked that we were safe with *this* agathos, but I wasn't about to let my guard down. People were desperate, and that made them dangerous. I thought the riots in Milton and Jersey had been bad, but that was nothing compared to the unrest we were living through now. Shit, things back then had been almost quaint in comparison.

There was a pause, the light from the person's torch illuminating the space as they paused on the threshold. A murmured word, then the shuffling sound continued, no claws this time.

An ancient woman sidled up next to me, bent double over the cane she was holding. I glanced at her out of the corner of my eye, but a thick shawl draped over her head hid everything except her tanned hands, the skin papery thin with age, shakily gripping the cane.

"Hello, daimon." Her voice was thin and reedy, heavily accented. This was the temple custodian we'd been waiting for? No wonder Grace and Bullet had managed a power nap; this lady was so old I was surprised she'd gotten here at all.

"Hello, agathos."

She made a dismissive sound in the back of her throat, unimpressed with my very literal nickname, and for an odd moment, I was reminded of my mom.

"Are you well, daimon?"

"Me? Uh, yeah. Sure, I guess. All things considered."

She stared at the healed statue of Sophia without any surprise on her face.

"These are not easy times to be well in," she said gravely. "We must all take care of one another."

That sounded deceptively reasonable. Why was she being so nice? She was an agathos, and an old one at that.

"Times were dark before the sky was. The agathos I've encountered weren't so keen on taking care of each other then," I remarked lightly, trying to gauge the woman's mood, while clinging tightly to Grace's hope and curiosity to keep my own temper in check.

I supposed they'd been sort of happy to look out for one another, but only for those who complied, who fit the mold.

She let out a rusty laugh, still staring at the ruins. "Most agathos are stupid, selfish, insolent little beasts. They have forgotten their purpose, the purpose of the original agathos. In Anesidora's centuries of silence, they grew cruel and petty. Most of the time, I am ashamed to be called an agathos."

201

The venom in her voice took me by surprise. I wasn't sure I'd ever met an agathos who was *ashamed* to be one. Not even Grace—not really. She wanted them to do better, she expected more from them, but Grace liked being a helper of humanity.

"My name is Eirene. As was my mother's name, my grandmother's before, and so on. My daughter and granddaughter are also named Eirene, and one day they will inherit my role as custodian of this temple the way I inherited it from my matriarch. If the Great Mother and Goddess of Night don't kill us all before then."

Eirene looked up at me, and I startled at her face before I could stop myself. She had agathos eyes, but they weren't flecked with color like Grace's. They were mostly a strange pale milky color, with only the faintest hint of gold. It looked like she had no irises at all. Eirene tipped her chin toward the pile of broken marble where the others were waiting. "My blood runs through this temple, allowing me to understand Sophia even when she's at her weakest. When the goddesses respond to her, she will communicate with you through me. In the meantime, please come back to my home to rest and eat. There is a room meant for visiting agathos, though in recent decades, those who have made the trip here preferred luxury hotels to my humble home."

Grace popped up before I could say anything, Wild and Riot scrambling comically behind as she moved towards us while Bullet wandered out with an amused smile on his face.

"We would be so grateful for a place to stay," Grace said, apparently swayed by Eirene's words. I wrapped an arm around Grace's waist before she could get any closer to the total stranger, pulling her into my side. Wild flicked on his flashlight, shooting me a questioning look. I shrugged apologetically—Eirene hadn't given me any cause to think of her as untrustworthy, except for the fact that she was an agathos, and therefore I didn't trust her.

Then again, Eirene had probably spent most of her life hating daimons, and here she was, opening her home to four of them that she didn't even know. Maybe I was being a little hypocritical.

"I'm Grace. This is Dare, Riot, Wild and Bullet," Grace said, gesturing at each of us in turn, her hands shaking with cold.

Eirene gave Grace a look that bordered on pity. "Oh dear girl, come, let's walk. You need a proper meal and a few hours by the fire. Come, come. These goddesses have nothing but time, it could be days before they come to a decision to meet. Weeks, even."

"We don't have weeks," Grace murmured, glancing at the statue of Sophia over her shoulder one last time before following Eirene, the four of us crowding in close behind her. "I'm not even sure we have days. People will die. They might be dying already."

Eirene shot Grace a sad smile. "If only the suffering of mortals was enough to sway the gods. This is Milos," she added as we passed through the protective shield in front of the library, gesturing at a large, pale Anatolian Shepherd dog, easily waist-height on me, and almost shoulder-height on Eirene. "I am the custodian of the temple, and Milos is the custodian of me."

Eirene cackled, and I felt a burst of amusement through the bond from Grace like a bright ray of sunshine that disappeared all too quickly.

"Wait, there were others—" I began, suddenly conscious of the fact that we weren't being that quiet, and the fact that Grace had lit the library ruins up like a Christmas tree.

"Don't worry, you'll get a chance to say hello," Eirene interjected, sounding as though she was rolling her eyes. Milos fell into step next to her, and Eirene absently scratched behind the dog's ears. "They're waiting for you."

I didn't even have time to lunge for Grace although she was right next to me—Wild was there first, banding his arms around her shoulders and pulling her into his chest, her face hidden by his bicep.

"I wouldn't lead you anywhere near them if they were a danger to you," Eirene said sharply. "Besides, Milos would tear them apart if they so much as whispered any negativity in your direction. She's a very clever girl," she added affectionately, patting a preening Milos again. I had to admit, it *did* look like Milos understood every word we were saying.

It wouldn't be the weirdest thing to happen to us. There wasn't much I questioned anymore.

"Why do you think the agathos aren't a danger to us? To Grace?" Riot pressed.

"Perhaps they were once." Eirene glanced back at the library. "They went to pray to the spirits for guidance, and the spirits wouldn't let them through. Their souls were judged and found wanting. Whatever nonsense they were fed by their Basilinna, by what they saw on television, there is no greater wake-up call than that."

It didn't seem to reassure Wild much, but Grace wriggled out of his grip, taking his hand instead and dragging him along behind her as Eirene began walking again. There was no chance of getting out of here unseen— there was a row of flames up ahead in front of the remnants of the theater. They were waiting for us.

"I have known you," Eirene said softly, just loud enough for us to hear. "You have been promised for generations. Whenever my ancestors and I despaired of the path the agathos have taken, Sophia would remind us that a new age was on the horizon."

"You're giving me too much credit," Grace replied with an awkward laugh.

"If anything, I'm not giving you enough. Certainly, no one else is. Perhaps you don't realize how powerful a Prophêtis really is—especially when you are faced with the actions of goddesses too powerful to fight back against. But not all wars are won on battlefields, Prophêtis. Sometimes—more often than you may think—they are won in private rooms, in secret meetings, in wealthy homes. Not all voices carry the same weight, Prophêtis. Don't underestimate just how powerful yours is."

Grace felt contemplative, but she didn't have time to think on Eirene's words because we were already approaching the waiting line of agathos. They were kneeling, heads bowed, holding candles out in front of them in perfect silence.

It was unsettling, and I didn't trust it. Neither did Grace, judging by the emotions I could feel through the bond—still very much a weird, foreign sensation in my chest.

Eirene broke the silence with a clipped speech in what I thought was Turkish. I didn't need to speak the language to know she was unimpressed, and the agathos on the ground bowed their heads further, thoroughly cowed by her telling-off.

"What did you tell them?" Bullet asked curiously as we moved away from them, toward the empty parking lot.

"The truth. That after meeting you, it is clear you will fight for the agathos who never fought for you. And that they don't deserve it. Come, let's go."

It must have been three miles at least to Eirene's home, which I was trying not to be resentful about it, but honestly, none of us were really up for another walk. Grace didn't complain, but she couldn't quite hide her winces as she traveled over the rocky ground in thin, worn sandals.

Hopefully, Eirene had some shoes that would fit Grace. Warmer clothes, too. It was a miracle Grace didn't have hypothermia yet.

"I hope this is okay to ask," Grace said to Eirene eventually, struggling to catch her breath as she talked. "But where are your bonded?"

Right, all agathos women had bonded. Grace had been the odd one out until she'd found hers.

"My final bonded made his way underworld just last week, joining the others. Over the past year, I lost all of them. I will join them soon, I'm confident."

"Oh. I'm... I'm so sorry," Grace rasped, stumbling slightly. Wild grabbed her arm, righting her. "That's... I can't even imagine what you're going through."

Eirene glanced back at Grace over her shoulder, a serene smile on her face, gnarled fingers buried in Milos' fur. "You are very young, Prophêtis, and when you are young, it is hard to imagine death as anything but a terrible ending. My bonded and I shared a very good life together. Our home was filled with love, our children and grandchildren are happy and healthy. There were bad days, of course, but those bad days never felt like they would go on forever because the love we felt for one another was stronger. The underworld is our next beginning, not a dreaded ending."

I glanced at Bullet out of the corner of my eye, finding him staring off into the distance with a sad smile on his face. He'd been saved from the underworld, snatched from the jaws of death by the bond that tied him and Grace together.

Was he happy? Relieved? He didn't *look* like a man who'd cheated death.

Eirene held up the torch, squinting at our faces before turning back around. "I hope you are as fortunate with your bonded, Grace. Agathos do not like to admit to it, not even to themselves, but many bonded are not happy with who the Fates paired them with."

I felt Grace's surprise at that, and it made me wonder about her own parents. Hadn't she said that two of her dads were kinder to her than the others? Surely, that was the kind of thing that would cause tension between bonded and maybe make for a not-so-happy union? It wasn't like anyone was able to hide how they were really feeling when their emotions were broadcast all the time.

"The Fates are busy," Eirene continued. "They had enough tasks before Anesidora gave them the responsibility of assigning soul bonds as well, and they don't have the luxury of taking time and care with it. If you love all of your soul bonds, then you should consider yourself very fortunate indeed."

"I do," Grace whispered as we passed a tall stone gate with barbed wire on top. Comforting. "I am very fortunate."

Did that mean Grace loved me too?

As always, the idea filled me with a mixture of dread and comfort. What was real and what wasn't? What was the bond and what was *us*? Did I love her? Did I know her well enough to love her?

Did that matter? Maybe I didn't know her favorite color or go-to pizza toppings, but I could feel Grace's *soul* through the bond, and it was the most beautiful thing I'd ever known. Was that love?

Eirene handed Grace the torch, and set to work unlocking a heavy wrought iron gate while Milos prowled behind us, eyes glinting occasionally in the firelight as she passed. Riot and I jumped in to help Eirene push the gates open, and it was reassuring to see Eirene go through the process of locking it up again after we'd filed inside.

"This is a very old home," Eirene explained as we approached the looming structure, the details impossible to make out with just the one

torch lighting our immediate surroundings. "My family has lived here for generations. Since the home was not so modern to begin with, I think I have gotten by better than some recently," she added drily, unlocking the front door and letting us inside.

Eirene took the torch back, leading us into a small living room. We paused at the heavy wooden door, and I ran my fingertips over the rough textured wall. Was it stone? This place really must be old.

"Come, I will stoke the fire," Eirene announced, kneeling in front of a cast iron fireplace in the corner and opening the door with a creak, stoking the embers and fussing with the wood until the flame was built higher again. Eirene climbed to her feet with a groan and lit some candles.

I'd been right about the stone—the entire house looked like it had been carved out of it. Low, uneven steps wound up behind the fireplace to a second level, and while the rock was smooth, it sort of undulated like waves from the wall to the floor, without any sharp lines separating them.

There was a bench built along one wall with some mismatched cushions on it, and a faded velvet couch and armchair, with a few rugs scattered on the ground to cover the stone floor.

"Upstairs is a suite for you to use. There is another fireplace in the bedroom, but one of you strong daimons will have to carry the wood up; my bones are too old for this."

"Of course," Grace agreed, taking the torch Eirene handed her. "Anything we can do to be of assistance."

Eirene gave her a weary smile, collapsing in the armchair. In this light, the deep lines in her face were more pronounced, as were the dark shadows under her eyes. I didn't see it before, but it was clear now that she was in mourning.

"I will be down here," Eirene said, gesturing toward double doors that presumably led to the rest of the house. "Once the fire is hotter, I will cook for us. Feel free to go explore, though there isn't much to see anymore. There was a beautiful garden, before the endless night..."

Grace moved to comfort Eirene again, but the old woman waved her off. "Go upstairs, rest, wash, relax. Hold one another tight and wait for the goddesses to decide if we all get to live or die."

CHAPTER 19

Eirene's house was small and ancient, yet it felt like a palatial mansion to us. The upstairs housed a surprisingly enormous bedroom, with a huge bed that Grace had blushingly explained was standard in agathos homes.

Wild got the fire going in the open hearth in the bedroom, illuminating the room, and we spent a couple of hours grazing on the snacks we had and heating water so we could each wash. Bullet had snuck downstairs to find Eirene fast asleep in the chair, and had topped up the wood on the fire she was sitting next to. She was pretty ancient to be making that long ass walk to and from the temple, and I wasn't surprised she needed a break.

Where were her kids? Did they all live far away from here? Why was she all alone?

"Still asleep?" I asked Wild as he came back into the room. He nodded once, pressing the door quietly shut behind him so we didn't wake her. I tended to the fire while he sat down at the head of the bed and Grace flopped down in the center, sighing happily.

"I've taken beds for granted," Grace announced, smiling dreamily at the ceiling. "Never again. I have a whole new appreciation for beds. And warmth. And running water and electricity."

"Hear, hear," Bullet replied, wriggling back against the pillows next to Wild. "I really hope the goddesses make up their minds soon, but I'm not going to complain about a few hours of rest and relaxation."

He was almost fully asleep the moment he stopped talking, and we all watched in silence for a moment, holding our breath. I was confident that I wasn't the only one waiting to see a trickle of blood from his nose, or see the color suddenly leach out of his skin again.

"He's okay," Grace whispered, watching him carefully, twisting the opal ring on her finger.

She glanced up as Wild signed to her, assuring her that he'd stay with Bullet.

Grace turned to face me, giving me an impressively stern look that made me want to bite her lip. "You and Dare need to sleep."

"Dare first," I replied, bumping him with my shoulder, making him stumble against the bed. There was probably enough room for us, but my mind was too wound up to sleep. "I'm going to walk around for a bit, check the place out."

"I'm coming with you," Grace said decisively, wrapping herself in the blanket she'd used to travel here.

"Grace, you need to rest—'

"I had a rest at the temple," she interrupted, tilting her chin up stubbornly. She wasn't the same agathos I'd met in Milton all those weeks ago—the one who'd hidden her blush behind her hands when we'd sat on her couch getting to know each other. She'd grown in confidence, and I loved that for her. What I didn't love was the world-weariness in her expression, but I wasn't sure there was anything to be done about that. The lived experiences that had put that look in Grace's eyes couldn't be taken back.

"Come on then, Gracie," I sighed, tucking the blanket tighter around her and draping an arm over her shoulders. "Though I want it noted for the record that I think you should be resting."

"Noted," Dare replied instantly, making Grace laugh quietly. I almost rolled my eyes at the satisfied look on his face—apparently making Grace laugh was a point of pride for him.

We made our way through the quiet house using one of the candles for light, heading out through the cozy dining room to a covered patio. I set the light down on a side table before sitting back on the outdoor day bed, encouraging Grace to lie down with her head on my lap. She sighed contentedly as I began working my fingers through her hair, tackling the tangles that had formed over the past few days.

What was beyond the patio? A garden? Or what would have been a garden, before the sun disappeared. If our little rendezvous with the deities went well and the sun came back, would the plants grow again or had the damage already been done? It'd be a real kick in the teeth to go through all this, convince Nyx to lift the darkness, then die of starvation.

"I used to go running a lot as the sun was rising," Grace said quietly, her thoughts mirroring my own. "Occasionally, I'd think to myself how pretty those early morning rays were, but that was about it. It was expected, you know? Whatever else was happening, the sun rose each morning and set each night. In hindsight, I wish I'd been more grateful for it."

I wasn't entirely sure I agreed. In hindsight, I wished I'd been more scared of Nyx, or at least had a greater appreciation for what she could do.

"Do you ever regret getting in my car that night?" Grace asked. My hands stilled.

"The night we met?"

She hummed in agreement, nudging my hand with her head. I snorted, resuming my combing.

"No. I've never once regretted getting in your car, or meeting you, or being bonded to you, or whatever train of thought you're following. Not once, Gracie. I love you like fucking crazy, okay?"

"I love you too."

"I know that," I scoffed. I felt it every day, and it was the best feeling in the world. "Where's all this coming from?"

Grace hesitated, fidgeting slightly. I'd drop it if she didn't want to talk about it, but I knew she did. She was just worried that it was trivial. That she wasn't allowed to be concerned about anything except the *big*, save-the-world things we had going on, even though it was all a waiting game right now.

"I know the bond with him is new," Grace began slowly. "But I think Dare has some regrets. Or maybe regret isn't the right word—maybe he's just concerned... Or he doesn't quite trust me? I guess I've been spoiled in that I *don't* recognize how exactly he feels about me, because I never experienced it from you or Bullet or Wild."

My immediate instinct was to protect Grace, and if that meant punching Dare in the face to knock some sense into him, then that seemed like a totally reasonable option.

"Stop," Grace commanded softly. "That's not the answer and not why I brought it up. Maybe I shouldn't have brought it up at all—"

"No, it's fine, I have myself under control." I exhaled heavily. "I can't speak for Dare, but I know that he's not the same guy he was the last time I saw him. He's suffered a lot in that time, and he was alone when he knew deep down that he wasn't meant to be. Maybe it's not about you, but trusting *this*. Trusting that this is actually real after he wanted it and wondered about it for so long." I shrugged. "That's how I'd feel anyway. I think."

"You're really wise," Grace breathed, snuggling further against me. I snorted. "Tell me, oh wise one, do you think we'll get called back to the sanctuary soon?"

"I doubt the goddesses will make things that easy for us." Besides, no matter when they called us back, it would always to be too soon and not soon enough. Enough people had been sacrificed on the altar of their anger, and yet the idea of willingly walking into a meeting between two all-powerful deities, of Grace going in there...

There wasn't enough time in the world for me to be okay with that.

Twenty-four hours later, we hadn't heard a thing. Eirene had fed us repeatedly with the abundance of vegetables she'd harvested from her garden before all the plants had died, and assured us that Sophia could speak to her whenever she wanted, and that she'd heard nothing.

By unspoken agreement, all four of us had been working to distract Grace. Maybe it was a little unfair of us to keep her in a low-simmering state of horny, but the big, multiple soul bonds-sized bed was making Grace *feel* things. Things she was probably too prim and proper to admit to out loud.

Maybe part of it was just 'what could have been'. In another life, a normal-ish life, we'd have had a bed like this. Not in Grace's apartment—now flattened—it was too small. I'd have lived at Underworld if the others wanted to, but I hated being around so many people all the time. Maybe we could have taken over the big house on the Oneiroi Estate again; it had a giant harem-sized bedroom with a bed that comfortably slept all of us in it.

That was probably the innocent, slightly wistful path her mind had started down. Unfortunately, she was bonded to daimons, and we'd all perverted that longing into something completely different.

Or maybe it was Dare's influence. She'd lost the sharp edge of shyness when it came to sex since he'd been around—it was the gift and curse of the Philotes. While his gifts couldn't *influence* agathos or daimons in the way it did for humans, it did draw sexual desire and arousal that was already there to the surface.

"You guys are out of control," Grace chastised, standing in front of the dark window as Wild wrapped his arms around her from behind, one hand cupping her throat. "This is so not the time."

"Why not?" Bullet asked cheerfully, laying back on the bed, arms crossed behind his head. "What else are we doing? Eirene asked me over a bowl of vegetable when your last orgasm was because you look so stressed."

"That was awkward," Grace laughed, the sound turning into a gasp of surprise, her head tipped back against Wild's shoulder. I had no idea what he was doing, but she was into it.

"Not awkward," I disagreed, throwing another log on the fire and perching on the edge of the hearth. "A very valid concern. You've got *four* bonded, Gracie. Granted, we appear to be living in the end times, but you should still be coming at least a couple of times a day."

I could feel her gearing up to protest, but I was pretty sure Wild's hand slid under her skirt at that moment. Grace curled forward, a soft sigh escaping her, arousal snaking through the bond. Through *all* the bonds.

Dare exhaled heavily, fidgety and restless as he paced in front of me, squirming under the weight of all the sexual desire. Even if he hadn't been bonded to Grace, his nature meant that he was tuned into arousal like it was his own personal radio frequency, and we were *all* in the mood. For Dare, he was practically being prim and proper, still holding himself back, trying to only show Grace the best sides of himself. Soon he'd realize that trusting Grace with his worst sides and watching her fall in love with him anyway was the best reward.

"That is..." Grace rasped, Wild's body blocking most of hers from our view. "That feels so *good.*"

"You're allowed to feel good, Amazing Grace," Bullet said quickly, picking up on her flare of guilt. "Take every moment you can to feel good. You deserve it."

"Hear, hear," Dare said, trying to act like his dick wasn't about to bust through his trousers.

"So, did they go over orgies in those Saturday morning classes?" I asked casually. "Or was it more of a 'figure it out as you go' kind of thing?"

"You are a menace to society," Dare grumbled, pausing his pacing and awkwardly adjusting himself in a feeble attempt to hide his hard-on.

"It's a genuine question," I protested, trying and failing to suppress a smirk. "Grace has all of her bonded now; I feel like group sex is an important issue to gain clarity on."

Wild shook with silent laughter, but Bullet was watching me with surprise and some hesitancy on his face, and I knew he and I were overdue for a chat, especially after we'd come so close to losing him. I didn't want to live with any regrets.

Grace came on Wild's fingers with a muffled cry.

I could chat with Bullet later.

Wild bent his head, kissing Grace's neck as she slowly came down from her peak, before withdrawing his hand and spinning them around so she faced us.

Grace blinked blearily at us, eyes glassy and cheeks flushed. Fucking beautiful.

"Well?" I teased. "What's the verdict on orgy lessons?"

"They did cover it a little. Sort of. They said that every group was different, that there was no right way of doing... things," Grace replied, her voice a little slurred.

"How open-minded of them," I replied drily, making Grace and Bullet laugh. "How would you feel about experimenting a little, Gracie? You know there's no pressure."

Well, Dare was breathing like he was in labor, but he could always go jerk off in the bathroom.

"Aren't we already experimenting?" Grace asked, shooting me a wry smile. "I just came in front of all of you."

"Hardly," I scoffed. "We didn't see anything. You shy, Gracie? If you want to just lie back and relax, and let those nerves disappear, I'll set Dare on you. You'll forget all about being shy."

"Set me on her," Dare repeated derisively, semi-doubled over next to the wall. "Riot, remember when you used to work for me and spent your days making me coffee and cleaning up after me? I miss those days."

Bullet grinned, eyes darting between us, giving me a sudden flashback to our school days when it had just been the three of us against the world. "Is this some kind of dominance test?" His voice lowered, mimicking a nature documentary narrator. "And here we see the Philotes daimon on the cusp of going into heat, asserting his dominance over the posturing Moros..."

"I'd laugh but my dick is about to fall off," Dare groaned, while Wild shook silently behind Grace as he encouraged her towards the bed, more amused than I'd ever seen him.

"Come here," Grace said with a soft smile, reaching for Dare as she perched on the edge of the mattress. "I never want you to be uncomfortable."

He tried to play it cool and saunter over to the bed, but it was hard to walk cool with a steel pipe between your legs, and in the end he did something between a strut and a waddle, shooting me a very clear 'shut the fuck up' look as he went.

Grace didn't make him wait though, scooting up the bed to make room for Dare as he crawled over her, a look of fierce hunger in his eyes. His mask of politeness was slipping slightly, showing the sex daimon underneath as he picked up her wrist, running his tongue possessively over the tattoo he'd inked on her skin.

"I need you," he rasped, lowering his hips and grinding against her. Wild, Bullet and I all seemed to be holding our breath, waiting for Grace's response, watching the bond like hawks for signs of discomfort.

"You have me. You can always have me," she murmured, spreading her thighs wider to accommodate him. "Take what you need from me, Dare. I want to be what you need."

"You are," he mumbled into her neck, still mindlessly humping her like an animal. This wouldn't do. I didn't hold it against him—he was practically OD'ing on lust—but Grace deserved a little more finesse than Dare currently had on offer.

"Get him on his back," I instructed Grace, making my way over to the bed. "He'll be embarrassed if he comes in his pants."

Dare made some muffled sound of protest, face buried in the crook of Grace's neck, sucking love bites onto her skin, but my Gracie was a good girl, and she listened to my instructions. She clamped her knees either side of Dare's hips, smoothly rolling them until she was straddling him, and Dare groaned loudly as her weight bore down on his cock.

"Let me take the edge off," Grace whispered, anticipating my suggestion as she shifted down Dare's body and pulled his cock free of his trousers. He bucked up eagerly into her hand as she spread precum over her palm before fisting his shaft, throwing her hair over one shoulder so it was out of her way before bending down to lick his tip.

Bullet exhaled heavily, fidgeting slightly as Wild prowled toward him, sitting right next to him on the bed.

I leaned my legs against the end of the bed, reaching forward to slide my hands up the back of Grace's legs, while she began bobbing over Dare's lap, a small surprised moan escaping her as I began sliding her dress up over her hips. She was quite a sight—ass up in a pair of *soaked* black cotton panties, no trace of shyness to be found. I crouched down, pressing a kiss against the globe of her ass that made her squirm, before sliding my hand between her legs and stroking the damp gusset of her panties.

As much as I wanted to dominate Grace's attention, Dare was thrusting wildly into her mouth, clearly running out of self-control, and I didn't want to distract her.

"I'm going to come. Shit, I'm definitely going to come. Grace—" Dare gasped. She swatted his hand away as he went to pull her head off, stilling to swallow. That was enough being patient on my part. I wrenched Grace's panties down to her knees, collecting her wetness and dragging it up to her clit. Grace released Dare's still-hard cock, letting out a breathy moan as I began rubbing circles around her clit just the way she liked, her hips rocking back against me.

"Need to taste you," I muttered, dropping to my knees and pulling her thighs apart to tongue her pussy.

"It's okay," Grace whispered. "I want you to."

It took me a moment to realize Grace wasn't talking to me, but to Bullet and Wild, though I had no idea why they needed the reassurance because there was no sense of hesitation coming from Grace at all.

I felt the mattress shift, and whatever those two were up to had Grace's arousal growing more potent.

"Is there any lube in here?" Dare asked, panting slightly. I paused, not knowing which of us he was asking on behalf of.

"Yes," Bullet replied breathily, and *very* quickly. "In the nightstand."

"What do you say, Grace?" Dare murmured, her excitement growing. "Want to play? Riot will take good care of you. He'll have you begging for a cock in your ass in no time."

There was no sense of shock, so I guessed Grace was at least familiar with the concept. At worst, there was some mild disbelief mixed with a sense of confidence that she'd *never* enjoy that.

Challenge accepted.

I straightened, catching the bottle of lube Wild tossed at me. Bullet looked equally doubtful, lying against Wild's chest between his spread legs, Wild's fist working Bullet's cock like he'd done it a thousand times before.

"I don't know what you're looking so doubtful about, I'm pretty sure you'll be begging for the exact same thing," I teased.

Bullet flushed red, but didn't argue. He did the opposite of argue, writhing restlessly as Wild tightened his grip, twisting his hand with each stroke.

221

I encouraged Grace up the bed, still straddling Dare, and sank my cock into her hot, tight pussy without any preamble, exhaling at the feeling of being *home*, being connected to her.

"Riot," she whimpered, wriggling, trying to fuck herself on me, but Dare's hands clamped down on her hips, keeping her in place.

"Patience, Gracie," I chided, popping open the capped bottle. "We want this to feel so good for you."

I almost laughed at her apprehension. She had no qualms about experimenting, but she seemed pretty confident that there was no way she was going to like this.

Fuck, I couldn't wait for the day when Dare and I were taking Grace together. She'd moan so pretty pinned between us.

She startled as the cool lube dripped between her cheeks, but Dare immediately captured her mouth, distracting her while I squeezed some of the liquid onto my fingers, my cock throbbing in anticipation.

Grace's cunt fluttered around me, a shiver going down her spine as I slid my thumb down to her back entrance, circling the tight ring of muscle and monitoring her responses.

A little shock, curiosity, arousal, followed by another dose of shock at the arousal. I took my time, letting her adjust to the sensations she hadn't expected to like, before pressing my thumb forward.

"Relax," Dare murmured, his hand disappearing between them to stimulate her clit.

"You try to relax when someone is touching your butt," she muttered, that bratty tinge to her voice that sometimes emerged during sex making an appearance, making my dick ache.

"Who's to say I haven't?" Dare laughed. "I'm an open-minded guy, Grace. There's not a lot I won't do. You can play with my ass whenever you want, I'm not too good for prostate stimulation," he added with a wink. Grace was a delicious mixture of shock and intrigue, and distracted enough to relax for me.

"Oh!" Grace gasped, pussy contracting around me. "Oh. That feels..."

"What?" Bullet asked, sweating slightly, his fingers digging into Wild's thighs. Was Wild edging him? Poor Bullet. "What does it feel like?"

"Good," Grace replied in a strangled voice. "Different. Full. I like it."

"Full?" I repeated with a grin, slowly thrusting my hips, dragging my cock through her slick cunt. "Wait 'til it's my cock in there. I wish we had some toys, but I guess I'll just have to use my fingers."

"Get him on his back," Dare whispered to Grace, parroting my words with a shit-eating grin on his face. "Let me play with your ass while you show Riot how good you ride his dick."

Taking all of us by surprise, Dare's words sent Grace over the edge, a soft, rolling orgasm ripping through her body, her cunt strangling my cock. Grace blossomed under all of our attention, learning to embrace parts of herself she probably didn't even know she had, and it was fucking *beautiful* to witness.

"Fuck," Dare groaned, that additional hit of arousal going straight to his head. I pulled out with some difficulty, lying on the bed and pulling Grace over my lap where she immediately impaled herself on my cock, pussy still fluttering around me as she bounced herself on my dick, chasing her next orgasm. Dare grabbed the lube, coating his fingers, and I glanced at Wild and Bullet out of the corner of my eye as they moved. Wild hauled Bullet up onto his lap, still jerking Bullet off roughly while grinding into his ass.

"Fuck, fuck, fuck," Bullet chanted, squirming restlessly, his desire fueling Grace's. She whimpered as Dare's finger breached her ass, his other hand tightly gripping her cheek, opening her up to him.

Grace fell forward, teeth scraping my chest.

"That's it," Dare encouraged, his voice low and rough. "I'm going to add a second finger. Let me in, beautiful."

I grunted at the added pressure, a bolt of lust shooting through the bond. She was close, she was definitely going to come again soon, and I didn't think I could hold off much longer either.

"Fuck!" Bullet yelled, collapsing back against Wild's chest as he came all over Wild's hand.

Grace's movements grew more erratic, her moans louder and more desperate than usual as Dare fucked her ass with his fingers.

"That's it, Gracie," I encouraged, gripping her thighs tight enough to leave finger-shaped bruises. "Come for us. Show us just how much you like being filled by your bonded."

The words were for Grace, but apparently my dirty talk worked on Wild too, since he pinned Bullet in place with a heavy exhale, movements stuttering to a stop. With a final, choked moan, Grace tightened around me again, and I gave up fighting my own orgasm.

"Can you pass out from pleasure?" Grace slurred, wincing slightly as Dare withdrew his fingers, patting her butt cheek affectionately.

"Definitely," Bullet slurred, pants pulled up but still splayed over Wild's body like a blanket.

We were a mess. A sweaty heap of tangled limbs and labored breathing, illuminated by the crackling fire that had turned the room golden and threw off enough heat to keep Nyx's chill away.

It was a rare moment of perfection. It couldn't last.

GRACE

CHAPTER 20

Nyx's garden appeared around me, only slightly less terrifying than it had been the first time I'd ended up here.

At least this time, I knew where I was. I dropped to my knees automatically, the thick velvet of the black dress I was wearing cushioning the blow. There was no doubt in my mind that Nyx knew I was here, so I bowed my head in readiness and waited.

I wanted Bullet because he always knew what to do, but me being here meant he was safe, didn't it? Right. No matter how afraid I was, this option was better. I could be brave.

'Do what scares you,' he'd said, what felt like a million years ago. Like I'd always stumble into the right option, the path I needed to follow, if I was just brave enough to take the first step.

It didn't feel brave to choose the scariest option. It felt idiotic.

"You have truly broken my connection with my Spirit of Dreams," Nyx grumbled, appearing out of nowhere. I flopped forward clumsily, prostrating myself on the ground before her. She didn't sound angry at least, just... curious.

"I wonder if you're an agathos at all any longer? Or are you something else?"

I opened my mouth to say of course I was still an agathos, but was I? I hadn't used my Eutychia gift recently, hadn't taken on any human's mental anguish as my own. I hadn't done anything agathos to check.

Was that what made me what I was? The gifts I had? Was being an agathos about what I could do or was it who I was?

Faced with the prospect of meeting both of the goddesses, the question suddenly seemed like a pertinent one. I was a child of Gaia, she'd made me what I was and punished me for it. And as angry as I was with Nyx, as much as I hated the actions that had brought harm to so many, without her there were no daimons. No Bullet, no Riot, no Wild, no Dare. I resented her, and I was furious with her, but my life would be lonely and miserable without them.

How did I reconcile that?

"My sister and I will meet you and your bonded at the agathos sanctuary at midnight. Wake up, Grace the Agathos."

I jackknifed upright with a gasp, waking Wild and Riot at the same time. Dare and Bullet apparently hadn't gone to sleep yet, both sitting by the low burning fire.

"What is it?" Bullet asked, eyes wide.

"What time is it? We need to go. They're meeting us there at midnight." I was already scrambling out of the bed, pulling on the warmer shirt and trousers Eirene had left for me, finger combing my hair before dragging on the woolen coat, glancing at the gloves and opting to leave them off. "Get up, get up," I insisted, grabbing Riot's arm and tugging him out of bed.

"I'm up, I'm up," he yawned, accepting the clothes Dare threw at him.

"It's eleven o'clock," Bullet said, squinting at the small clock on the mantle. "We'll be cutting it fine."

That got the rest of them moving. By the time we got to the bottom of the stairs, Eirene was there waiting for us, a somber look on her face.

"Sophia told me it is time, but it seems you already know that. Here, I dug out the flashlights and batteries," she said, handing us one each. "Not that you will need them when you enter the realm of the divine, but you have to get there in one piece. Milos will accompany you to make sure you find the way."

"Thank you," I breathed, giving her a hug on instinct. She froze for a moment before wrapping frail arms around me, squeezing me tight. "We'll be okay, Milos should stay with you—"

"No. Milos is a smart girl, her family line as intertwined with the sanctuary as mine is. She will return to me." Eirene moved back, cupping my face and looking into my eyes. "You are always welcome to return here too, young Grace, however this meeting goes. Even when you are old and gray like I am, my daughter and my granddaughter will always welcome the Prophêtis into this home."

"Where are your children?" Riot asked. "Why did they leave you alone?"

Eirene gave him a sad smile. "There are other sacred sites. My children dispersed to cover them all when the sky went dark, to pay homage to the goddesses, to pray for our salvation. We each have a part to play, young daimon, but none as important as what you all have to do. Go, don't keep the goddesses waiting."

We didn't. Fed and rested and dressed in warmer clothes, the journey back to the ruins felt like it went faster, even though the blisters on my feet still bothered me, especially since the boots I'd borrowed from Eirene were a size too big. Milos ran ahead, a pale blur in the darkness, keeping us on track.

Our steps slowed as we got to the long avenue that led to the library. I thought it had been quiet last time, with those few subdued agathos hanging around, but that was nothing compared to now. Idly, I wondered what visiting this place would be like if the world wasn't falling apart. In the time before, when there were human tourists and agathos or daimon pilgrims alike. I shivered in my wool coat, hands scrunched into fists inside the pockets, wishing I'd worn the gloves.

It was never a pilgrimage I intended to make, even though many agathos did. I'd always felt too twisted inside, too tainted to contemplate visiting such a sacred place.

And yet here I was, by invitation of the divine, to visit one goddess that I served, whose image I'd been made in, and one I was supposed to hate, but couldn't. One who'd given me life, but the other who'd given me *purpose.*

I was standing on a precipice from which I couldn't return, and I wasn't alone. I would never be alone again.

Maybe I'd walk out of this as the first agathos to fall from the light, or maybe I'd already fallen. Perhaps I might be the first daimon to be *made*, not *born*. As I looked between the four men standing stoically at my side, ready to face off against the divine without an ounce of fear, I wondered if that would really be so bad.

I was born to serve the light, but the dark had brought them to me. My friends. My lovers. My soulmates. The dark had given me life and hope and *meaning* when I'd had none.

Once upon a time, their kind had been my enemy. Now, it was my own people I had to fear.

There was no barrier as we entered the foreground to the library this time. No test of worthiness. There was a distinct sense of *keep away* though, and any sensible person would turn around and get as far away from here as possible.

The archway between Sophia's plinth and Arete's plinth emitted a faint golden glow, and the five of us climbed the steps as though we were in a trance while Milos paced in the courtyard. I gripped Bullet's hand on my left and Riot's on my right.

"Hold each other's hands," I whispered, coming to a stop in front of the archway. "I don't want us to get separated."

"Done," Riot assured me—Dare on his other side and Wild on Bullet's. "It's not too late to turn around, Gracie."

"Yes, it is," I replied softly, taking the first step across the threshold into the unknown with my bonded at my side.

BULLET

CHAPTER 21

It took a moment for our eyes to adjust. There was *light* here. A lot of it, in fact. It was a different kind of light to a bright sunny day in our realm, provided I was remembering correctly what sunshine looked like. The clouds overhead were the pinkish gold color of the sky at dawn, and everything had a sort of blush-colored tint to it.

"Where are we?" Riot murmured from Grace's other side. It was warm here, with soft grass beneath our feet and the soothing rush of a waterfall in the pool behind us. Where *we* were was some kind of pretty, Eden-like oasis, surrounded by lush trees and glittering pastel-colored flowers, but that wasn't what Riot was asking about.

He was asking about the looming mountain above us, every inch of it carved with statues of deities as tall as skyscrapers, with palatial Grecian-style palaces dotted around the sides of the mountain, right up to the biggest, most ostentatious one on top.

"We're at the base of Olympus," I said softly, staring up at the long abandoned palaces, their owners still very much imprisoned in Tartarus' domain. Despite how long it had been, they still looked pristine.

"So clever, my Spirit of Dreams," Nyx crowed, stepping out of the shadows in a thicker veil than usual, her silver crown glinting in the light.

"Yes, yes, brilliant." We all jumped as a goddess who could only be Gaia emerged from the very ground itself, growing from the earth like the Spartoi had, but with far more flourish.

Nyx had always been veiled, and the deities we'd seen in the underworld had been relatively human-looking, but there was no mistaking Gaia for anything other than a divine being. She wasn't made of flesh and blood, but *nature*. Her "skin" was the rough texture of tree bark, and thick, leafy vines sprouted from the top of her head like hair, draping and intertwining around her body like a shroud, leaving tree-like arms exposed. Both she and Nyx were at least ten-feet tall, easily dwarfing us as they came to stand facing one another right in front of our little group.

Grace's terror poured through the bond, and I attempted to squeeze her hand, though mine was shaking so much that I wasn't sure if my muscles had cooperated or not.

"Lift your darkness," Gaia ordered Nyx, skipping the pleasantries. "You've proven your point."

"And what point is that?" Nyx asked pleasantly, cocking her head to the side.

"You wanted the mortals to believe, they believe. We've both received more prayers and offerings in the past few days than we have in centuries."

"You wanted the mortals to believe," Nyx replied mildly. "I want them to suffer. Why stop now?"

"There won't be any left *to* suffer—"

"So much the better. You may care for prayers and offerings, but I do not. I have no need for mortals."

This... This wasn't going well.

I'd always known Nyx was ambivalent about mortals, but this was a lot harsher than ambivalence. It didn't make sense though—I'd seen futures for Grace and the others, seen futures for all kinds of people. I'd seen things that made me think the world wasn't quite the same place in the future as it was in the past, but there had definitely been *people*.

Were those visions wrong? Had Nyx planted them in my mind just to mess with me? Had she planned on wiping us out all along?

No. No, I couldn't believe that.

I had to believe that everything we'd been through hadn't been for nothing. That the waiting and the struggling and the suffering had *meant* something.

Gaia let out a growl of frustration that made us all jump. It sounded like two boulders scraping against one another. "Enough of this, Nyx."

"It's not as though you can undo what you did," Nyx pointed out cheerfully. "And if your punishment stands, why shouldn't mine?"

"Mine was not so severe!"

"An oversight on your part."

"What do you want?" Grace's voice was so soft compared to the goddesses', but there was power behind it. She was scared and shaking, but Grace was strong too. "Goddess of Night, I am begging you on behalf of humanity to lift this darkness. If there's something you want in exchange, then tell us, *please.*"

Grace was playing a dangerous game. There was nothing Nyx would want from us, and no guarantee Gaia would cooperate, even if it gave her what she claimed she wanted. Not if it was at the expense of her pride.

"You know what I want," Nyx replied, but she was looking at Gaia.

"You have your little Prophêtis for that," Gaia snarled.

Oh shit, maybe Nyx was on our side after all? Was she playing 4d Chess while we were playing Checkers? Or had she just seen an opportunity and taken it?

"My little Prophêtis with her impossible task," Nyx shot back. "One that you could make far easier, were you not so determined to hold on to a power you don't even exercise. You want the mortals to live? Give them back the gods that kept them in check."

"You think the Olympians will thank you for begging and scraping on their behalf? They're selfish and greedy, and no amount of time in Tartarus will change that."

Nyx scoffed. "I don't need them to thank me. They fear me, which is far more useful. So do you, whether you admit it or not. It seems that your precious earth doesn't do so well without sunlight."

There was that terrifying grinding, growling sound again, and I knew Nyx had her, but at what cost?

Gaia turned her coal black eyes on Grace, and my girl did her best to hide her shiver. "You are a foolish little girl, did you know that? The product of a foolish mother, whose hubris and arrogant prayers got you into this situation in the first place."

Wait, Grace had inherited this mantle of responsibility because of her *mother*?

"What is that supposed to mean?" Riot asked coolly, not a shred of respect in his tone. *Cool, cool, going to add fearing for Riot's life to my list of worries.*

"What about her mother?"

"Her *mother*," Gaia continued, not acknowledging Riot at all. "Her mother, mid-ungrateful prayer requesting a son instead of a daughter, complained to herself that one day her daughter would know what it was like to have her words ignored by the gods. How fortunate for you, that I am generous. That your voice reaches the ears of the gods when others don't, *Prophêtis*."

Grace was stunned, and I felt her indecision. She'd been conditioned her entire life to be grateful for divine gifts, and instinctually, she wondered if she was meant to be grateful now. If Gaia's claim of generosity was a genuine one.

It wasn't.

I'd interacted with goddesses enough to know that Gaia had been offended by Faith's complaining and rashly given Grace a voice that carried to the heavens and down to the underworld out of pure spite.

"You are the Fates' little experiment—one of many—but the only one stupid enough to tie yourself to a prophecy by praying to a goddess you were meant to hate. The only one lonely enough to actually go through with bonding a daimon. The only one cursed with a mother ungrateful enough to wish you extra divine attention."

Each insult landed like an arrow, piercing Grace's most vulnerable side. Every doubt she'd ever had about herself, every question about why she was different and what it meant, Gaia was validating them all.

Gaia scoffed. "You are the perfect mixture of tragic and desperate, Grace Bellamy. Everything you *think* is special about yourself can be boiled down to that."

"No, it can't," I replied quietly, throwing my own sense of self-preservation out the window. "Circumstance made Grace *what* she is, not *who* she is, and it's who she is that makes her special."

Gaia seemed to grow a little more in size, the vines draped around her body moving restlessly.

"*I* am what made her special," Gaia hissed. "I am what makes any of you special. I *created* mortal life. You should all be on your knees thanking me each and every day, the useless agathos most of all. Oh, they pay lip service to me, but their actions, their lack of respect for the earth I have given them, speak otherwise. You have all grown too confident, too assured of your own importance."

I glanced at Nyx, hoping she'd intercede and talk Gaia down, but she seemed perfectly content to watch her sister rage. Great.

"You think that the return of the Olympians and a so-called "second age of heroes" would somehow improve the lives of agathos and daimons, but it won't. Agathos are *helpmeets*. That is your role. Daimons are malevolent spirits, that is their role," Gaia clipped. "Most agathos are compensated for dedicating their lives to service with *soul bonds*, and yet you *still* have the nerve to complain. It's still not enough. You complain about agathos and daimons having no *choice*. That you somehow deserve more *freedom*. You make speeches for mortals and claim you deserve *more*. What would humans give to be presented their soulmates? You have *no* appreciation for the generosity you've been shown."

"Agathos are immensely grateful for their soul bonds—" Grace rasped.

"It doesn't seem like it to me," Gaia cut in. "Perhaps you'd rather be human. I wonder if you'd complain then."

With that rather ominous hypothetical, Gaia turned her back on Grace, returning her attention to Nyx. "Lift the veil of darkness, let the sun shine on my earth once more, and I will gift a direct path for one volunteer to go to Tartarus. Let your ungrateful little Prophêtis do with that what she will."

Oh no, I did *not* like the sound of that.

Firstly, because a path to Tartarus *and* the return of daylight were both things we wanted, and a gift from a goddess never came without a cost.

Secondly, I knew exactly what Grace would do with a path for one to Tartarus, and it wasn't an option that any of her bonded would be happy with.

We were going to fight about this for sure.

"You have a deal, sister mine," Nyx replied serenely. "The veil is lifted."

There was a split second pause before Gaia replied. "The path is open."

Grace attempted to rein in her burst of cautious excitement. The darkness was gone. It wasn't a magical fix for all the damage that had been done, but the earth would heal, wouldn't it? Humanity would survive.

We could rebuild. We had hope where there'd been none before.

"Happy travels, little Prophêtis," Gaia told Grace, her voice full of disdain. "Have one more gift before I go—a lesson in humility and appreciation. Perhaps, were you a better kind of agathos, it wouldn't have been a lesson you needed."

Grace's faint hope morphed into terror as Gaia disappeared, taking what felt like a part of us with her. There was a sucking sensation in my chest, like a vacuum had been shoved between my ribs and pulled out something essential, something I needed as much as I needed air to breathe or water to drink.

I doubled over, dragging Grace with me as my knees hit the ground. What was happening to me?

Grace let out a sound of anguish, releasing my hand, her nails scraping at her chest as though she was trying to claw through to her skin.

She felt it too. It wasn't *me*, it was all of us. It was the bonds.

Gaia had broken the bonds.

The bond that had been keeping me alive.

CHAPTER 22

My heart was gone. Ripped free of my chest.

There was no other way of describing the sensation of the bond being torn out of my soul. Grace was the center of my universe. The connection to her had given me hope and meaning when I'd had none.

And it was gone. How was it gone? What did it mean?

How did I get it back? I wouldn't survive without it. We wouldn't, not one of us.

I needed it back.

I'd do anything to get it back, and that was a promise. Nyx could hold me to that deal for the rest of my days.

CHAPTER 23

Grace clutched her chest, body curled into herself as she kneeled on the ground. A sound somewhere between a sob and raw scream escaped her, a pain so deep that I didn't need the supernatural bond to tell me how much she was hurting.

I was an idiot.

All this time, I worried that it was the bond that made me care about Grace. What a fucking *idiot*.

I looked at Grace and I knew that bond had just been a bonus. An added extra. I didn't care for her any less without it, despite the gaping, empty sensation in my chest.

All that suspicion, all that time wasted, for nothing. And now the bond was gone, ripped away by one of the most powerful goddesses in existence. There was nothing we could do.

It was too late.

GRACE

CHAPTER 24

"Stop this! Please, make it stop," I gasped, crawling towards Nyx with one hand, the other gripping my chest like it'd fall apart if I let go. That's what it felt like—like the very internal structure of my body had been disassembled, ripped apart and discarded. "Put them back. Fix it. *Please*."

I forced my gaze up, and even though Nyx was veiled, I could tell that her attention was directed behind me, head tilted thoughtfully to the side. I climbed to my feet, following her gaze, and my heart dropped. Or perhaps broke. Whatever it was, it hurt. Bullet's face was scrunched up in pain, his hands pulling aggressively at his pale blonde hair like he was trying to rip it out.

Wild reached for him like he was approaching a feral animal, moving to pull Bullet's hands away from his hair, but Bullet snarled at him in warning. Wild froze in place, agony and indecision written all over his face.

"Bullet," I breathed, turning fully to face him and stumbling into his space, not leaving an inch of space between us. *No, no, no, this couldn't be happening.* I'd saved him. I'd brought him back. Bullet was mine. Mine to keep, to *love*.

"I'm sorry," Bullet gritted out, the tendons in his neck sticking out from whatever it was he was battling. He looked up at me with so much regret in his eyes that it brought me to my knees. "I'm sorry, Amazing Grace."

"No, don't say that," I pleaded, gripping his elbows as he began to sway forward, taking his weight. Wild snapped out of his frozen state, moving behind Bullet and helping him to the ground, sitting between his legs. "Bullet, you're not going anywhere."

"Save him!" Riot yelled at Nyx. "You're a fucking all-powerful goddess. *Save him.*"

"I didn't set the length of his mortal thread, Moros," Nyx snapped, though there was a hint of sadness in her voice. "Take it up with the Fates. The Spirit of Dreams has already been saved from the Shears of Fate once. This is his time."

"It's not," I whispered, gasping for air. When had I started crying?

"Return to the mortal realm, Prophêtis," Nyx said quietly, her voice resigned. "The path you need is open for one of you to follow. The sun shines once more."

Before I could respond, we were back in front of Sophia's plinth, the soft ground beneath us now cracked and broken stone, glowing white in the moonlight.

Moonlight.

"We did it, Bullet," I rasped. "See? Open your eyes. The stars are shining again. There's a full moon, and it will be morning soon. And there's a path somewhere for us to go to Tartarus and fulfill the prophecy. And then we're going to live happily ever after, okay? We'll go back to your house in the countryside and we'll never do anything for anyone ever again. We'll just live in peace and be happy, just us. Bullet, open your eyes, *please*. Just hold on a little longer and then we can go home, okay?"

"Gracie..." Riot whispered, a hint of something I didn't want to hear in his voice. Acceptance. Resignation. Something I couldn't understand because there was no bond to tell me.

A breathy, slightly hysterical laugh of relief escaped me as Bullet opened his eyes. He was going to be *fine*. He was going to be fine. I'd find a way to get us back to his home, and we'd all live together in peace, prophecy or no. So long as Bullet was safe, I'd figure the rest out.

His gaze slid to Riot, giving him a weak smile. "You're like the brother I never had, you know that?"

"Stop that," I whispered, holding his hands with my shaky ones. "Stop saying goodbye."

"I know we haven't always seen eye-to-eye," Bullet continued, his voice barely above a rasp. "And I know I let you down—"

"You didn't," Riot interrupted, voice thick. "You couldn't. I'm sorry, so fucking sorry. You've always been the best of us, Bullet. You gotta stick around, because we can't keep it together without you."

"You can. You will. I've seen it. I've always known what you're capable of. What you'll *be*." Riot fell to one knee with a thud, clutching his chest, while Bullet turned his gaze to Dare.

Dare gripped the column at the top of the stairs, looking down at us on the ground and shaking his head in denial.

"Remember, you promised to make her smile," Bullet told him with a weak laugh. "I don't envy you that job over the next few days, but you can't afford Nyx's punishment right now, so don't screw it up."

"It'll be a lot more than a few days," Dare replied quietly. "Don't underestimate how much you mean to us, Bullet."

Wild let out a quiet gasp of pain, battling to keep his emotions under control, his arms trembling as he cradled Bullet's upper body. Bullet tipped his head back to look at him, and my wracking sobs felt as though they'd tear me apart.

"I wish we had more time," Bullet whispered, staring up at Wild. His lips were pale, and it looked as though he was fighting to keep his eyes open. "There are so many things I'd do differently. I *knew* this moment was coming, and I still let fear rule my actions. I should have made the most of the time we had—"

Wild bent forward, carefully lifting Bullet to press a firm kiss on his forehead. Telling him without words that this wasn't the time for regrets. That Wild wished he had more time too.

Wild lowered him back to the ground, and Bullet blinked slowly at me, the corners of his lips tipping into the softest of smiles. "You're going to save the world, Amazing Grace. I'm so glad I got to love you."

"I love you," I whispered brokenly, his eyes drifting closed. "I love you, and you can't leave me, can't leave us. Stay. Please stay, I'll do anything—"

Wild inhaled sharply as Bullet's form slackened with an ominous kind of finality.

"No, no, no, no," I chanted, furiously shoving the fabric of his coat aside so I could check for a pulse or breath or something. Anything. I refused to believe that Bullet's time had come. I'd saved him. I'd *saved* him.

"Let me," Dare whispered, gently wrapping his fingers around my wrist and guiding me away. "Your hands are shaking."

I shuffled back, scraping my palms on the stone as I moved down one of the steps to give Dare room, the glittering stars above *mocking* me.

I tipped my head to the sky and screamed.

Screamed at the unfairness of it all, at the sacrifices we were expected to make, at the goddesses who did what they wanted with no regard for the suffering of those they considered beneath them.

"There's a pulse," Dare said, grabbing my arm and tugging me forwards. "It's faint, but it's there."

He gripped my wrist to keep my hand steady, pressing two fingers against the pulse point in Bullet's neck. I held my breath, waiting. There was the very faintest thud—too weak and too delayed. He needed medical attention, medicine, *something*—

"Fuck," Riot hissed from behind me. "We've got company."

"Keep him safe," I instructed Wild, grabbing his hand where it rested on Bullet's chest and giving it a squeeze. I wanted to say more, but I couldn't even meet Wild's eyes.

He'd cared for Bullet too. Maybe even loved him, though it was a struggle for Wild to identify that emotion.

Gaia had ripped them apart too, even without a bond directly between them. In a decision that had probably taken Gaia half a second to make, she'd caused so much destruction, so much heartbreak, and we had to live with that somehow.

How were we supposed to live with that?

I forced myself to stand, knowing I'd need to face whoever was here. Probably more agathos.

No, I realized as I turned around, looking down the steps to the courtyard. No, it was much worse than that.

"You can't take him," I shakily told a glittering Thanatos, his gaze unusually somber compared to the last time we'd seen him. "No. You can't. I won't let you."

I glanced back to make sure Wild still had him, finding him clutching Bullet tighter, as though he was readying himself for another wrestling match with the God of Death.

"I felt his heartbeat," I insisted, turning back to Thanatos while Dare made a noise of agreement. "He's not dead. You can't take him."

"He has a better chance of surviving if he comes with me," Thanatos replied evenly. "I'm not going to take him to the underworld, but he can't stay here."

"What does that mean?" Dare asked, he and Riot taking up protective positions either side of me.

"Your Oneiroi isn't dead, but he isn't alive either. He's somewhere in between, and where he goes now *matters*." Thanatos paused, watching us carefully. "You need to accept that this might be the end though."

"Well, I don't accept that," I snapped, drowning in helplessness. There had to be a way. If I could just... get the bond back somehow...

"Where will you take him?" Riot asked.

"The Isles of the Blessed in the Atlantic Ocean. There's a mirror location in the underworld, and the isle sits somewhat between the veil. Until we can be sure which way his soul will go, that is the safest place for him."

"Which way do you think his soul will go?" My voice was hoarse, and I hated myself a little for even asking the question. For even contemplating that this was truly the end. Tears slid down my face, and Riot and Dare pressed closer, keeping me upright.

Thanatos hesitated. "That's above my paygrade. I can't force him to live. The tether connecting him to this world, this life, was *you*. Your bond."

"So we get the tether back," Riot stated. "Re-bond. Somehow."

Thanatos shrugged. "Find the Fates—Clotho the Spinner, Lachesis the Allotter, and Atropos the Inflexible. I have no idea *how* you'll find them unless they want to be found, but things like bonds are under their remit. They won't be happy that Gaia undid all their hard work."

"I doubt the Fates care that much about our bonds," Dare scoffed. Thanatos narrowed his eyes at him.

"You're the new one, aren't you? I doubt the Fates care all that much about *your* bonds specifically, but Gaia broke *all* the bonds. That's a lot of work on the Fates part, gone."

"All... She broke *all* the bonds?" I repeated, horrified.

Thanatos gave me a strangely pitying look. "Release your Oneiroi to me, Prophêtis. There were many of us who hoped today would go differently. Who hoped that Mother Gaia would choose to release the Olympians and put an end to all of this madness. I am on your side, Grace the Agathos. Let me help you."

"Can we go with him?" I asked, dreading the answer that I already knew was coming.

"You have important work to be doing here, I won't take you." A lead weight settled in my stomach. "Pick two others. Daimon, agathos, mortal, whatever. They will be his *phylakes*—protectors, guardians, that sort of thing."

"What will they need to do?" Riot asked suspiciously.

"Care for the flesh," Thanatos replied, gesturing at Bullet. "It's an honor, really. I will collect them from wherever they are on earth, transport them to the Isles where they will be completely safe from Gaia's rage, and once their task is complete, they can return to their regular lives."

"Is it dangerous there?" Dare pressed.

Thanatos shook his head. "It is a paradise. There is food there, no starving, desperate people. Even with the veil lifted, food is scarce. You would be doing two people a great favor."

I was already going through everyone I knew in my head, trying to figure out who was the most trustworthy and who could go as a couple. Foster and Estrella were my first thought, but I doubted they'd want to leave the group. The kakodaimonistai would be happy to serve, but who to send?

"What about a child?" Dare asked, drawing all of our attention.

"Sure." Thanatos shrugged. "So long as there's someone to care for them since the Oneiroi is, you know. Indisposed."

I shuffled further in front of Bullet, shielding him from Thanatos' gaze.

"Dare?" Riot prompted. "What are you thinking?"

The reminder that I no longer had any idea made the hollow place where the bonds had been ache fiercely.

"Quinn," I replied quietly. "Rogue and Quinn."

"You'd entrust Bullet's care to Rogue?" Riot asked dubiously.

Rogue. Rogue who'd called Riot for me at the convenience store. Who *hadn't* ratted Mercy out when she'd been at her home visiting Dice.

I didn't think she was as empathetic as my daimons, but I'd also felt a sense of *something* from her. Some kind of kinship. And provided they were both alive—which I had to believe—she'd been caring for a baby in the freezing cold and darkness for days.

"She'll have to swear an oath of protection, if that helps you make your decision." Thanatos' voice was impatient as he tapped his foot irritably. We were running out of time.

"Grace?" Dare said softly, grabbing my free hand and giving it a squeeze. "I wouldn't suggest anything that I thought would harm Bullet."

"I know. And keeping a baby away from all of this carnage is a blessing I can't turn down."

Dare gave Thanatos a long look. "Will you tell us if Bullet goes to the underworld?"

My head swam. I didn't want to acknowledge that was even a possibility. No, no, it *wasn't*. Bullet wasn't going to the underworld. Bullet was coming back.

My love for Bullet had saved him once before. It would save him again.

"Fine, I'll let you know," Thanatos clipped, snapping his fingers before he disappeared. There was a thud behind me, and I whirled around to find Wild's arms empty, his fists pounding furiously on the stone where Bullet had laid.

I slumped down on the stairs, out of energy to cry or rage at the unfairness of it all anymore. I had to believe that this wasn't the end, that Bullet hadn't just vanished into thin air before I'd even had a chance to say goodbye. I had to believe that, or I would never get up again. I crawled forward, toward the line of fire, but Wild's beating against the ground didn't cease. Before I could reach for him, Riot snatched me around the waist, dragging me back down the stairs.

While I didn't *need* the bond to understand that Wild was as distraught as I was, the loss of insight into his state of mind was distressing. For Wild, the bond was more than just a tangible confirmation of our relationship. It was a means of communication.

"Wild," I rasped, trying to reach for him while Riot held me in place. Wild's already crimson eyes looked darker and less focused than usual, though maybe it was just the sudden influx of starlight throwing off my vision.

"Gracie, you need to get out of here. He's not safe right now," Riot warned, voice tight.

"Wild," I tried again in a coaxing voice, my alarm growing as his knuckles split, spilling blood onto the stone. The look on Wild's face... I'd never seen it on him before.

"Wild, come back to me," I whispered.

CHAPTER 25

My rage tore through me like an inferno I couldn't control. Rage at Gaia, at Nyx, at the unfairness of it all. Rage at goddesses who treated us as though we were disposable and at our inability to stop them.

Bullet was gone. Taken by the very same god who'd humiliated me and stolen my voice. How was I supposed to trust *Thanatos* with Bullet's care? He hovered on the verge of life and death, the scales poised to tip in either direction, and there was nothing I could do.

I pounded my fists against the unforgiving stone that had sat here for centuries, hating this place, the task Grace had been given, the gaping wound in my chest where the bond had been, myself. Hating *everything*.

"Dare," Riot clipped, standing taller than I'd ever seen him as he held Grace back. "You need to—"

Milos skidded to a stop in the courtyard, barking furiously, running back and forth between the base of the steps and the entrance to the courtyard.

Whatever. The dog wanted something, but I didn't have it in me to care what. Not when Bullet...

Bullet.

"Time to go," Dare said quietly as I hit the ground again. Grace protested as he gently dragged her out of Riot's embrace. "If there are others here, we're not exactly in a position to defend ourselves right now. I vote we follow Milos, to be safe."

This was the last place Bullet had been. I didn't want to leave. It felt too much like goodbye, even though he wasn't here anymore. I'd fight, I'd bleed to bring him back.

I shouldn't have let Thanatos take him. Maybe I could find the so-called Isles of the Blessed myself. There was nowhere Bullet would be safer than with us.

"Wild," Grace whispered. "Come back to me. I can't leave here without you."

It took everything in me not to bare my teeth at her. At the beautiful soul bond I'd loved and lost. But I couldn't go with her. My control was in tatters. It wasn't the time. It *wasn't* the time.

I needed blood. More than just my own, which was dripping in red rivulets onto the stone ground after I'd attacked it.

I needed an opponent. I needed to feel the crunch of bone beneath my fists, the thud of flesh against flesh. *Needed it.*

Maybe those agathos who'd been hanging around, unworthy to cross the threshold to the courtyard, could provide the outlet I needed.

What had they done for anyone? Why did they deserve to walk around unharmed?

Would the world have gone dark if the agathos had just openly supported Grace from the beginning? If they'd backed her words and put human minds at ease? They shouldered some of this blame too. There were deaths on their conscience.

"Alright, let's go," Riot said harshly, standing over me and shoving my shoulder.

How fucking dare he.

I climbed to my feet slowly, seeing Riot through a dark-red cloud of anger. Did he have a death wish?

"You need to beat the shit out of someone, Wild? You can beat the shit out of me. It's not going to help. It's not going to bring him back."

"Riot, no," Grace gasped, struggling against Dare as he encouraged her down the stairs. "Please don't fight, not now—"

Milos' incessant barking drowned out her pleas. The dog bounded up the stairs, gently taking Grace's coat sleeve between her teeth and tugging.

"Grace, go," Riot said firmly, moving between me and her, blocking her from my sight. "Wild isn't going to be any use to anyone until he gets this shit out of his system, and Milos obviously wants you out of here. *Go.*"

"Come on, I've got you," Dare said quietly, while Milos continued to drag her away. Away from *me*. "They'll catch up, okay? They'll *both* catch up. They'll be fine."

I flexed my fingers at my sides, itching to give Riot the fight he was asking for, *needing* Grace to leave. Somewhere, in the back of my mind, I realized that I was grateful that I couldn't speak in that moment, because I would have definitely said something I regretted to make her go.

I couldn't be Wild, Grace's Bonded right now, not when I was Wild, The Keres Daimon.

I'd never be Wild, Grace's Bonded ever again.

GRACE

CHAPTER 26

Everything was a blur. I felt like I was moving through sludge as Dare and Milos dragged me away from the temple. We'd all come here together. I'd had all four of them at my side, I thought nothing was strong enough to tear us apart.

How could this be happening?

Someone was shouting up ahead, and Milos released me, running back and forth to check what was up ahead before returning to us. Dare was saying something, and I got the feeling it was important, but my ears wouldn't cooperate enough to listen.

How had it all gone wrong? The sky was lighter than it had been in days, despite it still being night. It was mocking me. An infuriating reminder of what I'd had to give up in order to save people who mostly despised me.

It wasn't fair. It wasn't right.

"Stop!" Dare yelled, shoving an arm in front of me as we passed the ticketing booth into what was once the parking lot. What *should* have been the parking lot.

Milos yipped incessantly, pacing back and forth as though we hadn't seen the giant hole where solid ground had once been.

A hole that was growing larger by the second. It was at least a football-field across, but it was burrowing into the ground, the walls crumbling and smoothing, into a perfect cylinder, deeper and darker than the naked eye could see.

"This is the path." It was my voice, but it wasn't. It felt so far away.

"This isn't a path," Dare shot back harshly. "This is a death pit. Milos, go back and make sure Wild and Riot don't fall in. I know the way back to Eirene's house, Grace is safe with me."

Milos yipped, brushing her body against mine as she sprinted back into the ruins.

"Don't let go of my hand," Dare ordered, snatching my hand tightly in his grip. "And don't get any ideas about going in there."

But I should, shouldn't I? It was a path. Nyx had fought to get me this path so I could go to Tartarus and fulfill the prophecy.

Bullet had...

Bullet was gone, in service of *this*. All of it was leading to this entryway to Tartarus, this pit of darkness that was apparently our path to salvation.

I should jump into it. Otherwise, what had all this suffering been for?

Dare's grip tightened as he dragged me around the edge, clambering over the occasionally felled tree or broken ruin. Nothing was safe from the pit.

Dare pulled the hood of my coat up over my head before tightening his grip on my hand and resuming his punishing pace. The agathos we'd seen before were gathering on the opposite side of the pit—far enough away from us that we weren't in any immediate danger, but who really knew anymore what was safe and what wasn't? They'd kneeled to me not that long ago, but now the immediate threat of global extinction had passed, perhaps all the agathos would return to blaming me for everything.

Did it matter anymore?

Did any of it matter?

The journey back to Eirene's passed in a blur of numbness. I felt *nothing*. A few hours ago, I had the constant feedback of four bonds. Four sets of emotion that weren't mine, giving me insight into the four men I'd fallen in love with.

And now, all I had was the hollow misery of my own thoughts.

I was on the day bed somehow, though I had no recollection of sitting down. Of even coming through the front gate. I could remember the conversation I'd had with Riot in this exact spot perfectly though. *Why wasn't he here? Where did he go?* There was a blanket on my lap, keeping away the chill, but it wasn't nearly as cold as it had been.

The first rays of sun hit my skin, and it was almost too much. Too warm, too intense after what felt like years without it. In the early morning light, I brokenly hummed *Empty Chairs at Empty Tables* under my breath, trying to recall the exact cadence of Bullet's voice when he'd sung it. It was a song of grief and pain, of sacrifice and futility, of the guilt of surviving.

I'd never been much of a singer, but Bullet had lived a life filled with music, and I'd carry on his traditions until he was back to carry them on himself.

He'd be back. He *would* be. He had to be.

God, it *hurt*, but somehow it didn't. Like whenever I felt myself inching closer to that sharp blade of devastation, a protective instinct I didn't know I had shrouded me and pulled me back. It kept me numb, floating through the motions of whatever it was I was supposed to be doing without registering what it was.

I reached for the cup of water someone had given me, knowing logically that I had to stay hydrated, even though I didn't feel thirsty. There was bread too—when had that gotten here?—and I picked it apart with my fingers, occasionally going through the motions of putting a crumb in my mouth and chewing it until it disintegrated. Eating. Eating was a thing that I was supposed to do.

Someone sat down next to me, close enough to let me know they were there, but not touching me. One of my bonded. My ex-bonded. Without the connection tethering us, I couldn't tell without looking anymore. I'd never again just *know* where they were or what they were thinking but not saying. I'd never feel what they felt, what they felt for me, never know if those feelings changed.

Would they? I didn't love them any less, but maybe I was stupid and naïve to hope that they'd still care about me without the bond forcing them to. Not one of them would have given me—an agathos—a second look if we hadn't been pushed together. They hadn't expected this for their lives, hadn't asked for it.

Maybe they'd been willing to put up with me and everything that came *with* me when they'd felt like they didn't have a choice, but they did now. They could walk away.

They didn't owe me anything.

That well of agony loomed again, tears that I didn't want to shed threatening to fall. *No, no, think of something else. Anything else. Pretend it's not happening. Pretend it's still yesterday, when we were all together and the bonds were strong. When all four of them were unequivocally mine, and I was stupid enough to believe that there was no force strong enough to tear us apart.*

I missed being stupid. I'd been happy when I was stupid. Now I knew better, and it *hurt*.

My hands shook with the effort of containing all the emotions I wasn't ready to feel. Warm, strong fingers carefully lifted the glass I hadn't realized I was holding out of my grip, setting it on the table.

If I let myself fall apart, I wasn't sure I'd ever put myself back together again, and I had *things to do*. There was a gaping pit in what had once been a parking lot that attested to that. Everyone and everything relied on me keeping it together.

"Breathe, Grace." Dare's voice was low and even, his palms warm where they rested against the back of my hands.

I was breathing. Wasn't I? The world was spinning and it was hard to concentrate. The sunlight was too much after so long without it, it was going to my head.

"Breathe with me." Dare gently tipped my chin up, encouraging me to look at him. He looked agonized, and I realized that those hands on me weren't as steady as I'd first assumed. "Breathe with me, Grace. I know it feels impossible right now, that *everything* feels impossible right now, but I promise you, you'll feel better when you get some air in your lungs."

Would I? I *did* want to feel better. That sounded nice.

With a painful amount of effort, I focused on the rise and fall of Dare's chest, regulating my own breath to match. The tight, panicky feeling around my airways eased, so I supposed he'd been right.

Except everything still felt incomprehensibly awful, like I was walking a tightrope above a sea of vicious sharks, but the sharks were me. Or rather, the things inside of me.

"Kiss me," I demanded hoarsely, barely recognizing myself.

"What?"

"Kiss me. Kiss me and make love to me. Maybe we can get the bond back," I insisted, talking through the idea as it occurred to me. Maybe that was all we needed to do?

"Grace..."

The hesitancy in his voice was unmistakable.

"Right, right. Sorry, that was a stupid suggestion. I shouldn't assume that you want—"

"Oh, I *want*," Dare interrupted, tightening his grip on my jaw. "I want the bond back. I want it even more than I did the first time, knowing what it is that I've lost. But you're very raw and vulnerable right now, Grace. I don't want you to do anything you'll regret."

He swiped his thumb under my eye, catching the stray tear that fell.

"Okay," I replied, my voice hollow. Some part of me registered that he was probably right, and that I wasn't in the right frame of mind for that. That Dare deserved better than sex as an experiment. Still, the rejection stung. I looked around, belatedly realizing I hadn't heard Riot or Wild come back yet.

"They're still not here," Dare said, swallowing nervously. "Milos hasn't come back yet either."

"What if they fell in the pit?" I asked, sitting up straight and pulling away from him. "I wouldn't know! There's no connection any more. If they... If they..." I couldn't say it, couldn't get the words past the tightness in my throat. "I wouldn't know."

"I'm sure they're fine," Dare assured me, his voice remarkably calm. "But even if they're not, I'm not going back to check on them. Not if it means leaving you alone. Riot would kill me if I did that, and so would Wild, once he's back in his right mind. They'll be okay, Grace."

"I've never seen Wild like that," I whispered. He'd looked at me like he didn't even recognize me.

"Don't take it personally," Dare said firmly, hands flexing as though he was struggling not to reach for me again. "Honestly, that restless energy had probably been building up for a long time—it's been days where the most physical energy Wild used was walking. That's not enough for a Keres, especially when we've been witnessing violence at every turn, triggering his bloodlust."

My heart hurt, a fresh wave of grief washing over me. Wild always seemed so strong, so immoveable. I'd been vaguely aware that the violence we'd witnessed was hard for him to deal with, but even through the bond, he'd locked down the full extent of his struggle.

261

"Don't feel guilty, Grace," Dare said in a low voice, scanning my face. "There's nothing you could have done. Losing Bullet…"

Dare sucked in a pained breath, his gaze dropping to his lap. *Don't cry, don't cry, don't cry,* I chanted, looking up at the porch ceiling and blinking rapidly to keep the tears at bay. Riot and Wild were who knows where, I *had* to keep it together.

"He was right to keep me away," Dare rasped. "He knew his future was uncertain after I showed up—"

"No." I shook my head. "No. I *saved* him. We avoided that fate. This… This is Gaia. This is all her."

I gulped down oxygen, trying to keep the tide of feeling at bay, but the warmer my skin grew under the sun's morning rays, the more everything inside me hurt.

"Let it out, Grace." I didn't protest as Dare pulled me back into his embrace. "Don't fight what you're feeling. It's scary and it's painful, but it's only going to hurt more if you keep it bottled up inside."

I gasped, a sob tearing free of my body before I could help it. Then another, and another. The hurt I'd been trying to hide had escaped, and I'd never be able to run from it again.

MERCY

CHAPTER 27

I couldn't sleep.

The guys shared the two big rooms in The Lodge, equipped with bunk beds, but Harbor had set up a trundle for me in the enclosed front porch so I had some privacy as the only female who lived at the campsite.

That was before the endless night.

It wasn't safe for me to sleep there alone after the sky turned dark—not when the campsite, already self-sufficient, had become such a tempting target for people who needed supplies. We'd filled the lodgings with human families, shared everything we had, but it hadn't been enough to keep the peace.

Everyone was hungry. There wasn't enough wood to burn to keep the chill away. And no matter what Harbor said about protecting myself, I couldn't *not* use my gifts. If the world was ending, what was the point holding back? If I could ease the physical suffering of the humans who had only the faintest understanding of what was going on, then I would.

But the stars had returned. The sky had gone from pitch black to dusky twilight. The freeze was finally ending.

For all the good it did. Everyone was still starving and desperate. They'd turned to violence to survive, and that instinct wouldn't disappear just because the sun was shining again.

Whichever goddess had done this—we were leaning toward the Goddess of Night—had forever ended life on earth as we'd known it.

"Mercy?" Harbor whispered, slipping into the hallway where I'd been pacing at midnight after his watch shift ended. "What are you still doing up? Is Sterling snoring?"

I shook my head, almost managing a smile. My trundle had been moved to one of the boys' bunk rooms for the time being. It had been empty most of the time since one or two of them were always on guard duty. I'd wanted to help, but they were all far too over-protective, insisting I manage the supplies inside the camp instead.

"What is it?" Harbor pressed. "You've been off all evening. Did you... Did you not want the darkness to lift?" he asked hesitantly.

I blinked at him. "Of course I did."

It wasn't the first time he'd said something like this. Sometimes, I felt like Harbor didn't know what to make of the fact that my soul bond was a daimon. If he thought it made me a little daimonic too.

"It's just... I don't know. I feel weird. *Off.* There's a sort of... emptiness in my chest, that I can't explain." I frowned to myself, massaging the spot above my breastbone.

Harbor stepped into my space, resting his palms on my shoulders. It wasn't unusual for him to touch me this way, offering comfort, but I startled at the strangeness of the sensation today. It felt different, somehow. He smelled so good—like pine trees and fresh lake air. I was eye-level with his chest, a small peek of tanned chest visible where the top two buttons of his plaid shirt were undone, his jacket unzipped.

His breathing was labored, and I realized that mine was too, my breath catching in my throat.

I was...

I was *attracted* to him. Harbor wasn't my soul bond. It shouldn't be possible, and yet I wanted nothing more than for those hands on my shoulders to pull me close, for him to kiss me like there was nothing in the world he wanted more.

"Harbor," I whispered, watching the rise and fall of his chest, too scared to look up in case I didn't see those feelings reflected in his eyes. "What is happening to me?"

"I have to let go," he replied, voice pained. "I don't know... Something is wrong."

His *jeans*. There was a *bulge* in his jeans. For me? I'd experienced desire for Dice, I knew what it felt like, but Harbor had never found his soul bond. This was his first time, and it was for *me*.

Dice.

That's what was missing. The pull to Dice that had hounded me day and night, that I'd fought to ignore from the moment I ran, it was gone.

I looked up at Harbor in shock. "The soul bond pull to Dice has disappeared."

Was he dead? Was that the reason? No, it couldn't be. I refused to accept that. Dice was strong, and fierce, and *fine*. Free of me, at long last.

I swallowed thickly. Despite the nightmares that haunted me where I watched Dice die a thousand different ways each time, I'd seen him fight off multiple agathos single-handedly. I *knew* he was strong, that he'd practically raised himself. He could handle anything. He'd probably been just fine through the days of darkness. Excelled, even.

I ignored the small voice in my head that told me I was lying to myself.

"Are we... Are we soul bonds now?" Harbor asked hesitantly, fingers flexing on my shoulders. "Is this what it felt like for you before? I don't know how that would be possible, but I've never experienced desire before. Shit, Mercy. I *desire* you a lot."

I didn't question it. I didn't *want* to question it.

Harbor had cared for me and helped me when he had nothing to gain and everything to lose from it. He was safety, and home, and peace. He'd never judged me for the terrible things I'd done, and night after night, I'd lain in my trundle and wondered why the Fates couldn't have given me him instead.

I grabbed the front of his shirt, closed the distance between us, and kissed him.

CHAPTER 28

Grace had sobbed for the rest of the day, throwing up twice before passing out on the daybed where we'd spent the night. I hadn't been able to bring myself to leave, not even for a second, though as the hours passed without Riot or Wild returning, I was growing increasingly panicked.

What if one or both of them was seriously hurt? Without the bonds connecting them, Grace had no internal warning system, no way to know if they needed help. Shit, it was almost a certainty that Riot was seriously hurt. Wild was a Keres daimon lost to bloodlust—no Moros stood a chance against him.

Eirene appeared at the open door as the sun rose, illuminating the remains of her garden. Would Gaia take pity on the ground and heal it? It didn't seem like it, or surely she'd have done it already. Maybe the Olympians could fix it, though if it meant Grace entering that pit, then it would never happen.

I wouldn't let it.

Eirene silently beckoned for me to follow her inside, and I carefully extricated myself from where Grace had been lying on my lap, tucking the blanket tightly around her. Her skin was brighter and healthier than it had appeared yesterday after a day of sunlight, and yet I'd never seen her look so fragile.

Losing the bonds had hurt her. Losing Bullet had broken her.

None of us would never be the same.

"Milos still hasn't returned," Eirene said quietly, leading me inside to sit down with the bowl of artichoke hearts she'd cooked for me. "She will be fine—she comes and goes from the temple regularly on her own, though staying away all night is slightly unusual. If you told her to watch over your friends, then that is where she will be."

She stared out the window, and perhaps it was the harshness of the sunlight compared to the glowing firelight I was used to seeing her in, or perhaps it was the stress of the past few days, but Eirene looked a lot more drawn and frail than I'd expected.

"I can't leave Grace," I muttered, feeling ten years older than I had yesterday. "And I don't think they'd want me to."

"Sophia communicates to me in feeling and intuition, rather than words," Eirene replied slowly, giving the bowl of food a pointed look, encouraging me to eat. I knew I should, but I had no appetite. "I don't *feel* as though I should go to the temple, or that I should encourage either of you to go. I think you can take that as a good sign."

It wasn't particularly reassuring.

Eirene gave Grace's sleeping form a pitying look through the window. "I thought there was no greater pain than feeling the life of my bonded slip away, but this... This might be worse. Not only losing one, but knowing the others are right in front of you, but the connection is gone. I wouldn't have been able to survive it."

"Grace will survive it," I replied absently, pushing my food around my plate. "Not easily. Not without fighting for that survival every day. She'll be angry soon, though. That anger will keep her going."

That anger would save us all. It wasn't Grace's compassion that would see the prophecy fulfilled, but her rage.

Loud barking from outside the gate startled me and Eirene, and I cursed under my breath as Grace sat upright, looking around with panicked eyes and a tear-stained face.

"Milos," Eirene said calmly.

"Let's go!" Grace yelled, half falling off the bed and rushing away from the house through the dead garden. I shoved away from the table, scrambling to follow, leaving Eirene behind.

Grace fumbled with the lock, and I gently grabbed her shoulders, moving her out of the way to get the gate open, finding Milos standing there alone.

Where the fuck were Riot and Wild?

Milos ran to us, nudging Grace's arm before darting back to the path, pausing and looking back at us.

"She wants us to follow," Grace said quietly, worry written all over her face. Shit. Grace hadn't even eaten yet, and I was pretty sure she was dehydrated from crying, not to mention we both needed to bathe.

But there was no way she was going to wait around to wash and have a decent meal if she thought for even a second that the others were in trouble.

"Then let's go."

Grace and I ran after Milos, stumbling to a stop a few feet in front of what had been the parking lot when it became clear what we were looking at. A merry band of agathos, daimons and humans had set up camp nearby, lounging around with bottles of wine in hand, laughing and sunbathing.

"You're here!" Vasileios called, spotting us. "Everyone—Grace is here!"

Grace was frozen, staring at the cheering crowd like a deer in headlights. They were so happy to see her, so relieved that the sun was shining. This was a moment of joy for them, and they wanted her to share in it, not realizing that she was falling apart inside.

Further around the pit were the agathos we'd seen earlier, some of them watching Vasileios' group warily, others... praying? They looked as though they were *worshipping* the pit, which... Yeah, that tracked, actually. They'd been desperate and scared, and the pit had appeared at the same time the darkness had lifted.

Vasileios gave a stunned Grace a one-armed hug before clapping me on the shoulder while Milos hovered at Grace's side. Where were Wild and Riot? Why hadn't she stayed with them?

She's a dog, I reminded myself. *She can't exactly understand complex instructions.*

"How did you guys get here?" I asked. Grace trembled slightly and I shifted behind her, wrapping my arms around her shoulders, hoping she knew that I was here for her no matter what. "Where are, uh, the Spartoi?"

A hundred soldiers clad in bronze armor were pretty hard to miss.

"About that..." Vasileios rubbed the back of his neck, giving Grace an apologetic look. "Turns out the Spartoi didn't really want to listen to me? Once we worked out where you were, Theras gave the order and they just marched off. I assume they're walking here." He shrugged.

Walking here? I had no real concept of how far away things were, but the boat trip had been hours.

I scanned the group again, realizing it was a little smaller than I remembered. "Did everyone come along for the trip?"

"All the daimons. We ran out of kykeon, and even though the Kakodaimonistai know about us now after Grace announced us to the world, they were... I don't know how to say it. Unsettled, maybe? Without the kykeon, they couldn't see our true eyes, and our gifts affected them more. Most of the agathos stayed with them, feeling drawn to care for them. It is good, I think. If they managed to keep the villa safe over the past few days, then we have a base not far from Athens."

After the carnage we'd seen in the smaller city where we'd gotten off the boat, I wasn't optimistic about that.

"How did you work out where we were?" I asked. "Not that we're not happy to see you, but we thought you were going back to Leonidio."

"Ah, Marek heard Hygeia's offer while she was healing you, and the agathos worked out pretty quickly you were probably coming here. We stole a couple of boats and decided we didn't want to be apart from the

Prophêtis. Especially now you've fixed the agathos; they are all horny for everyone now. It's amazing," he added with a laugh, throwing Grace an easy wink before frowning at the somber look on her face. "That's good, isn't it?"

Foster and Estrella approached hand-in-hand, watching Grace with matching expressions of concern.

"Are you okay, Grace? Where are the others?" Foster asked carefully, looking between Grace and me. Grace trembled in my grip, and I tightened my arms around her.

"Riot and Wild are here... somewhere. Wild got hit with bloodlust, they're fighting it out. That was yesterday," I admitted uneasily, glancing at the ruins in the distance. "After we met with the goddesses."

Estrella blinked at me. "What goddesses?"

"I'll ask some of our group to go look for them," Vasileios said at the same time. "We even practiced ASL on the boat ride over here so we can all communicate with Wild better."

That act of kindness was enough to tip Grace over the edge again. She turned in my arms, burying her face against my chest to hide her tears.

"We met with Gaia and Nyx," I explained as Vasileios waved over a couple of semi-drunk daimons, relaying the instruction to head into the ruins and look for Wild and Riot. "Nyx lifted the darkness in return for Gaia opening a path for one person to travel to Tartarus."

Foster glanced over his shoulder at the pit, eyes wide.

There was a moment of heavy silence between the five of us, their unspoken question hanging in the air.

Where is Bullet?

"Grace..." I prompted, unsure if she wanted me to tell them or not. From the limited amount of time I'd spent with them, I felt like they were good people who wouldn't push for information if she wasn't ready.

She wiped her eyes on my shirt, blowing out a long breath against my chest. Before my eyes, Grace seemed to transform, pulling her shoulders back and tipping her chin up, a mask of stoic calm falling over her face.

It was awe-inspiring to watch, and it broke my fucking heart. Grace's grief was fresh and painful, and she shouldn't have to suppress it for anyone or anything.

But she would.

She would, because she'd been given a job to do and Grace would see it through to completion, no matter how much she was suffering.

Grace turned to face everyone, an inch of space between her back and my chest. The rest of the group had drawn closer, probably wondering what it was that had gotten the Prophêtis so upset.

"Bullet..." Grace began, pausing to take one more steadying breath when her voice shook. "Bullet isn't here. It was the bond between us that had been keeping Bullet alive."

"He's dead?!" Estrella gasped, slumping into Foster's side, while Vasileios frowned.

"What do you mean?" he asked. "What does the bond have to do with it?"

Grace paused, studying the assembled group again. "Oh. Oh. None of the bonded agathos are here..."

"No," Foster replied slowly, wrapping an arm around Estrella's waist. "They all stayed back in Greece. Grace, what's going on?"

273

"Gaia broke the bonds. All the bonds." Grace's voice shook again, and one of her hands drifted to Milos while the other found mine behind her back. "I wish I could explain it better, but I can't. All I know is that the bonds are gone and in their place are full gaping wounds in my chest." She swallowed thickly. "I don't know if it's permanent—Sophia mentioned that the Fates might be able to fix it, but if agathos can feel desire for other people..."

Right. That did sound like it was pretty permanent.

"And Bullet?" Vasileios asked, all traces of amusement gone.

"He's not dead," I said firmly, *needing* that to be true. If Grace was feeling hopeless, then I was going to maintain hope for both of us. "He's in some kind of in-between."

"Like a coma?" Foster asked, wincing. "Sorry, that was inappropriate—"

"That's probably the closest comparison," I agreed. "A coma, but with a little more divine influence. He has been taken by Thanatos to a safe place until... Until we can figure out how to fix it."

"He's safe with the God of Death?" Estrella sounded about as comfortable with that idea as I felt.

"It was the best option we had." The words sounded weak to my own ears. It was the best option we had, but it was still a shitty one.

"Do you want to get drunk with us? We, er, *borrowed* a lot of wine from people celebrating the sunshine." Vasileios held up a half-drunk bottle of red wine almost apologetically. "We thought... Well, we didn't know it was this bad."

Grace smiled weakly. "I think my stomach is a little empty for wine, but I'd love to hear about your journey here while we wait for Ovie and Fox to come back with Wild and Riot."

The internal battle was written all over her face as we followed Vasileios over to where the others had set up a rough makeshift camp. She glanced over at the other side of the pit, and I'd wager she was debating whether to go and track down Wild and Riot herself, but struggling with the idea of going back to where she'd last seen Bullet.

Just in case it really was the last time.

It wasn't. I'd made a deal with Bullet, and I intended to honor it. If he ended up in the underworld, I was going to drag him back. I didn't think telling Grace that would help though. First, because I didn't want to get her hopes up in case I failed. Second, because she might object to me visiting the underworld and I didn't want her to worry.

"I think we should not tell you about our journey as we did many things you wouldn't approve of," Vasileios told Grace as we all sat down on a blanket a few feet away from the pit. Milos dropped down next to us, resting her enormous head on Grace's lap, very much to Grace's surprise. She stroked Milos' head a few times, and the poor pup fell asleep almost instantly. "And then we were wondering if we'd ever find you, and suddenly the stars appeared and the agathos lost their minds. It is only because Foster and Estrella wanted to see you so badly that they have clothes on right now. They have been fused at the—"

"O-kay, thanks for that," Foster interjected, blushing an impressive shade of beetroot. "At first, I thought I was feeling the soul bond pull somehow, that Estrella had meant to be mine all along." He cleared his throat awkwardly. "But we realized pretty quickly that *all* the agathos with us were experiencing desire for the first time, even if they didn't have a specific *person*, you know."

"General lust," Estrella added, giving Foster a seductive smile like she couldn't help herself despite the generally terrible conditions. "We were in a makeshift campsite and all of a sudden all the agathos men had their dicks out to explore their hard-ons while the stars twinkled above us."

There were six agathos there, including Foster, all squirming slightly where they sat. The other group of agathos further around the pit were far enough away that they wouldn't be able to hear us, and I vaguely wondered if they'd had a sexually liberating twenty-four hours too.

"It was a perverted kind of magical moment," Vasileios agreed. "It's been a long time since I've had lovers I needed to be so gentle with. Don't worry—we made sure to dedicate our orgy to Dionysus. It was a hasty prayer, but I think we got the job done."

"Very thoughtful of you," I replied drily, imagining a roadside orgy with a bunch of daimons, humans, and virgin agathos, while also recognizing the terrible truth that Grace wasn't stuck with me anymore. She could have anyone.

Why would she choose me when she'd absolutely sensed my wariness about our relationship while we'd been bonded? Yes, she'd asked for sex in the hopes of reestablishing the bond, but that may have just been a moment of weakness.

Grace was the Prophêtis. She could have anyone she wanted.

If she could choose anyone in the world, would she still choose me?

CHAPTER 29

"Wild! Riot! Where are you guys?"

The faint, vaguely familiar voice penetrated the fog in my mind, and I forced my eyes open. When had I closed them? The ground beneath my cheek was cool, but nowhere near the frigid temperatures it had been. No, the sun was shining overhead.

The sun.

The goddesses.

Bullet.

My throat felt like sandpaper, and each swallow hurt as I forced myself onto all fours, muscles aching like I'd just been ten rounds in the ring.

Where was I? I was definitely surrounded by ruins, but I couldn't see the statues of the agathos, just crumbling archways and the remains of what had probably been walls. How the fuck did I get here?

Bullet had...

Bullet...

Thanatos had shown up. Taken him away.

My head pounded as I sifted through memories tainted by bloodlust. I knew I wasn't seeing things as they had happened—I was seeing what my Keres side had seen. When bloodlust hit, everyone and everything was a threat.

Riot.

Fuck! Where was Riot?

I scrambled to my feet, my hands stinging as the movement aggravated every cut and scrape.

Come on, Riot. Where are you?

I clambered up the ruins to get to a higher vantage point, desperately trying to catch a glimpse of Riot's dark hair or colorful tattoos. We'd been fighting, I remembered that now. He'd antagonized me on purpose, drawing my attention away from Grace and Dare.

Grace...

Where was Grace?

I wouldn't have hurt her. Would I?

My bruised and bloodied knuckles seemed to mock me, and I shoved my hands out of sight, clenching them into fists as I searched for Riot. For my *friend*.

It was a foreign term for a daimon to use, but it fit. Riot was my friend, and he'd helped me through my haze and I'd...

What had I done to him? Fear had me in a chokehold. I was a champion fighter, a Keres daimon, and the bloodlust made me stronger. Fuck, fuck, fuck.

I jumped down to the ground, ready to run back to where I thought the library was, but a strange movement caught my eye. The blood dripping off my knuckles seemed to be... traveling?

Instead of sinking into the ground, the droplets were running over the ground like strange, shiny red ants. I followed, both mesmerized and horrified. *Please let this lead to Riot*, I thought helplessly. How long had I been out here?

Where was Grace?

She'd left with Dare and Milos, so I was guessing she'd gone back to Eirene's house. I had to get back there. Dare was fine and all, but he wasn't strong enough to protect Grace alone. And without Bullet... She'd be heartbroken. The empty space where the bond had been ached like a stab wound to the chest.

She needed me. She'd needed me from the second the bond had broken, and I'd let her down. Worse, I'd taken Riot away from her, too.

I picked up my pace, jogging along next to the droplets of blood as every muscle in my body ached in protest. Occasionally, I'd hear the faint voices of others calling for me or Riot, but I ignored them.

It wasn't as though I could yell back.

A few minutes later, I found myself back at the library, stepping through the invisible barrier to the courtyard in front of the agathos statues. In front of the entrance to the realm of the gods. The fucking *gods*, who heaped one trial after another upon us.

Riot.

I stared at his still form in the corner of the courtyard in horror.

His face was swollen, so smeared in blood that he was unrecognizable. *No, no, no.* I'd killed him.

I'd *killed* him.

In my anger, in my *grief*, I'd killed him. Grace would never forgive me for this. I'd never forgive myself.

What would Bullet think? He'd be so ashamed of me. Horrified that I'd done this in the name of grief.

How was I meant to fix this? How could I tell Grace? She couldn't see Riot like this, it would devastate her.

His sweater lay to the side, torn into shreds, and I stumbled towards it, my limbs uncooperative. Maybe I could staunch the bleeding, bandage him up.

It's too late.

Maybe I could pray. Except I was voiceless. Fuck! How had I let myself get so out of control?

How could I have hurt Riot? I had in the past, *before*. Before Grace, before I knew what he meant to her. Before he'd come to mean something to me. Riot was my friend. He understood me, he'd been learning ASL for me, he read my moods well enough to know when I needed to burn off some tension, or what I was trying to say when I couldn't speak. He'd been a good friend to me, and I'd never appreciated how much.

Not appreciating what I had until it was gone seemed to be the theme of my life. I never appreciated Bullet enough, never found a way to tell him how much I cared, that it was more than just sex.

Never told Grace I loved her.

I'd never have a chance now. She'd never see me as anything other than Riot's murderer.

The sweater felt scratchy against my fingers as I picked it up. The fresh blood from the wound at Riot's temple was also running over the ground in steady rivulets, but I used the fabric to gingerly wipe away the older stuff. Was he breathing? I couldn't tell. Fuck, fuck, fuck.

A flash of silver caught my attention, and I startled, dropping the sweater on the ground. The blood we'd shed was sinking into the plinth of the statue to the right of Sophia's, the one that read Αρετη—Arete, perhaps? I knew vaguely that she was an agathos too, one of excellence, virtue, of fulfilling potential.

That ship had long since sailed for me.

Instead of lighting up gold the way the temples had with Grace's blood, it was silver light that healed the broken stone. *Riot's blood* had done that. Riot's and mine.

We had no idea what we were truly capable of.

Did this mean Riot was still alive? With shaking hands, I moved to look for his pulse, but Thanatos stepped out of midair in front of me, knocking me back onto my ass.

No.

I nearly choked on a desperate gasp, an agonizing attempt to speak, to beg.

Don't take him, please don't take him. I'm sorry. I'm so sorry, I regret it so much.

Thanatos stared at me impassively, arms crossed over his chest, before turning his dispassionate gaze on Riot, silver flashes still illuminating the ground.

"How the mighty have fallen, Keres. You didn't cry this much when I took your voice."

I'd happily give up all of my senses if it meant I could take back the past twenty-four hours.

"But I haven't come for him," Thanatos continued, tipping his chin at Riot. "I've come for you."

My head snapped up, fear making it impossible to breathe. Me? It was my time? No, that couldn't be. I still had so much to do. And Grace, Grace needed me. Even if she could never forgive me, even if she never looked me in the eye again, I could still help her, be there for her. I'd spend the rest of my life doing whatever it was she asked me to do, anything to make her happy, even just a little.

Thanatos' gaze was unwavering, his expression totally unreadable. "I hate you, you know. Why the Fates decided *you* were worthy of the Prophêtis, I'll never know, but here we are. Come along, Keres. You have work to do."

GRACE

CHAPTER 30

I watched the other side of the pit as discreetly as I could, waiting obsessively for Wild and Riot to return. I should have never left them, no matter what they said. I'd been there, I could have stopped it. Now that I was out, the idea of going back into the ruins, back to where Bullet...

Nausea churned in my gut despite my empty stomach.

Vasileios and his band of followers were singing loudly, drinking and celebrating next to the pit. When Dare had explained what it was, where it likely led, they'd taken it as a sign to ramp up their excitement. After all, this was what we'd been waiting for, wasn't it? This was the path to Tartarus we needed, the way in. The way *out*.

Thanks were given to the gods before every drink was poured, and I joined in each dedication with the water I'd been sipping on. I should be pleased.

Be grateful, I commanded myself. *This is what we worked for. This is what our sacrifices were for. The least you can do is be grateful.*

"They're back," Dare said shakily.

My head shot up, and I watched in alarm as Ovie and Fox returned alone, expressions grim.

"Dare," I whispered, my hand trembling as I reached for his forearm.

"Don't panic," he replied, without a shred of confidence in his voice. "There could be a totally fine, not-terrifying reason. Don't panic."

"Too late," I rasped, spotting the beige wool sweater in Ovie's hand. The one Riot had been wearing when we'd left Eirene's house.

Ovie approached with his eyes downcast, unfolding the torn sweater and holding it up for me.

Showing me the bloodstains.

I was going to be sick.

"I'm so sorry," Fox whispered. "This is all we could find. They're both gone."

"How can they be *gone*?" Dare asked before I could voice that exact same question. "There's another gate. Maybe they got confused and went out that way."

Fox hesitated. "There was a lot of blood outside the agathos temple. Too much for someone to just walk away…"

"No." I shook my head. "No, neither of them would *really* hurt each other."

I glanced up at Dare, finding him pressing his lips together like he was trying not to say something.

Perhaps to remind me before I'd met either of them, Wild *had* beaten up Riot. But that was a long time ago, before they really knew each other. Wild wouldn't do that now.

I tightened my grip on Dare's arm, dragging him away from the now subdued group so I could talk to him in relative privacy.

"Dare, what if they fell in the pit?" I whispered urgently. "What if that's why Milos dragged us back here?"

He glanced uneasily back at the chasm, wanting to object, but not quite able to, knowing I might be right. The pit was for me, it was my path. I had to follow it eventually, and if Riot and Wild had ended up falling into it, then I had even more reason to leave.

"I have to go," I told Dare, my voice sounding hollow even to my own ears. "The prophecy was for me. I was the one told to rescue the treasure held in the deep."

Well, me and Bullet, but he wasn't here. I'd failed him and I didn't intend on failing anyone else.

"The pit is for me—" I began.

"The pit is a power trip," Dare snapped. "An egotistical statement from a maniacal goddess. Don't play her games, Grace. You go into that pit, you're never coming back."

"It's the path," I insisted. "That's the way to Tartarus. The *only* way."

It wasn't as though I trusted Gaia, of course I didn't, but she and Nyx had come to an accord. Nyx wouldn't have told me to take the path if it didn't lead to where it was meant to go.

"Leaping to certain death or imprisonment isn't the answer." Dare paused for a moment, giving me an unreadable look. "Bullet wouldn't want you to do that either. None of them would."

"I know," I replied, a sense of calmness overtaking me. No, not calmness. It was like the darkness I'd always fought against, but *more*. A well of rage as deep and black as the pit in front of us.

There was no breathing through the anger this time, no fighting against it. The rage was the fuel I needed to keep going. To keep myself from collapsing onto the ground and never getting up again.

"The path is for me, Dare. I need to follow it—more than I already thought I did if Riot and Wild are down there too."

Dare made a sound of discontent. "Obviously, I'm not going to let you go alone."

"You don't have a choice." I remembered Gaia's words, her pronouncement that only one could volunteer themselves to go to Tartarus.

Because of course she'd make me go alone. Whatever the hardest option was, that was what Gaia insisted on. However she could punish us, whatever would hurt the *most*, that was what she did. Why she hadn't just killed me yet, I wasn't sure. Perhaps she couldn't, maybe the Fates had determined it wasn't my time yet, and there was nothing she could do.

The rage in my chest where my bonds had been burned hotter. I hadn't asked for this. I'd inherited a battle I wasn't qualified for, that I didn't want to fight, and I'd done my best to do the right thing and it had cost me *everything*.

The soul bonds were one of the few things I *didn't* resent about being an agathos, the one thing I'd always longed for, and she'd destroyed them, taking Bullet in the process. Maybe taking Wild and Riot too.

Gaia wanted me to go into that pit and lose Dare too. If she couldn't get rid of me, she'd get rid of anything that mattered to me if I let her. If I couldn't find a way to stop her.

How was I supposed to walk this impossibly fine line between being Grace the Prophêtis, Grace with a job to do whether she wanted to do it or not, and Grace who loved Bullet, Riot, Wild and Dare? The more I tried to fulfill the Prophêtis, the more they suffered.

No, no more. If there was a way to get them back, I'd find it. I'd find the Fates, I'd *demand* an answer. Or I'd find the Olympians and demand they fix this if they wanted to be free from Gaia's prison.

Hadn't I sacrificed enough? Hadn't I done enough to ask for something in return for everything I was forced to give up?

I held onto Dare's arm, savoring the warmth and strength of him under my palms. He was here and whole and healthy. Strong. I had to keep him that way, had to keep him from coming to harm too.

In the short time I'd known him, Dare had helped me grow into myself, in the way that Wild had made me stronger, and Bullet had made me wiser, and Riot had given me a sense of belonging. I hoped I'd given them each something just as important. I hoped that me being in their lives had made them better.

"Grace—"

"I love you." Dare's mouth slammed closed at my pronouncement, eyebrows darting up. "I just want you to know that, Dare. I *need* you to know that."

"This isn't goodbye, Grace, so don't talk like it is," he shot back fiercely. His indignant rage rising to match mine. "I love you. I wish I'd realized earlier just how much, trusted that what I felt was real and that it was *good*, but I know now. I'm not making that mistake again. I love you, and I'm not letting you go off alone. Not into that pit, not anywhere. Whatever trials we have to face, we face them together."

I couldn't lie, so I didn't. I didn't tell him that I couldn't risk it, that I couldn't lose him too. Instead, I pulled Dare close and kissed him like there was no tomorrow.

Just in case there wasn't. Not for us.

Milos interrupted our moment, barking loudly before shoving into us when we took too long to respond, knocking us back a few steps.

"Hey, chill," Dare chided, giving her an affronted look while pulling me back another couple of steps. Milos continued to bark, darting back and forth frantically in front of us. Between us and the pit.

"Listen," I whispered, grabbing Dare's elbow, ready to drag him away. There was a noise coming from the earth—a faint, scraping sound, like boulders rubbing together. "They need to move. They need to move! Everyone! Get away from the pit!"

I tried to get closer to them, but Milos and Dare held me back. Fortunately, her barking had caught their attention anyway. Both Vasileios' group and the agathos on the other side of the pit stood, scrambling clumsily back as the scraping noise grew too loud for anyone to miss.

Please, please, please, don't let Riot or Wild be down that hole.

"What the fuck," Dare breathed, yanking me a few more steps backwards as something emerged from the pit. Something huge. I stared at the dark mass for a long moment before realizing what I was looking at was *hair.* Thick, dark, hair matted so tightly it looked more like a blanket sitting atop an *enormous* head. The tops of wings followed, covered in dark red and black scales that looked sharp enough to cut through steel, but I didn't even have a chance to be terrified of that because the *thing's* face appeared. And its eyes...

Its eyes were *flames.* Twin pools of fire, staring right at me. The creature grinned, exposing rows of sharp teeth, and as its wings carried it further into the air, I was vaguely aware that it had a human-like torso, but its legs were two coiled serpents, the same black and red as its wings.

The beast was the size of a building, casting us all into shadow as it hovered above the opening to Tartarus, grinning at me.

And not in a friendly way.

The others were running, their screams of terror catching the creature's attention. It twisted its head towards my friends, and a deep sense of calm and purpose washed over me.

Gaia had called me "the perfect mixture of tragic and desperate," and maybe she was right. Maybe that was all that *was* special about me.

It was all I *needed* to be special about me.

"Hey!" I yelled, slipping out of Dare's grip and rushing for the pit. He cursed, his footsteps thudding against the dirt as he ran after me. "Hey! Over here!"

The monster turned its hungry gaze back on me, flame-eyes flashing even brighter. Dare planted himself firmly at my side, linking our fingers together.

"Who are you?" I called, mustering all of my bravado. "Why did you come here?"

The creature watched me in silence for a long moment, before tipping its head back and spewing a stream of fire into the sky.

THANK YOU

Firstly, I need to thank Steph from Rawls Reads Edits for dev editing, and Lorie Collins for proofreading. I also need to thank Lucy—my friend, alpha reader, and sounding board for this series. You're all amazing, thank you!

But mostly, reader, I need to thank you.

I wrote Dare Not during one of the most difficult periods of my life, and this book was where I poured all of those hard, painful feelings into. That I have this creative outlet that I adore and I'm passionate about and that I get to do for a living is such an incredible privilege, and I'm so grateful to all of you for taking a chance on my books.

There is one final book in the State of Grace series—Saving Grace—which will be out in early April 2023. I hope you've enjoyed this series so far—feel free to reach out and let me know your thoughts, I always love hearing from readers!

For the latest news and teasers, join the Colette Rhodes Facebook Group or subscribe to my newsletter.

Colette x

GLOSSARY

TYPES OF AGATHOS MENTIONED:

Arete = Virtue

Eusebia = Piety

Eutychia = Good Luck

Hygeia = Good Health

Sophia = Wisdom

Sophrosyne = Self-Control

Soteria = Safety

TYPES OF DAIMONS MENTIONED:

Apate = Deceit

Ate = Delusion

Dolos = Trickery

Geras = Old Age

Keres = Violent Death

Moros = Doom

Oizys = Misery

Oneiroi = Dreams

Philotes = Sex, Affection

APRIL 2023:

SAVING GRACE

ALSO BY COLETTE RHODES

STATE OF GRACE:
Run Riot
Silver Bullet
Wild Game
Dare Not
Saving Grace

SHADES OF SIN:
(MF monster romance)
Luxuria
Superbia

THREE BEARS DUET:
Gilded Mess
Golden Chaos

LITTLE RED DUET:
Scarlet Disaster
Seeing Red

KNOTTY BY NATURE:
(RH omegaverse with T.S. Snow)
Allure Part 1
Allure Part 2

Printed in Great Britain
by Amazon

47826568R00175